THE MAN
WHO LOST
HIS SHADOW

and

NINE OTHER
GERMAN FAIRY TALES

RETOLD BY

Gertrude C. Schwebell

ILLUSTRATED BY

MAX BARSIS

DOVER PUBLICATIONS, INC.
NEW YORK

Published in Canada by General Publishing Company, Ltd., 30 Lesmill Road, Don Mills, Toronto,
Ontario.
Published in the United Kingdom by Constable
and Company, Ltd., 10 Orange Street, London WC 2.

This Dover edition, first published in 1974, is an
unabridged and unaltered republication of the work
originally published by Stephen Daye Press, New
York, in 1957 under the title *Where Magic Reigns:
German Fairy Tales Since Grimm.*

International Standard Book Number: 0-486-21151-7
Library of Congress Catalog Card Number: 74-78682

Manufactured in the United States of America
Dover Publications, Inc.
180 Varick Street
New York, N. Y. 10014

Contents

A True Fairy Tale

Many fairy tales once well known are missing from children's books published today. Poor imprisoned stories, they lead a dreary, dusty life on the shelves of libraries, labeled as reference books. This is an awful fate for fairy tales, so one day I decided to retell my favorite German fairy tales in modern English.

I soon found out that I had started something much more difficult than I had expected. There was an enormous number of stories to choose from. As I stood one day in the spacious book-lined Children's Room of the New York Public Library, I felt weary and somewhat discouraged, not sure how to go on. Suddenly it came to my mind how, as a little girl confident of the power of magic, I would wish for things difficult to obtain. I even remembered the words of the magic spell. Why not try again?

I closed my eyes and held my breath till I heard a faint whirring sound, the wheel of Time turning back. To tell

the truth, it was quite a while before it turned back far
enough! Then, suddenly there I was, a pigtailed little girl
again who—sometimes—had been able to make the world
do her bidding.

I murmured:

> *What I wish for shall come true!*
> *From witches' fat I cooked a brew,*
> *I threw in toads, and rats, and bats,*
> *And the tails of three black cats.*
> *I wish!* . . . . *I wish!* . . . . *I wish:*
> I WANT A PUBLISHER!

I waited seven seconds, then opened my eyes.

Of course! It still worked.

There he was coming toward me, earnest and quite in-
tent on his purpose. Thank goodness he did not know he
had to come because I had put a spell on him. I only hope
he never finds out. What would he think of me?

Well, he came. He bowed and said:

"I want to publish a book of German fairy tales no
longer known to the children of today. Not just pretty
stories—they have to be beautiful, and ethical, and a pleasure to read. Will you help me do this?"

"Gladly," I said. "There is nothing I would rather do."
And I took a deep breath. After all, it is not so easy to conjure up a publisher out of a city of eight million people!

He went on to explain what he wanted. "None of the
Grimm's Fairy Tales," he warned. "People would say they
know the stories, because they think that German fairy
tales and Grimm's fairy tales are one and the same. I would
like children to know how many other beautiful stories
there are."

That was exactly what I wanted too—how delighted I was! Isn't a library a wonderful place to go to and conjure up the impossible?

I had a glorious time after that as slowly the book took shape. It was a special pleasure to discover that Max Barsis, who did the charming illustrations, has also been familiar with these stories since childhood.

Here it is now, the book about the happy land where wishes come true. Let us cross the rainbow bridge and go into the land *where magic reigns.*

G.C.S.

The Story of
Little Mook

*

WILHELM HAUFF

In Nicea, my home town, there lived a man whom every-one called "Little Mook." I was only a boy then, but I still remember him very well because I once received a sound thrashing on his behalf.

Little Mook was a queer-looking old man when I knew him. He was only three or four feet tall, and his delicate little body had to carry a head which was bigger than most peoples' heads are. He kept house for himself, and lived all alone in his big house which he left only once a month. People would not have known he was dead or alive except for the fat clouds of smoke which arose from his chimney at noontime. In the evening he liked to promenade on his flat roof, and wasn't that a strange sight! Since he was so very short, his body was hidden behind the roof's balustrade. The story got around that it was only his big head that took a walk there, all by itself.

We were wild boys, my friends and I, and enjoyed taunting and teasing everybody. Little Mook was easy prey for our pranks. The day he used to take his monthly walk, we would gather at his house waiting for him. First came his big head, covered by an even bigger turban, then the small body, dressed in a worn-out short cloak and baggy pants. A long dagger hung from his wide silken cummerbund. The dagger was so long it was hard to tell whether Mook was fastened to the dagger or the dagger to Mook! We broke into wild cheers when he finally emerged from his house. We threw our caps in the air and danced around him like maniacs. Little Mook greeted us with grave politeness as he shuffled down the street, wearing the largest and widest slippers I ever saw.

Yelling, "Little Mook, Little Mook!" we followed him. We had a funny little verse which we sang, and which was more loud than melodious:

> *Little Mook, Little Mook!*
> *Lives alone in his big house,*
> *Once a month just he goes out.*

Like a mountain is his head,
For a dwarf he's not so bad!
Turn around and take a look,
Try and catch us, Little Mook!

I must confess we often went too far with our silly jokes. I remember that I pulled his little cloak, and once I stepped on his big slipper making him fall down. I thought it wildly funny, but I stopped laughing when I saw him going into my father's house. He stayed a long time, and when he finally left I saw from my hiding place near the door that my father shook hands with Little Mook and bowed very politely. I stayed in hiding for a long time. At last I became so hungry that, full of misgivings and with hanging head, I went to my father's room.

"I hear you have been abusing Little Mook," my father said severely. "I am going to tell you his story and I'm sure you won't tease him any more. But first you'll get the usual."

"The usual" was twenty-five strokes which he dealt out whenever I deserved it. For this punishment he always used his long pipestem after having removed the amber mouthpiece. This time I received an extremely well-administered thrashing. After having doled out "the usual" most conscientiously, my father sat down. He said, "Now listen carefully," and told me the story of Little Mook.

The father of Little Mook, whose real name is Mukrah, was a well-esteemed but rather poor man here in Nicea. He lived almost as withdrawn a life as his son does now. He was ashamed of having a dwarf for a son and disliked his only child, letting him grow up without proper education. In his teens Little Mook was still a merry child. His father always scolded him for behaving as if he had not yet grown out of his baby shoes though he was already sixteen years old.

One day the old man took a bad fall. He died soon after, and left Little Mook poor and ignorant. Mukrah had been head over heels in debt to his relatives. Those hardhearted people now chased Little Mook from his home, advising him to go into the wide world and seek his fortune.

Little Mook answered proudly that he was already on his way! He only asked for his father's clothes, and they were handed over to him. Father Mukrah had been a tall, strong man and his clothes did not fit his dwarfish son at all. But Little Mook knew what to do. He cut off what was too long and then put on the garments. He seemed to have forgotten, though, that they were not only too long but also much too wide for him. But he did not care, and till this very day he is wearing his father's clothes. The large turban, the wide belt, the baggy pants, the voluminous blue cloak, were all his father's. He also took his father's long Damascene dagger, shoved it in his cummerbund, and then left his home town.

Cheerfully he wandered along, for he was sure he would soon meet with splendid good luck. If he saw a broken piece of glass glitter in the sun, he picked it up, sure he had found a jewel; if he saw the dome of a mosque gleam like fire, if he saw a lake sparkle like a mirror, he rushed there full of expectation, convinced he had reached the Land of Miracles. But alas! All these lovely images disappeared as soon as he came near. And his empty stomach and his tired little feet reminded him painfully of the fact that he still lived on earth and not in Dreamland. He had traveled thus for two days—hungry, sad, and despairing that he would ever find his good luck. Wild fruit was his only food, the hard ground was his bed.

On the morning of the third day he saw from a hill a large city, not too far away. The crescent moon shone brightly from the pinnacles, colorful buntings waved from the roofs and seemed to lure him to the city. He stood still in happy surprise, taking in the marvelous sight.

"This is where Little Mook will make his fortune," he said to himself. "There or nowhere!"

Cheerfully he trudged on. It seemed so near, but it was a long, long walk for him, and his short little legs nearly gave out on him. Every so often he had to rest in the shadow of a palm tree. Finally he reached the city gate. He straightened out his cloak, tied his turban more neatly around his head, folded his belt still wider, thrust his dagger through it at a more daredevil angle, dusted his shoes, gripped his little staff more tightly, and courageously entered the large city.

He passed through several streets, but no door was opened inviting him in. Nobody called to him—as he had dimly imagined—"Little Mook, come on in! Eat and drink and rest your poor little feet." Nothing like that happened!

He was just scanning the front of a stately house anxiously when one of its windows was opened. An old woman thrust out her head and called in a singsong voice:

Come on, come on!
The food is done,
The table is set
For dog and cat.

Now take your pick!
Come on! Come quick!

Little Mook saw a great number of cats and dogs rush to the house. He hesitated a few moments, wondering if he should take advantage of this strange invitation. Starved as he was, he took heart and decided to follow a pair of pretty little cats. He was sure they would know the way to the kitchen better than he. In the hall he met the sour-looking old woman who had called from the window.

"What do you want here?" she asked sullenly.

"Why! You invited everybody to your meal!" answered Little Mook. "I came because I am dreadfully hungry."

The old woman laughed and said, "The whole town knows that I cook only for my darling cats. Once in a while I invite company for them from the neighborhood, as you see. Now, where do you come from, little stranger?"

Trustingly Little Mook told her about his hard luck since his father's death, and asked permission to eat with the cats that day. The woman was quite taken with his frank tale, and gave him plenty to eat and to drink. When he was satisfied and feeling much better, she said to him, "Little Mook, you ought to stay with me as my servant. There is little work, and I'll pay you well and treat you nicely."

Little Mook had enjoyed the cats' food. He was willing to stay, and thus he became Mrs. Ahavzy's servant. His duties were easy enough but very strange. His mistress owned two tomcats and four tabby cats. Every morning Mook had to brush their fur and rub them with precious salves. He had to take care of them all day, serve them their food, and in the evening he had to bed them down on silk pillows and cover them with little velvet blankets.

There were also a couple of dogs in the house, and he was in charge of them too. But they were not fussed over half as much as the cats, which Mrs. Ahavzy kept as if they were her own children. Little Mook's life was just as solitary as it had been in his father's house, for he saw nobody but his mistress, and cats and dogs.

For a while he was well contented. He had plenty to eat and little work, and Mrs. Ahavzy was quite pleased with him. But by and by the cats became mischievous. Whenever the mistress left the house, they darted and capered through the rooms like crazy, upsetting everything and breaking many a nice piece of china. But as soon as they heard Mrs. Ahavzy enter the house, then those two-faced little demons retreated to their pillows. Purring contentedly and wagging their tails, they looked as if they could not hurt a fly. Mrs. Ahavzy always flew off the handle when she saw her rooms in such a deplorable state. She blamed it all on Little Mook. He pleaded his innocence most ardently, but she would not believe him. She trusted her darling cats, who looked so gentle and so innocent, more than her little servant.

Little Mook was very sad that, after all, this was not proving to be his lucky chance, and he decided to leave. But he remembered very well how miserable he had been when he had to travel without money. Mrs. Ahavzy had promised him good pay, but he had never seen a single dinar. He made up his mind to obtain his wages somehow.

There was one room in Mrs. Ahavzy's house that was always locked. He had often heard her rumbling around there, and he would have given anything to learn what she kept in there. But he never had a chance to satisfy his curiosity. He was convinced she kept her money there and now, being determined to leave, he watched anxiously for a chance to get in. But he was never able to.

One morning, after his mistress had left the house, his favorite little dog came running up to him and tugged at his baggy pants. Mook followed his little friend, and behold! the dog led him to Mrs. Ahavzy's bedroom. Wagging its tail, the little dog scratched at a narrow door which Mook had not noticed before. The door was ajar. Little Mook pushed it open and with pleased surprise realized he was in the forbidden room. He looked high and low for money, but he did not find any. Only old clothes and strangely formed glasses and chinaware were displayed. A crystal beaker attracted him more than anything else he saw. It was finely cut and embossed with lovely figures. He lifted it up for a closer look but, oh, he had not seen that the cover was only loosely resting on it. It fell down, shattering to a thousand pieces!

Little Mook was half dead with fright. Now his fate was sealed; he had to flee or the old woman would surely kill him! He looked around for something useful to take with him. A pair of large slippers caught his attention. They were not very pretty, but his own slippers were too worn out for a trip. He was also attracted by their size. Surely, now everybody would see that he had indeed outgrown his baby shoes!

Quickly he shed his little slippers and stepped into the large ones. A walking stick with a beautifully carved lion's head was leaning idly in a corner. It certainly was out of place here in the old woman's house. He took it and left the room. He hastened to his small chamber, put on his father's turban, slung his cloak over his shoulders, put the dagger into his belt, and, as quick as his feet would carry him, he bolted from the house and out of the city. He was so afraid of the old woman that he dashed on and on till he was all out of breath. Never in his life had he run like that; it seemed he could not stop. A strange power propelled him forward. He tried every way he could to come to a standstill but he did not succeed. At last it struck him there might be something the matter with his new slippers, for they sprinted on, dragging him along. In great distress he finally called out, "Wo—back! Har! Whoa!" the way one curbs a horse.

The slippers stopped at once, and Little Mook threw himself on the ground, utterly exhausted. But he was happy. Now he had gained something which should help him to make his way in the world. He fell asleep at once; his frail body, constantly overburdened by his big head, was easily fatigued.

In his dream he saw the little dog that had helped him to the slippers. It said to him, "Dear Mook! You don't know yet the secret of the slippers. Turn around on the heels three times, and you can fly wherever you want to. Your walking stick is really a divining rod. Wherever gold is buried, it will knock on the ground three times, and twice if it is silver." That was Little Mook's dream.

When he woke up, the dream was still very vivid in his mind. "Well, I could try it," he thought. He put on the slippers, lifted up one foot, and tried to turn on a heel. Wow! That was easier said than done! Those unwieldy slippers came off, or he stepped on one when he tried to catch his balance. His big head pulled him this way and that way, and dozens of times he lost his footing! He stumbled, fell over, got up, tried it again and again. It was quite a stunt for the poor little fellow. But he was deter-

mined not to give up. After a couple of downfalls, he got
the hang of it. Arms outstretched, he whirled around three
times, coattails flying. Huzzy, hey! He made it! Quickly he
wished to be in the next big city, and there, his slippers
lifted him up into the air. Like the wind he flew through
the high clouds, and before he had caught his breath, or
had noticed how it all happened, he found himself in a
big market square. There were many stalls and colorful
tents; a gay crowd milled busily around. Highly pleased,
Little Mook walked up and down, but soon he thought it
advisable to take refuge in less crowded streets. He was
so short, and his slippers were so long! People would step
on them so that he almost tumbled over, or his long pro-
truding dagger would poke people's sides so that they became incensed. He had to beat a retreat.

Walking in the quiet side streets, Mook realized that he
really had to make up his mind how to earn a living. He
owned a magic stick, but how should he find a place where
gold or silver were buried? If the worst came to the worst,
he could join a side show as a freak, but he was too proud
for that! Finally he thought of his great ability in running.
"My slippers ought to make a living for me," he said to
himself. "I'll hire myself out as a runner."

He was sure the king of such a big city would pay
very good wages, and soon he was on his way to the palace.
The mameluke at the gate brusquely asked what he wanted
here. Mook said he was looking for work, and he was
shown to the overseer of the slaves.

"I would like to become the king's runner," Little Mook
said modestly.

The overseer gave him a long, appraising look.

"Indeed! Is that what you want here? Become a runner

with those tiny feet of yours? . . . Get out of here!" he shouted, enraged. "I'm not a fool's fool, or am I?"

"I certainly meant what I said," replied Mook with great dignity. "Why don't you give me a try? You can match me against your very best man. I'll bet my turban I'll beat him."

The overseer thought this was too good a joke to miss. "All right! Tonight we'll have a great running match," he said and grinned. "Now come along with me, little fellow," and he took him to the big kitchen and ordered a nice meal for Little Mook. Then he rushed to the king and told him all about the dwarf and his ridiculous proposal.

The king was a merry man, who enjoyed nothing better than a good joke. He said gratefully that it was very thoughtful of the overseer to have retained the manikin. He ordered him to prepare the large meadow behind the palace for the race so that his whole court could easily watch it. The king told the princes and princesses what a jolly spectacle was in store for them this evening, and they in turn told their servants about it. Everybody was looking forward to it, and when evening drew near a cheerful crowd was waiting to see the big-mouthed dwarf live up to his boastful talk. A raised dais was put up for the kingly family—and bleachers for the courtiers. As soon as the king, the princes, and princesses were seated, Little Mook stepped forward and made a most deferential bow to the illustrious personages.

Loud cheering greeted him because most people had never seen his like. The queer figure so strangely enveloped in bulging garments, the wide slippers on those tiny feet—certainly, that was a unique costume for a runner! Ah! he was too funny for words and people laughed aloud and clapped their hands. Little Mook was not in the least little bit disturbed by their laughter. Jauntily leaning on his little cane, he calmly waited for his adversary. In accordance with Little Mook's special request, the overseer had chosen the king's best courier for the race. The runner now approached, a tall man with powerful limbs. They took their places, waiting for the starting signal.

Princess Amarza, as arranged, waved her veil and, like two arrows heading for the same goal, the two competitors flew across the smooth meadow.

The long-legged runner had a considerable start over Little Mook in the beginning, but the little one with his magic slippers soon caught up with him, overtook him— there! . . . He whizzed past the runner like a flash! Ah! Little Mook stood at the goal, cockily leaning on his little cane, coolly waiting for the arrival of the other man, who ran and ran with all his might, embarrassed and panting. The startled onlookers were rendered motionless by surprise, but when the king applauded wildly, the crowd broke into hilarious yelling and waving.

"Three cheers for Little Mook, victor of the race!" they shouted lustily.

Little Mook was brought before the king, and threw himself on the ground.

"Most glorious King, my heart and my feet are at your command," he said eagerly. "I showed you only a small sample of my art. Do give me permission now to be one of your runners."

But the king answered graciously, "You shall be my Courier-in-Chief and always near my kingly person. One hundred gold pieces a year are your salary and you shall dine with my first servants."

Small wonder Mook was convinced he finally had found the good fortune he had so ardently pursued. His heart was glad within him. He also enjoyed the king's special favor, and was always used for his most urgent and most important messages. And Little Mook acquitted himself each time with greatest efficiency and with unbelievable speed.

But the king's attendants disliked Little Mook heartily. Why, he was only a dwarf, who knew nothing except how to run faster than anybody else! And such a one was outshining them with their lord and master! They planned many a plot against Little Mook, but all plotting was nought. The king fully trusted his Secret-High-Courier-in-Chief, which was the gorgeous title bestowed on Little Mook ere long.

Mook was well aware of these enmities and he fell to brooding. He was much too goodhearted to want revenge. Oh no! He tried hard to think of something that would turn their hatred to friendship. He remembered his magic wand which he had never used, being so lucky anyhow. But now Mook thought, "Maybe I'll find a treasure and they'll like me better when I'm rich."

Often he had heard people talk about the treasures which the king's father had buried somewhere when an enemy had threatened the country. The old king had died before he could disclose his secret to his son, and nobody knew where to look for the gold. Little Mook decided to carry his magic stick with him always, hoping he might one day chance upon the hidden treasure. And so it happened. One evening, while he was walking in a lonely part of the immense palace gardens, he felt the stick twitch in his hand. And then it struck the ground three times. Well he knew what that meant! He took his big dagger and marked the trees. He returned to the palace after hiding a spade from a gardener's shed. Now he had only to wait for night to come.

Treasure digging was much harder work than Little Mook had anticipated. His arms were weak, the spade was big and heavy. He had toiled for two hours before he struck something sounding like metal. Eagerly he dug away, and soon he uncovered the lid of a big iron chest. He crawled into the hole he had dug and tried to lift the lid. It was so heavy! "Oh dear, oh dear," he sighed, wiping the sweat off his brow. But finally he succeeded. There was gold in a big jar, gold aplenty. Of course he was too weak to move the earthen pot. Therefore he filled his pants, his belt, and his wide coat with gold, covered the spot with earth, and lifted the coat, after having it tied into a bundle, upon his back. Indeed! Without his slippers he would not have been able to take a single step, so heavy was his load. But he made it. Unnoticed, he finally reached his room and hid the gold under his pillows.

Little Mook was sure that now it would be easy for him to turn his enemies into friends and protectors. Really! That shows that poor Little Mook never had the luck to have a good education. For then he would not have assumed that one can buy true friends with gold. He should have oiled his slippers then and there, taken his bundle of gold, and just disappeared!

Little Mook squandered gold with full hands. Of course, everybody took it, and everybody became envious. Ahuly, the Cook-in-Chief, said, "He's a forger, a counterfeiter!" "He cajoled the king out of it," grumbled Achmet, overseer of the slaves. But the treasurer Archaz, Little Mook's worst enemy, said bluntly, "Why! He stole it!" Then they made a plot to find out how Little Mook had got the money.

Korchuz, the king's cupbearer, took to sighing and walking around with a most dejected face. The king could not help noticing it and soon he asked kindly, "Tell me, Korchuz, has ill luck befallen you that you look so woebegone?"

"Alas and alack!" sighed Korchuz. "I am sad because I have lost my lord's favor."

"What nonsense, friend Korchuz," replied the king. "The sun of my grace is shining upon you as always."

"If I may make bold to speak, oh, most gracious King," said Korchuz humbly, "I am disheartened because my lord lavishes his gifts upon the Courier-in-Chief, but his old and faithful servants are forgotten."

"What are you hinting at, Korchuz?" the king shouted impatiently. "Out with it!" He was beginning to be annoyed by so much mysterious talk. Korchuz told him then how Little Mook dealt out good gold to all and sundry, and the king was very surprised. He was easily convinced that Little Mook somehow was robbing his treasure house, and he became very angry with Mook. This turn of events suited the plotters and especially the treasurer very well indeed. Archaz hated to render account of the treasures, for he was not above filling his own pockets. Now he was happy to have found a scapegoat.

The king ordered his Courier-in-Chief to be watched carefully. Soon, late one evening, the report came in that Little Mook had slunk into the garden, carrying a spade. Unfortunately Little Mook had, all too soon and all in vain, depleted the little treasure under his pillows. Now he was on his way to get a new supply from the iron box in the ground. Stealthily the guards followed him, led by Archaz and Ahuly, and when Little Mook was about to fill his cloak with gold, they fell upon him. They seized and bound him and took him to the king.

Sullenly the king gazed upon his poor Secret-High-Courier-in-Chief. He felt betrayed, and anyhow he hated to be awakened from his sleep in the dead of night. The mamelukes had lifted the pot of gold from the ground. Now they put it in front of the king as proof, together with the spade and Little Mook's blue cloak, half filled with gold. The treasurer declared they had seized Little Mook while he was burying the gold in the ground.

"Is that the truth?" the king asked scornfully. "Where did you get the gold?"

"I found it in the garden a few weeks ago," Little Mook answered truthfully. "I was not going to dig it under. I was going to dig it out!"

They all burst out laughing at this flimsy excuse. Greatly vexed by Little Mook's supposed impudence, the king cried, "You miserable little wretch! You dare to lie to my face after you robbed me! There is no good faith left among men!" He turned away in great wrath. "Treasurer Archaz! Tell me, is this the gold that is missing from my treasure vault?"

Archaz prostrated himself before the king.

"Oh, King of the Age! This is the stolen gold," he cried boldly. "I'll take that on my oath!"

"Put my Secret-High-Courier-in-Chief in chains and throw him into the dungeon," the king said grimly.

"Hearing is obeying," replied the chief mameluke, and poor Little Mook was dragged away.

The jar of gold was sent to the treasurer's house with

the king's order to store it away again. Highly pleased with this state of affairs, Archaz had gone home. Now he greedily counted the glittering coins, putting aside a nice heap for himself. The treacherous man never told anybody that he found a slip of paper at the bottom of the jar. It read: "The enemy is approaching the capital, and I am hiding part of my treasure. The king's curse fall upon him who finds it and does not deliver it to my son. King Sadi."

Poor Little Mook had a most distressing time in the dungeon. He knew that stealing the king's property was punished by death. He could prove his innocence only by disclosing the secret of his lion-headed cane, yet he hesitated to do so. He was worried that his cane and slippers would be taken away from him. He tried to turn on his heels, but he was so closely chained to the wall that it was impossible, hard as he tried. So his magic slippers were no help to him in his predicament.

But when on the very next day the death warrant was read to him, he decided it was wiser to live without the magic wand than to die in possession of it. He asked for a private interview, and when the king granted him this, he told him his secret. At first the king did not believe him, but Little Mook promised to prove his words if the king would grant him his life, and the king gave him his word of honor. Some gold was then buried in the garden and Little Mook was led out and he walked around. As soon as he came upon the spot, the cane twitched in his hand and knocked on the ground three times.

Now the king realized that Little Mook's story was true and that his treasurer had betrayed him. He sent him—as is the custom in the Orient—a silken cord that Archaz might take his own life by hanging himself with it.

But to Little Mook he said, still wrathful, "I granted your life. But I shall keep you a prisoner to the end of your life if you don't tell me the secret of your speed."

One single night in prison had been quite enough for Little Mook. He confessed that his magic slippers enabled him to travel at such tremendous speed. He did not mention anything about turning on the heel, but, wisely, kept that to himself. Full of curiosity the king stepped into the slippers and whizz! There he went! The slippers raced around the garden with him like crazy. In vain he tried to halt every so often, but he did not know how to control the magic slippers. Enjoying his revenge, Little Mook let him run till the king, completely played out, fell to the ground. The king was in a white rage, and as soon as he had caught his breath, he shouted, "I granted your life, and I granted you your freedom. I gave you my word of honor," he went on, boiling with fury, "and a king has to keep it! But you are expelled from my country, and if you are found in my boundaries after the next twelve hours, you'll swing from the gallows!"

So maddened was the king at Little Mook who had made him gallop through the palace gardens like one possessed, that the slippers and the lion-headed cane were confiscated and stored away in the king's treasure house.

Poor as ever, Little Mook wandered away. A curse upon his foolishness that had made him bold enough to believe he could play an important role at court! Luckily the country he was expelled from was quite small. After only eight hours he reached the frontier, though walking was very hard on him; he was so used to his dear slippers.

After having left the king's country, he fled into the

wilds, determined to live like a hermit, for he had taken
a dislike to people. In a dense forest he chanced upon a
place suitable for his purpose. A clear brook, overshadowed
by large fig trees, and soft turf invited him to rest. He
cast himself down on the grass, resolving never to taste
food again, but to await death here. Thinking sad thoughts,
he fell asleep.

He awoke in the evening, tormented by hunger, and
realized that it was most dangerous and most unpleasant
to abstain from food. Pretty soon Mook was looking around
for something to eat. Exquisite ripe figs hung from the
tree which had sheltered his sleep. He clambered up the
tree to pick some. Weren't they luscious and sweet! He
ate his fill and went to the brook to quench his thirst.

Nobody can imagine his horror as he saw his image in
the clear water. Lo and behold! ass's ears stuck out from
under his turban, and a long, ungainly nose adorned his
face! Terrified, he put his hands to his ears, and, really,
they were more than half an ell long.

"I deserve ass's ears!" he cried out in bitter dismay. "Like an ass I trampled upon my good luck!"

Woefully he wandered away, but when he became hungry he ate some more figs since he could find nothing else. Munching the second portion of savory figs, he turned it over in his mind that his long ears might fit under his big turban. He would not look quite so ridiculous then, he thought. With his hand he felt for his appalling ass's ears —they were gone! All gone! He rushed back to the brook and, eagerly bending down, he looked into the mirror-clear water. It was true! His monstrous ears, his long unsightly nose had assumed their usual forms once more.

Joyfully he realized how this had come to pass. The first fig tree had bestowed the horrid nose and ears on him, the second tree had healed him. Fate had favored him once more and given him the means to better his condition. From those two marvelous trees he gathered as many figs as he could carry, and then he returned to the country which he had left only yesterday. He bought new garments in the next small town and changed his appearance altogether. Then without any further delay he went to the capital. It was the season when ripe fruit was still a rarity and Little Mook sat down at the palace gate. He knew the habits of the Cook-in-Chief who used to buy delicacies for the king's table from vendors and peasants at the gate. Ere long Ahuly came, critically scanning the wares displayed. Soon the choice fruit in Little Mook's basket caught his eye.

"Ah! that's a dainty tidbit for this season." He was very pleased. "The king will surely enjoy them. What is the price for the basketful?"

Little Mook named a moderate sum and soon the deal

was on. Ahuly handed the basket to a slave and went on his way. Little Mook took to his heels and hid himself. He was sure they would try to find this particular fruit vendor as soon as misfortune befell the heads of courtiers, princes, princesses, and *the king!*

At table the king was in high good humor. Frequently he praised his Cook for his good cuisine and the pains he took to attain the rarest tidbits for his lord. Ahuly, thinking of the splendid figs he was going to serve as a dessert, grinned smugly. He dropped a few hints like, "All is well that ends well," or, "The evening crowns the day," till the princesses were very curious indeed as to what he would bring forth next. When he finally signaled to a slave to bring on the dessert, all present ahed and ohed at the tempting figs.

"How exquisite," marveled the king. "Ahuly, you are a splendid fellow and deserving of our most special favor."

Usually the king was inclined to keep such little extras mostly to himself. But today he smiled. "To every man his due," he said grandly, and cheerfully he doled out the delectable fruit. Each prince and each princess received two figs, the court ladies, the viziers, and agas only one. The rest of the figs the king put in front of him and started to devour them with greatest pleasure.

Suddenly Princess Amarza raised a loud cry. "By Allah! Oh, my Father, how strange you look!"

They all stared at the king. He was disfigured with monstrous flapping ears, a coarse, drooping nose almost touched his chin. They looked at each other in fright and bewilderment. Every one of them had grown the strangest headgear; it was a grotesque sight!

Who can imagine the panic that befell the court. All

the doctors of the city were summoned; in droves they flocked to the palace, they ordered pills and mixtures—but ears and noses remained the same. One prince was operated on, but his ears grew back.

Little Mook in his hiding place heard all about it; and he knew his time had come. He had a scholar's garment ready for himself, now he donned it; a large beard of goat hair completed his disguise. He went to the king's palace with a bagful of figs and offered his help as a foreign doctor of great experience. At first nobody believed that he could help, but Little Mook persuaded the desperate Grand Vizier to let one of the princes try it. The young man ate a fig; his nose and ears were reduced to their former size! Of course, everybody wanted to be healed now by the marvelous foreign doctor.

The king took Little Mook by the hand and led him to the treasure house.

"Here are my treasures," spoke the king. "Choose among them. Whatever you want is yours, only relieve me of this disgraceful misshape."

That was music in Little Mook's ears. Right away he had spied his dear slippers, and his little cane was lying there too. He walked around in the treasure vault as if he were admiring the king's wealth. But when he came near his slippers, he quickly stepped into them, grasped his cane, and tore off his false beard. Perplexed, the king looked into the well-known face of his cast-off Mook.

"Treacherous King!" Mook exclaimed. "You repaid my loyalty with ingratitude and you well deserve to be punished! Your ears shall remain as they are and remind you daily of Little Mook!"

Before the stunned king could utter a cry for help, Lit-

tle Mook had whirled around three times on his heels. He wished to be far away, and he vanished from the king's sight.

"Since that time," my father concluded his tale, "Little Mook lives here in his home town, a wealthy man, but he is lonely for he despises his fellow men. His marvelous experiences taught him wisdom, and he is always willing to help people in distress. He deserves your admiration and not your mockery."

This is Little Mook's story as my father related it to me on that day. I felt sorry for my rudeness toward the good little man. I told my friends about Little Mook's extraordinary fate and we never again abused him. On the contrary, we honored him as long as he lived, and when he went out we bowed to him as deep as to the cadi and mufti.

Undine

*

FRIEDRICH DE LA MOTTE FOUQUÉ

Hundreds of years ago a good old fisherman lived on a beautiful point of land which stretched far into the glassy blue waters of a large lake. He lived there all alone with his family. Nobody ever came to this lovely place, for behind the peninsula lay a wild wood, gloomy and pathless. People were afraid to cross it, for fear of goblins and frightful apparitions. But the pious old fisherman had never been molested when he walked through the forest to carry his delicious fish to the large city beyond the haunted wood.

But one lovely evening, as he sat before the door of his hut mending his nets, he became frightened. He heard strange rustling sounds stir in the darkness of the forest, and everything he had ever heard about the secrets of the wood rushed through his mind. Especially he recalled the image of a gigantic, thin, snow-white man, who kept nodding his head mysteriously. As he raised his eyes to the forest, he imagined he saw the nodding man advance toward him through the screen of leaves. He became alarmed, but soon he pulled himself together, remembering that nothing evil had ever befallen him in the forest. He murmured a short and fervent prayer, and he almost laughed when he saw how mistaken he had been. The white nodding man, he could see now, was only the well-known foaming brook which burst forth from the forest and flowed into the lake.

The rustling sounds had been caused by a knight in gorgeous attire, who emerged from the dark wood and came riding toward the hut. He wore a scarlet coat over a violet-colored, gold-embroidered jerkin; scarlet and violet-blue feathers waved from his gold-colored barret. From his sword belt hung a beautiful, richly adorned sword. The old fisherman lifted his cap courteously, but continued his work calmly, though he still felt uneasy. The knight halted his white charger and asked if he and his horse might have food and shelter for the night.

"As to your horse, dear sir," replied the fisherman, "I know of no better shelter than this peaceful meadow, and of no better food than the grass growing in it. But you yourself are heartily welcome to supper and lodging in my poor hut."

The knight was well contented. He dismounted, and together they unbridled and unsaddled the charger. Then he let it graze in the verdant pasture, saying to his host, "Even if I had found you less kind and hospitable, dear fisherman, you would not have been rid of me tonight. I see a large lake stretches before us, and Heaven forbid that I should ride back into the haunted wood after nightfall."

"We won't talk about the woods," answered the fisherman, and led his guest to the hut. The fisherman's old wife sat in a big chair by the hearth, where a scant fire lit the clean but dusky room. She rose at the entrance of the noble guest, and greeted him kindly.

"Sit down, young lord," she said. "We have quite a comfortable chair for you, but you must be a little careful with it, for one of its legs is a bit unsteady."

Cautiously the knight drew forward the chair and gingerly sat down. The three then started to talk in a friendly manner. The knight inquired several times about the enchanted wood, but the old man would not talk about it.

"At least let's not speak about it in the evening," he said. But the old folks did enjoy listening to the knight as he told about his travels. They learned that he hailed from South Germany where he had a castle at the source of the Danube, and that his name was Sir Hugo of Ringstetten.

In the middle of their talk the stranger heard a noise as if somebody were dashing water against the windows. Each time this happened, the old man would knit his brow. Finally a big gush splashed against the windowpanes, and water trickled into the room through the ill-fitting frames. He jumped up.

"Undine! Won't you stop this childish behavior," he called indignantly toward the window. "We have a noble visitor."

There was silence and then a suppressed giggle. The old man turned back to the room.

"You must pardon her for this, my honored guest," he said. "It's Undine, our foster child. She won't give up her mischievous ways, though she must be eighteen years old by now. But at bottom her heart is good."

The door flew open, and a beautiful fair-haired child slipped laughingly into the room and said, "You're only teasing me, Father! I don't see any guest."

At that moment she noticed the knight and stood transfixed. He was equally delighted with her lovely aspect, and looked at her steadily, as if to engrave her exquisite face on his mind. He was sure only her astonishment would give him time to do so, and that in the next moment she would turn away bashfully.

But it turned out quite differently.

After Undine had gazed at him for a long time, she came nearer. She knelt down before him and said, playing with a gold ornament which he wore around his neck on a rich chain, "Oh, you kind, you beautiful, guest. Have you finally come to our poor hut? How many years did you roam the earth till you found your way to us? Did you come through the wild woods, my handsome friend?"

He had no time for an answer. The old woman started to scold, and told Undine sharply to get up and do her work. But Undine, without answering, drew a little footstool near to Hugo's chair. She sat down there with her needlework and said cheerfully, "I will work here."

The old man did what parents of spoiled children sometimes do: he pretended not to notice Undine's bad manners and started to talk about something else.

But Undine would not let him talk. She said, "I asked where our lovely guest came from, and he has not answered me yet."

"I came from the forest, you pretty little elf," Hugo replied with a smile.

"Then you must tell me how you got there, for most people are afraid of it. Did you have strange adventures? Something queer always happens in the haunted woods."

The knight shuddered at the remembrance and involuntarily glanced at the window. He felt as if one of the bewildering specters he had met in the wood might be grinning at him, but he saw nothing except the deep, dark night. He pulled himself together and was going to tell his story, when the old man interrupted him, "Don't, Sir Knight! This is no time for such tales."

Passionately Undine jumped up from her footstool. Her arms akimbo, she stood before the old man.

"He shall not tell his story, Father? He must not? But I want to hear it! He must, he must indeed!"

She stamped her little foot, but all was done so prettily and playfully that Hugo could not take his eyes from her in her anger. She seemed even more bewitching than before when she had been friendly.

But the long-suppressed anger in the old man broke out now in full force. Fiercely he scolded her for her disobedience and ill-bred behavior to the stranger. His good wife joined in his reproaches, but Undine only scowled at them. Then the girl said, "If you want to scold me and won't do what I want, you can sleep alone in your smoky old hut!"

And like an arrow she shot through the door and ran out into the dark night.

Hugo and the fisherman leaped up from their seats. But before they had even reached the door, Undine had disappeared in the misty darkness. No sound of her light feet betrayed the direction she had taken. Hugo almost felt the whole fair vision had been only a continuation of the strange apparitions which had vexed him in the forest. But the old man murmured angrily, "That's not the first time she's done that! It means another sleepless night for me, for where could we go to seek her?"

"At least let us call her and beg her to come back," said Hugo. He started to call anxiously, "Undine! Oh, Undine! Do come back!"

The fisherman shook his head. "You don't know how wilful the child is. It's no use!" But he, too, called into the darkness, "Undine, Undine! I beg of you! Come back!" But no trace of Undine could be seen or heard.

Finally they returned to the hut, where they found the fire on the hearth almost burned out; the good wife had already gone to bed. The fisherman laid dry wood on the embers.

"You, too, are anxious about that silly girl, Sir Knight," he said, while he fetched a flagon of wine. "Let's sit and talk awhile. We wouldn't sleep anyhow."

Hugo agreed, so they sat and drank and talked. But whenever there was the least sound outside, they would look up and say, "There she is now!" They would be perfectly still for a moment, but Undine never came.

They could not think of much beside Undine, and soon the knight asked how the girl had come to live there. This is what the old man told his guest:

"More than fifteen years have passed since one beautiful day when I was on my way to the city to sell my fish. My wife stayed at home as usual, for God had blessed us with a lovely babe. Nothing extraordinary befell me on my way through the haunted woods, but at home I found my wife in desperation.

" 'Oh, dear God,' I asked anxiously, 'where is our little girl?'

" 'Gone, dear husband,' was all she could say for weeping. Later on I learned what had happened. My wife had been sitting on the shore with the child, playing with it. Suddenly the baby leaned over, smiling, as if she saw something most beautiful in the water. Then, with a sudden movement, she darted out of her mother's arms and down into the smooth water. I searched and searched for the poor little corpse, but in vain. No trace of her was ever found.

"That same evening we were sitting silently in our cottage, too desolate to speak. Suddenly there was a noise at the door. It sprang open, and a beautiful child of three or four years stood there, smiling at us. We were struck dumb with surprise. We could hardly believe she was real. But then we saw that her golden hair and her rich clothes were dripping wet. We undressed her and put her to bed. She never said a word but kept smiling at us with her large sea-blue eyes.

"Next morning we asked her who her parents were and what had brought her to our shore. But she gave only strange, bewildering answers, and we never found out where she came from. Every now and then she will talk of the most extraordinary things; you might think she must have lived on the moon. She will speak of golden castles, of crystal roofs, and what not.

"We had her baptized to ward off all evil spirits, and wanted to name her Dorothea, for I once heard that meant God's gift. But she would not hear of that name. Her parents had called her Undine, she said, and Undine she still was. I talked it over with the priest who came through the dark forest to christen her, and at first he objected to her name. But his heart warmed toward her when he saw how gay and charming she was. She begged and coaxed so sweetly that he forgot all his good reasons against the heathenish name. She was baptized Undine and behaved well and gently during the sacred rite, although usually she is wild and unruly. My wife was right, we have indeed our troubles with her. If I were to tell you . . ."

The knight interrupted the fisherman. "Listen to that noise! I've heard it for some time. Is that water, that furious roaring?"

They both ran to the door.

By the light of the newly risen moon they saw that the brook had broken wildly over its banks. Branches and stones whirled in the eddying waters. A heavy rainstorm had broken loose, the lake howled under the lashing of the wind, the trees groaned and bowed deep over the whirling water.

"Undine! For God's sake, Undine!" the cried.

But no answer came back to them. They rushed into the storm, calling her in frantic anxiety.

The longer Hugo searched and wandered in the shadows of the stormy night, the more bewildered he became. The thought that Undine might be a wood sprite returned to him with double force. Was everything just a mocking delusion, the hut, the fisherman, the whole peaceful point of land? Real enough were the howling storm, the crashing trees, the roaring waters. Yet, in the distance, he still heard the fisherman's voice calling anxiously, "Undine!"

Hugo came to the banks of the torrent at the edge of the haunted woods. In the moonlight he saw that the water had made an island of the fisherman's peninsula.

"Dear God," he thought, "maybe Undine strayed into the wild forest and is unable to get back. I must cross the stream and rescue her."

All the fearful apparitions he had met in the forest during the day came back to him. With special clarity he recalled the image of a tall, ghostly, white man, who now seemed to be grinning at him from the opposite bank, nodding his head. The thought of the specters urged him on. Was Undine there, weeping with fear among the threatening apparitions? Was she lying alone in the shadow of death?

"Undine," he groaned, "beloved child," while he frantically tried to cross the eddying river in the deceptive moonlight. He could scarcely hold his own in the rushing flood, but he stepped boldly forward. Suddenly he heard her sweet voice: "Trust him not, trust not! The old fellow is tricky—the stream."

The moon was just disappearing behind clouds. He stood in the deepening shadows, dizzy from the rolling waters, and he cried out, "Where are you, beloved? Are you a

will-o'-the-wisp dancing around me? I do not wish to live if you are gone!"

"Look around, then, look around, fair youth," he heard just behind him. By the returning light of the moon he saw Undine on a small island. Protected by sturdy interlaced branches, she was nestling in the grass, all smiles and loveliness. A few strides brought him to her side. Undine drew him down beside her in the soft grass.

"Have you come, my own friend? Now you shall tell me your story," she whispered softly. "Those cross old folks can't hear us now. Isn't this better than their smoky old hut?"

"It is heaven!" he cried, and he pressed the lovely creature to his heart and kissed her.

Meantime the old fisherman had reached the stream.

"There you are, Sir Knight, making love to my daughter!" he shouted angrily. "And I have been seeking her all night, alone and terrified."

"I just found her, old Father," cried the knight in reply.

"Well, I'm glad of that," answered the old man. "Now bring her back to me at once."

But Undine would not hear of it. "I won't come," she pouted. "I'd rather go right into the wild forest with this handsome stranger than return to the hut. I never have my own way there." She clung to Hugo's neck, her fathomless eyes shining strangely.

"Come back, Undine, come back to me!" the old man called in a pleading voice. But Undine was not moved by his sorrow. She embraced and kissed the knight, till he drew back. "Undine, the poor old man's grief goes to my heart. Does it not touch you? Let us go back to him."

Astonished, she raised her deep blue eyes to him. "If you think we must, all right!" she answered reluctantly. "I'll do whatever pleases you. But he must first promise to let you tell your story."

"Come, child! Oh, come back!" cried the fisherman. Determinedly Hugo took the wilful girl in his arms and carried her through the foaming flood. The old man, happy to have her back, embraced and petted Undine. His good wife came and kissed her tenderly. In the joy of their hearts they did not reproach her, and Undine overwhelmed her foster parents with caresses and kind words. All her defiance seemed to have been left behind.

The storm had worn itself out. Dawn began to glimmer over the lake, the little birds sang merrily. Undine insisted the knight should keep his promise right away, and the old folks indulged her cheerfully. Breakfast was set out under the trees before the cottage, and they all sat down to it with glad hearts. Undine sat down in the grass at the knight's feet, and he began his tale.

"About eight days ago I rode into the imperial city beyond the forest. A grand tournament was being held, and I spared neither lance nor steed. At one time when I was standing quietly at the lists during a pause in the noble game, my eye fell upon a most beautiful maiden on a balcony, who was looking at me steadily. I asked who she was and learned she was Bertha, adopted daughter of one of the great dukes in these parts. I had not been slack before, but, now that her eyes were upon me, I put all my heart into the game. That evening I was Bertha's partner at the ball, and we were together every evening during the tournament."

A sharp pain in his left hand made the knight stop in

his tale. He looked at his hand and saw that Undine's pearly teeth had bitten his finger sharply. She was giving him black and spiteful looks, but the next moment her angry eyes were tender and soft. She whispered softly, "It's your own fault!" then hid her face, and the knight went on with his tale, astonished and a little embarrassed.

"Bertha was a proud, strange maid. I stayed with her, and though she charmed me less in the following days, she was more gracious to me than to any other knight. One day I asked in jest for one of her gloves.

" 'You shall have it,' she said, 'if you will ride through the haunted forest alone and tell me your adventures.'

"I did not care much about having her glove, but as an honorable knight I could not back out of the adventure."

"I thought she loved you!" interrupted Undine.

"It looked like it," smiled the knight.

"She must be a fool to send away the man she loves," cried Undine, and laughed. "And into danger, too!"

"Yesterday morning I set out on my adventure," continued Hugo, and smiled at Undine. "The forest was so bright and lovely in the morning sun that I laughed at all those who could imagine evil in such a lovely place. I rode on and soon was deep in the wood. Then it occurred to me that there was a real danger. One could easily lose one's way in the pathless forest. I halted and looked up at the sun, and saw something black in the oak tree above me. I took it for a bear and drew my sword, but the hoary beast said in a coarse, human voice, 'I'm breaking off twigs up here to roast you with, Sir Simpleton!' He cackled and sniggered and gnashed his teeth. My terrified horse ran away with me before I could make out what kind of a devil he was."

"You should not mention that name," said the fisherman, and crossed himself.

"Go on," said Undine impatiently.

"I could not stop my horse. Wet with fright and heat, he rushed on madly, almost dashing me against the trees. Finally he stormed toward the brink of a rocky pit, and I thought my life was lost. But a tall white man threw himself in front of the maddened horse. It reared up high and stopped, trembling. I gained control of it again, and only then did I realize my savior was not a tall white man but a bright, silvery brook gushing down from the hillside."

"Thanks, dear brook!" cried Undine, and clapped her hands. But the old man shook his head wearily.

"Scarcely had I got firm hold of my reins again," continued the knight, "when a hideous dwarf sprang up beside me. He was ugly beyond compare, brownish-yellow, and his nose almost as big as his whole body. He grinned at me idiotically, bowing and scraping. 'Make way!' I cried impatiently, 'The horse is unruly and may run you over!'

" 'First give me some gold for saving your neck!' snarled the imp, grimacing. 'But for me, you and your pretty little horse would be lying in the pit. Whew!'

" 'That's a lie,' said I hotly, throwing a gold coin into his cap. 'It was the honest brook that saved me, not you, you spiteful little thing.'

"I trotted on, but the goblin sprang round like lightning and stood in front of my horse again. I pulled my still trembling horse another way; he was running at my side, screaming and laughing. I galloped; but he kept pace with me, jumping and shrieking, 'Bad coin! Bad gold! Bad gold! Bad coin!'

"I finally stopped. 'What do you want? Take another coin, take two. But let me alone!'

" 'Not gold, it's not gold that I want of you, my pretty little sir!' he grinned. 'I have more than enough. Wait, I'll show you!'

"Suddenly the ground became transparent. It looked like a smooth globe of green glass, and within I saw a crowd of goblins, playing with gold and silver. They pelted each other with the precious metal, rolling and tumbling, powdering their faces with gold dust. My ugly companion stood half above, half below the surface. Gold and more gold was reached up to him by the others, and he flung it back into the fathomless depths. He showed them the gold coins I had given him. They shrieked with laughter and hissed at me in scorn; pointing at me with their gold-stained fingers. Wilder and wilder, louder and louder, grew the turmoil as the crowd climbed up to me, till not only my horse but I, too, was terrified. I put my spurs to my steed, and in a mad gallop I raced through the woodlands.

"When at last I halted, it was evening. I thought I saw a white footpath and rode in its direction. But a dim, dead-white face peered at me through the leaves. Wherever I went, there it was. Angry, I pushed my horse against it. White foam splashed all over us, and we turned, blinded for the moment. Glancing around, I saw an indistinct head set on a gigantic body, equally white. The head nodded and nodded when I rode straight ahead, but water was dashed over me when I tried to turn. Thus it drove us on, farther and farther in one direction. Wearily I rode on till I reached your point of land and saw the cottage. And here the white man vanished."

"Thank heaven, he's gone!" said the fisherman. "Now, the best way back to town . . ."

Undine giggled softly, and the knight said, "I thought you wanted me to stay. Are you pleased now to see me go?"

"You cannot get away!" laughed the girl. "Try and cross the swollen river and you will be dashed to pieces! And Father can't take you across such a large lake in his little boat."

They went to see if it were true. And, indeed, they were, truly isolated, on an island! The knight would have to stay until the flood subsided. As they returned to the hut, he whispered into Undine's ear, "Well, what about it, little Undine? Are you angry because I have to remain here?"

"Never mind," she replied sulkily. "Heaven knows how much you would have raved about Bertha if I had not bitten you."

The days went by. The forest stream seemed to become wider and broader, but Hugo did not mind. For him the whole world was contained within this flowering little island. He felt as if never again he would cross its charmed borders, never again join his fellow men. He was content to stay because of Undine; Undine filled his heart!

The old folks were pleased to have him. There was plenty of food; they had fish and crab and some fowl besides their staple provisions. At length, however, their pleasure was disturbed. Every evening the two men were accustomed to sitting cheerfully with a bottle of wine, and now they had exhausted the fisherman's meager stock. Undine laughed at their long faces, but they did not think it very funny. Scolding them for their bad humor, Undine left the hut one evening but she was back quickly.

"The water has washed a barrel ashore. I bet it's a barrel of wine!" she announced merrily. The men followed her, and she led them to the barrel. They rolled it toward the hut as fast as they could, for another storm was brewing. The heavy clouds threatened to break, and a few drops fell. Undine looked up. Playfully she threatened the big clouds. "You, up there! Don't you dare to drench us! We are still some way from home."

The fisherman scolded her for such sinful presumption, but she only giggled, and they reached the hut, unharmed. Then the rain broke forth in torrents, and the storm roared wildly, but they did not mind. Soon they were comfortably seated at the fire, enjoying the excellent wine. The old man suddenly paused to exclaim, "Dear God! Here we are enjoying Thy goodly gift unmindful of its owner who perhaps has lost his life."

"Oh, never mind him," laughed Undine, and filled the knight's glass. But Hugo replied, "If I knew how to find him, good father, I would not hesitate to go out into the storm. No fear of danger would hold me back, on my word of honor!" He continued, "If I ever get back to the world beyond the wood, I'll search for him or his heirs and pay them double its price."

That pleased the old man, but Undine said half angrily, "You may do with your money as you please. But what a stupid idea to run out and search for him. I would cry my heart out if you got lost! Isn't it much nicer to stay here with me and this good wine?"

"Why, indeed it is," laughed Hugo.

"Well, then don't talk so foolishly. Everyone has to take care of himself. What do other people matter?"

The housewife looked at her sadly and sighed. But the fisherman forgot how fond he was of the pretty girl and reproved her sharply. "One would think you had been brought up by heathens!" he finished angrily. "God forgive you and me for it, you heartless child!"

"But that's what *I* really think," Undine pouted. "All your fine words won't change that."

"Be silent!" the old man cried sternly. Undine was frightened. She clung trembling to Hugo and whispered, "Are you angry, too, my fair friend?"

The knight pressed her soft hand and stroked her curls. He was unable to make any reply, but, although he was distressed and blamed it on the old man's harshness toward Undine, in his heart, he felt the old man was right. So the two couples sat there in a moody silence, angry with each other.

A gentle tap at the door broke the silence. They started up in terror. No human being could have crossed the wild waters. The knight grasped his sword, but the fisherman said quietly, "If it is what I fear, no sword can help us."

Undine ran to the door and said, boldly and crossly, "If you are up to mischief, you earth spirits, then Cooleborn shall teach you manners!"

The terrors of the others increased at these strange words, and they looked at the girl with dread. But somebody answered from the outside, "I am not a spirit of the earth. If you fear God and if you want to help me in my distress, let me in!"

Undine opened the door, and they saw an old priest. He started back at the radiant beauty of Undine. Suspecting magic and witchery here in the howling wilderness, he crossed himself and began a canticle: "All good spirits give praise to the Lord!"

"I am no ghost, reverend Father," Undine said, smiling. "Do I look so frightful? I worship God, too, and I praise him in my own way. See, your canticle did not frighten me. Come in, Father, you'll find good people here."

The priest entered. He was dripping wet. They led him into the bedroom and gave him dry clothes; then seated him in the most comfortable chair at the hearth and brought him food and wine. Undine waited on him very gracefully, then sat down at his feet on her little stool. Hugo teased her in a playful whisper about her good behavior, but she answered gravely, "He serves Him who made us all. That is too serious for a joke."

When the priest had recovered he told them that he had been on his way to the city to report the ravages of the flood. His boat had capsized in the storm, and he had not seen his two boatmen again, but he himself had been carried by the waters, unharmed, to their island.

"Island, indeed!" cried the fisherman. "It was a point of land till the flood came. But now we are quite cut off from the outside world."

"God forbid!" The good wife shuddered and crossed herself. The old man smiled at her. "That should make no difference to you! How many years is it since you saw the city? And we five would be able to live here all right."

"Then you would stay; you would have to stay with us," whispered Undine, half singing, and pressed closer to Hugo. But he was lost in deep strange thoughts.

The land beyond the wild waters seemed to recede farther and farther; dimmer and darker it appeared to his fancy. But the flowering island grew fairer and greener. And Undine was its sweetest rose, fairest flower of the whole wide world, indeed! Here was the priest to unite them. Why hesitate?

He turned to the priest.

"You see before you a betrothed pair, reverend sir," he started gravely. "If this girl and these kind old fisherfolk will consent, you shall wed us this very evening."

Now and again the old people had thought of this possibility, but they never had put it in words. Now it seemed strange to them and quite preposterous. Undine sat very still, her face grave and thoughtful. The priest inquired about the circumstances and asked the old couple's consent, which they gave after some deliberation. The housewife went to prepare the bridal chamber and to fetch forth two consecrated tapers for the wedding. The knight pulled two rings off his gold chain for them to exchange in the ceremony.

The priest lighted the holy tapers, placed them on the table, and called the young pair to him. With few but solemn words he joined their hands. The old couple blessed the young ones; and the bride leaned trembling against her husband, lost in thought.

But as soon as all was over, Undine's wild spirits rose again. She played all kinds of childish tricks on her husband, her parents, and even the venerable priest. No hint of displeasure or reproof would stop her. Her new husband was far from being pleased by her childish behavior. He gravely called her his "wife," and then she would be subdued for a moment and whisper in his ear to make him smile. But then some wild nonsense would dart through her head, and all would be worse than before.

At last the priest said kindly but very earnestly to her, "My sweet young lady, no one who beholds you can be severe with you, it is true. But remember, from now on it is your duty to keep your soul forever in harmony with that of your wedded husband."

"Soul!" cried Undine and laughed. "That sounds fine, and your advice may be excellent for other people. But if one has no soul at all, pray, what is to be done then? And that is the case with me."

The priest was deeply hurt and turned away from her in sorrow and anger. But she said beseechingly, "Don't look so cross. It hurts me, and you must not hurt a creature who has done no harm. Have patience with me, and I will tell you everything."

Suddenly she stopped as though some inward horror had stricken her, and burst into a flood of tears. They did not know what to make of this and looked at her in alarm. She dried her tears and said earnestly to the holy man, "To have a soul must be marvelous, but most fearful too. In God's name, Holy Father, tell me, would it not be better to have nothing to do with it?"

Breathlessly she waited for an answer, and her expression was one of vivid and strange curiosity. It made the others recoil from her in terror, but she had eyes only for the priest. "Heavy must be the burden of a soul," she continued as no one answered. "Heavy, indeed! The mere approach of mine overcomes me with sorrow and fear. And, oh! I was so joyous, so lighthearted!" She burst into tears again and covered her face with her hands.

The priest stepped nearer. He adjured her to confess the truth, to tell if any evil lurked in her and to throw off her lovely disguise. She fell on her knees, repeating his prayers. She praised God, thanking Him that she was at peace with all the world.

Finally the priest turned to Hugo.

"Sir Knight," he said gravely, "I leave you alone with her whom I made your wife. As far as I can see, there is no evil in her, although there is much that is mysterious. Be kind to her, and loving, and faithful."

He went out, and the fisherfolk followed, crossing themselves.

Undine was still on her knees. Looking shyly at Hugo, she said sadly, "Ah, now you will cast me off! And I have done no wrong, poor wretched child that I am." She looked so gentle and so touching that her husband forgot the terror that had chilled his heart. He drew her into his arms and kissed her. She smiled through tears. "You cannot forsake me," she whispered and caressed his face.

Had he married a fairy, an elf? Resolutely he shook off all his gloomy forebodings. But he could not prevent one question slipping out. "Dear child, tell me just one thing," he asked. "What did you say about Cooleborn and earth spirits when the priest knocked at the door?"

"Fairy tales! Children's fairy tales!" said Undine, and laughed with her usual gaiety. "First I frighten you with them, and then you frighten me. That's the end of the song and of my wedding."

"Oh no! That's not the end!" said the infatuated knight. He blew out the candles and led his lovely bride to their bridal chamber.

Next morning the old couple and the priest were sitting uneasily in the kitchen. But their expressions brightened when, beaming with happiness, the young couple appeared for breakfast. They looked at Undine with astonishment. She was the same, yet so different. Tenderly she kissed her foster parents, thanking them for all they had done for her. Humbly she greeted the priest and asked his blessings. Then she went to the hearth to prepare the meal and would not allow the good wife to trouble herself. She was like that all day, quiet, sweet, and attentive. They waited in vain for a return of her childish pranks and wilful ways. The priest said more than once to the bridegroom, "God has bestowed a great treasure upon you. Cherish and love her always."

In the evening Undine asked her husband to go with her to the little island. He was astonished to see the wild torrent had changed back into a gentle brook.

"Tomorrow the waters will have subsided," said Undine in a trembling voice, "and you can go wherever you wish."

"Not without you, my little Undine," answered the knight and laughed. "Remember, if I forsook you, Church and State would step in to bring your truant back to you."

"It all depends on you," murmured Undine, half anxiously. "You will not cast me off, beloved? My heart is bound to yours forever!"

She drew him to her side in the soft grass, but then she said, "Sit down here, where I can see your face. Then I can read my fate in your eyes before you have spoken. Now I will tell you all." And she began her strange tale.

"You must know, my own love, that beings exist in the elements who hardly differ from mankind. It is very seldom that they appear and let themselves be seen. In the flames glitter and sparkle the wondrous salamanders. In the depths of the earth dwell the spiteful race of gnomes. The woods are inhabited by nymphs who are also the spirits of the air. And in lakes, streams, rivers, and brooks live the numberless water sprites. They live in sparkling crystal halls, and sun and moon cast their shimmering light upon them. In their gardens grow beautiful flowers and lofty coral trees. Silver-bright is the sand, multicolored are the pearly shells. Fair and lovely is their world beneath the silver mantle of the deep! There they dwell, the water sprites, fairer and gentler than mankind. Sometimes a fisherman catches a glimpse of a mermaid, riding the waves and singing. Men called them Undines and spread the tale of their wondrous beauty all over the world.

"You see before you, my beloved, an Undine!"

The knight tried to persuade himself his lovely wife was in one of her silly moods and was teasing him. But a strange foreboding chilled his heart. He could not utter a word, but stared at her in awe and wonder. Undine sighed sadly, then she went on.

"We would be much happier than you mortals but for one great drawback. We, and the other children of the elements, vanish; we disappear when we die. Not a trace remains of us. When you, one day, arise from death to eternal life, we will be gone like the fire, the waves, the winds of yesterday. We have no souls. We live our merry lives, as carefree as the birds and fishes and all children of Nature.

"But no creature is content with its place. My father is a mighty prince of the Mediterranean Sea, and he was determined that his only child should win a soul, even if it must be at the cost of much suffering. For suffering is forever the lot of a soul, as we well know. We can acquire a soul, but only if we are united to one of you by the strongest ties of love.

"Now I have a soul, and I owe my soul to you. Do not forsake me, oh, my beloved! I could not deceive you, now that I have a soul and a conscience. But I beg of you: do not let me spend my human life in wretchedness.

"If you shrink from me, if you are repulsed by me, say it now! I will plunge into the water, and my Uncle Cooleborn will take me home to my parents in the deep sea, a loving, a suffering, forsaken woman."

Hugo pressed her to his heart. With tears and kisses he swore he would never leave her. He declared himself the happiest man in the world to have won her, and they returned to the hut completely happy.

When Hugo awoke next morning, he was alone. And again he feared that all he had experienced had been just a dream. But soon Undine entered the room, kissed him, and said, "I was out early to see if my uncle had kept his word. He has recalled all the waters and is flowing through the woods as quietly as always. All his friends in the lake and in the air have gone to rest. All is at peace around us, and you can ride home as soon as you please."

Hugo felt he was dreaming with his eyes open, but he did not show his astonishment about his strange in-laws. Later on as the two stood in the door of the hut in the sunshine Hugo said, "Let us stay here a few days more. Never again will we be as peaceful as here."

"As my lord wishes," replied Undine. "But, you see, now my foster parents think my gentleness is just a whim like a calm on the lake when the winds are quiet. If I leave them, now, they will soon love some flowers or trees instead of me. If they learned that I have a soul, that I feel love and affection for them, now at the time I am leaving them, would it not break their hearts? And how could I hide my love from them?"

Hugo agreed with her. After an affectionate farewell from the fisherfolk they started out on their journey. The priest accompanied them, and it was a pretty picture as they passed through the sun-dappled green of the wood. Undine sat gracefully on the noble steed, guarded on one side by the venerable priest in the white habit of his order, on the other by the youthful knight with his gorgeous attire and splendid sword.

The young couple had eyes only for each other and paid no attention to their surroundings till a low murmur caught Hugo's ear. Astonished, he saw the priest in eager conversation with a tall man, a stranger dressed in a white robe, his hood almost covering his face. His overlong garment flowed around him in vast folds, and he constantly had to gather it up, throw it over his arms, or rearrange it; yet it did not seem to hinder him in walking. The priest interrupted himself to ask the stranger's name.

"My name is Cooleborn," the odd man replied readily. "And I might well call myself Lord Cooleborn since I am the Lord of the Forest, free as the birds in the woods, and a little freer. By the way, I have something to say to that young lady."

He was suddenly at the other side of the priest, close to Undine. He stretched up to whisper in her ear.

Frightened, Undine turned away. "I want nothing more to do with you," she said coldly.

"Ho, Ho!" laughed the stranger. "What a grand marriage you must have made to cast off your relations so readily. Have you forgotten Uncle Cooleborn who, long ago, carried you all the way here on his back?"

"I beseech you never to come to me again," pleaded Undine. "Now I am scared of you, and my dear husband might become estranged when he realizes I have such odd relations."

"My little niece," replied Cooleborn, "please, remember that I'm here to protect you from the wicked earth spirits. Otherwise they might play some nasty tricks on you, my child. Let me go on with you through the woods." Undine was silent, and Cooleborn continued, "The old priest has a better memory than you have. He just told me I was so familiar to him, he must have seen me before. It's true, for I was the wave which capsized his boat, and I myself washed him safely ashore in time for your wedding."

Hugo and Undine looked at the priest, but he seemed to be walking in a dream and did not listen to them.

Soon Undine said to Cooleborn, "I can see the end of the wood. We want no more of your help; there is nothing that can frighten us more than you do. I entreat you, be-gone, and let us go in peace!"

This angered Cooleborn. He made a hideous face and hissed at Undine, and she cried out for help. Quick as a flash the knight was on the other side of the horse, swing-ing his sharp sword against Cooleborn's head. But, instead of the head, he struck a waterfall which suddenly gushed down a cliff at their side. The splashing sounded almost like laughter as they were all drenched to the skin.

The priest, as if suddenly awakened, said, "I was ex-pecting that, the brook runs so close to us on the hillside. At first, it almost seemed to be a man speaking to me."

The waterfall whispered distinctly in Hugo's ear:

Rash young knight,
Dashing knight,
I scold thee not,
I chide thee not.
Quick thy sword thou hast to wield
When thine precious wife thou'lt shield.
Rash knight,
Dashing knight!

A few more steps, and they were in the open. The city lay glittering before them. The evening sun, gilding the roofs, quickly dried the soaked garments of the wanderers.

The sudden disappearance of the young knight had made a great stir in the city, for he had been very popular. His retainers would not leave the place without their master, but none had the courage to seek him in the haunted woods. They stayed at their inn, hoping for his return. When, soon after his disappearance, the flood raged, nobody doubted that Lord Ringstetten was lost forever, and many grieved for him. Bertha was especially disconsolate, reproaching herself that she had dared him to ride into the haunted woods.

When now Hugo returned so suddenly, everybody rejoiced but Bertha. Everyone else was well pleased that he had brought home such an exquisite bride, but Bertha, naturally, was greatly embarrassed to see him come home a married man. She had really fallen in love with the handsome knight and she had not hidden her feelings. People knew a great deal more about her feelings than she now wished, and her pride was hurt. The whole town adored Undine. People assumed she was a princess, released by Hugo from a wicked magician in the enchanted wood.

Bertha behaved like a clever woman and was as kind as possible to Hugo's lovely bride, so that Undine grew daily more fond of fair Bertha.

"We must have known each other before," she often said to her, "or else some strange secret bond must exist between us. For I have loved you from the very moment I met you."

Bertha too could not deny that she felt true affection for Undine, although she had strong reasons to dislike her victorious rival. Their friendship became so great that they did not want to be separated. Undine even wished Bertha to accompany the young couple to Ringstetten Castle.

They were discussing this one pleasant evening as the three of them were strolling round the market place. The deep-blue night sky shone with stars, the magnificent fountain in the center of the square murmured peacefully, the glimmering lights of the surrounding houses gleamed through the leaves of the linden trees. A quiet noise of children at play and of other happy human beings hummed around them. They were so pleasantly alone, yet so near the very heart of the cheerful and living world. All was serene and at peace. It seemed a natural decision that Bertha should travel with them.

They were just fixing the day of their departure when a tall man came toward them from the middle of the square. He bowed respectfully to them and murmured something to Undine. She seemed displeased with the interruption, but stepped aside with him. They whispered to one another in what appeared to be a foreign language.

Hugo thought he recognized the tall man and stared at him, scowling. All at once Undine joyfully clapped her hands and left the stranger standing there. He shook his head and walked away hastily and angrily, and stepped into the fountain. Hugo was convinced he was right in his guess as to the man's identity, but Bertha asked curiously, "Was that the master of the waterworks? What did he want of you?"

Undine smiled mysteriously. "On your birthday, day after tomorrow, I'll tell you, sweet friend," she replied gaily. And she would say no more.

"Cooleborn?" asked Hugo with a secret shudder, as they walked home alone through the darkening streets.

"Yes, it was he," answered Undine. "He tried to tell me all sorts of nonsense. But against his will he delighted me with a lovely piece of news. If you wish to hear it now, my dear husband, I'll tell you every word. But if you wish to give your Undine very, very great pleasure, you'll wait two days and be surprised too."

She looked so sweet in her eagerness that the knight readily granted her wish. Even as Undine fell asleep, she murmured, "How delighted she'll be, dear, dear Bertha."

The guests were seated at table. Bertha, adorned with jewels and flowers like a goddess of spring, sat at the head. Undine and Hugo were at her side. When the rich meal was ended and the desserts served, the doors were opened after the old German custom, to let the common folks see and share the gaiety of the rich. Servants offered wine and cake to the spectators.

Bertha and Hugo were impatiently waiting for Undine's promised announcement. But she remained silent, smiling

happily to herself, anticipating the joy she would be able
to bestow on her friend. Some of the guests asked Undine
for a song. She was pleased and sent for her lute and sang
the following words:

> Morning so bright,
> Flowers so sweet,
> Fragrant and tall
> Is the grass at our feet.
>
> What shimmers so white,
> So wondrous and gay?
> Hath a blossom burst forth
> To greet the new day?
>
> A lovely, fair child!
> Oh tell us who brought thee?
> From unknown shores
> The lake hath borne thee.
>
> Mute and elusive
> Strangers they are.
> The flowers can't tend thee,
> And thy mother is far.
>
> Thy smile's fresh from heaven
> But bereavèd thou art,
> Thy life's just beginning:
> But thy mother is far!

More quickly she struck the chords as she went on:

> See! A gallant duke comes riding,
> Pities thee and takes thee home,
> Tends thee in his noble castle,
> Lucky child! Thou'rt not alone.

Thou hast gained love and pleasure,
The fairest art thou in the land.
Yet alas! The greatest treasure
Is left upon a distant strand.

Undine put down her lute with a melancholy smile. The eyes of the duke and the duchess were filled with tears.

"So it was when I found you, poor sweet orphan," said Bertha's foster father, deeply moved. "The fair singer is right; we have never been able to make up for your loss."

"Now you must hear of the poor parents," said Undine. She struck the chords and sang:

Mother searches all the rooms,
Restless walks she in and out,
But her tearful eyes behold
Nothing but an empty house.

Empty house! Oh, words of sorrow
For a mother's loving heart.
The sun returns when night is over,
But thy child from thee departed.

When the evening descendeth
Father seeks his fireside,
Tries to smile. But 't is in vain,
Scarcely he his tears can hide.

Father knows that in his home
Never childish laughter peals,
Deathlike stillness reigns alone.
Grief is all that mother feels.

"Oh, Undine! For God's sake, where are my parents?" cried Bertha, weeping. "Surely, you have discovered them, you wonderful woman. Otherwise you would not tear my heart like this. Perhaps they are even here? Can it be . . . ?" Her eyes glanced over the splendid company and rested on a royal princess who sat next to the duke.

But Undine bent forward to the door. Her eyes brimmed over with happy tears as she waved her hand to the crowd of spectators.

With faltering steps, the old fisherman and his wife stepped forward. They looked at Undine. Shyly they glanced at the lovely lady who, as they had been told, was their long-lost daughter.

"It is she!" cried the delighted Undine. The old couple rushed forward. Hugging their child, they wept aloud and praised God.

Enraged and frightened, Bertha freed herself. This was more than her proud spirit could endure, especially since she had expected an increase in splendor. A horrid suspicion flashed through her mind. Had her rival contrived this on purpose to humiliate her before Hugo and all the world? She hissed, "Treacherous creature!" to Undine, and "Bribed wretches!" to the old couple, and reviled them with ugly words.

The old woman whispered desperately, "Oh, God! She has grown up a wicked woman, yet my heart tells me she is my child!" The fisherman prayed quietly this girl might prove not to be their daughter.

Deathly pale, Undine looked from the parents to Bertha, from Bertha to the parents. She did not understand these people. Out of the heaven of her dreams she had suddenly been flung into a terror such as she had never before known.

"Have you a soul, then? Have you really a soul, Bertha?"

she exclaimed in agony. Surely her dear friend was caught in a kind of a nightmare and had only to be awakened. Had not everyone told her that mother love was the highest treasure of mankind? Why, oh why, this disaster?

But Bertha only stormed more violently. The poor old people lamented piteously, and the assembled company started to take sides, disputing angrily.

Undine stepped forward. With gentle dignity she asked to be listened to in her husband's house. In a moment all was quiet around her, and Undine said:

"You all look at each other with such hostility! I know little of your strange, heartless ways of life, and I think I shall never understand you. I can see I have gone about this affair in the wrong way, but that is not my fault. It is your own doing, believe me! I have little more to say, but this one thing has to be said: I have told no lie. I can give no proof beyond my word, but I will swear to it. I heard the facts from him who stole Bertha from her parents and then laid her down in the meadow in the duke's path."

"She is a sorceress!" shrieked Bertha. "A witch who deals with evil spirits! She says so herself."

"I am no witch," replied Undine, and innocence and guilelessness shone in her face. "Only look at me and see."

"Then she lies! She cannot prove I was born of these base folk." Bertha turned to the ducal pair. "Lead me away, my noble parents, and protect me from this treachery."

But the old duke stayed where he was, and the duchess said, "We must know the truth. God forbid that I leave this room before we know the truth."

The old fisherwife approached the duchess and curtsied deeply. "You give me courage to speak, noble lady. I must tell you that if this wicked maiden is my daughter, then she has a birthmark like a violet between her shoulders. If she would come with me to another room . . ."

"I will not undress before that countrywoman," replied Bertha, proudly turning away.

"But before me, you will," the duchess insisted gravely.

They withdrew, leaving the party in silent suspense. After a few moments they returned. Bertha was as pale as death.

"Right must be right," the duchess said. "Bertha is the fisherman's daughter, and our noble hostess spoke the truth."

The ducal pair departed with their stunned foster daughter. Upon a sign from the duke the fisherman and his wife followed them. Murmuring among themselves or in silent embarrassment, the guests took their leave.

Undine sank into Hugo's arms, weeping bitterly.

The Lord of Ringstetten was quite displeased with the unexpected turn of events. Yet he was touched by the guileless simplicity of his lovely bride. "She told me I gave her a soul," he thought. "But I must admit her new soul is much purer than mine ever was." Tenderly he consoled the sobbing Undine, determined to take her home the next day.

At daybreak the carriage was waiting for Undine at their hostelry. The steeds of the knight and his squires were pawing the ground. As Hugo was leading his fair bride to the carriage, a fishergirl stepped up to them.

"We want no fish," said Hugo. "We are just going away."

The girl started to sob, and only then did they recognize her as Bertha. She told them that the duke had been so angered by her rudeness that he had cast her off. She had been given a handsome dowry, though, and the fisherman too received a generous gift. He and his wife had returned to their home.

"On departing my father, if that is what he is, said to me, 'You shall not live with us till you have proven that you really wish to. Take courage and come across the haunted wood to us. But come as a fisherman's daughter for that's what you are.' I will do as he bids me, but I dread the forest! They say it is full of grim specters, and I'm so afraid! But what else can I do? The whole world has forsaken me!" She burst into bitter tears. Then she went on, "I only came to ask your pardon for my rude behavior, Lady Ringstetten. I know you meant kindly, noble Dame. You did not know what it meant to me, and in my surprise I said such wicked things. Forgive, oh, forgive me! I am so unhappy! Think what I was yesterday and what I am now!"

Undine embraced her affectionately. "You shall go to Ringstetten with us," she said, "and all shall be as it was before. Only call me Undine again, and not 'Lady' and 'noble Dame.' Aren't we sisters though we are not related?" she asked earnestly. "We were exchanged in the cradle, and we share our parents. I always wanted a sister. Now I have my wish, how happy we will be!"

Bertha looked shyly at Hugo. He felt sorry for the poor, forsaken maiden, and held out his hand to her. "Trust yourself to us," he said kindly. "We will send word to your parents to let them know where you are."

He placed the two ladies in the carriage, and gaily they rode through the beautiful countryside.

After a few days' traveling they arrived at Ringstetten Castle. The young lord was occupied with his steward and his retainers, and Undine and Bertha were left much to themselves. They took a walk on the high ramparts of the stronghold, admiring the beautiful Swabian landscape. A tall man approached them, greeting them respectfully. Somehow he reminded Bertha of the ominous fountain man. Undine waved him away, displeased, even threatening. He went away with hasty steps and nodding head.

"Don't be afraid, dear Bertha," Undine said consolingly. "That ugly man cannot harm you here." With that she told Bertha her whole story, from beginning to end. Bertha was alarmed. First she thought Undine had gone out of her mind. But soon she became convinced that this tale was true, for it explained all the strange events of the last months. She was bewildered to be a part of a living fairy tale, and as wild a tale as she ever heard of. She gazed at Undine with awe, but she shuddered. Her feelings for Undine grew cool. That evening at suppertime she wondered how the knight could so love and cherish this strange creature. To her Undine was more like a ghost than a human being.

After his long absence the Lord of Ringstetten found many tasks waiting for him and was busy all day. Neighbors came calling and many claims were made upon his time. Soon the castle bustled with life. Bertha thrived amidst these activities; her eyes flashed, her red mouth smiled. With great ado she moved about, eager to catch Hugo's attention. Her humble role was now quite forgotten. Indeed, soon she was in the foreground, and Undine was slowly being pushed into an inferior position. With Hugo, Bertha made no secret of her aversion to the strange being from the other world, and his heart, too, became estranged from Undine. He was drawn more and more toward Bertha, the child of earth, and Bertha did not bother to disguise her ardent love for him.

Undine went through each day with an absent expression on her pale face. She felt helpless and lost in a world she did not understand. She suffered. Suffering came to her swiftly and terribly as a blow, for she had not learned to suffer as all mortals do from infancy. Her first tears were not for a toy that eluded her groping baby hands, but for the unexplainable cruelties and wrongs in our world. Hugo did not understand her when she sought his protection against evil. How could he? Right and wrong were for him natural events of everyday life. But Undine's pure soul had not learned to compromise. In her bewilderment she clung to the man who had bestowed upon her the bitter sweetness of being human, of having a soul. It made him impatient. Sometimes he tried to be kind, but soon a cold shiver would creep over him, and he would turn away from her.

Poor Undine was very sad, and the other two were not happy either. Their uneasiness was greatly increased by the strange sights and sounds which haunted Hugo and Bertha. Nothing like that had ever happened in Ringstetten before. Restlessness and rumors spread in the castle. Hugo blamed this intrusion of the uncontrolled forces of nature on his connection with a mermaid, and he shrank from Undine. The language of the heart was forgotten.

One day Undine was sitting at the edge of the stone

fountain which stood in the middle of the castle courtyard. She looked down into the dark-green mysterious depths with a puzzled frown. "I did the right thing when I invited Bertha to live with us, didn't I?" she wondered. "Why does it turn out wrong whenever I try to do right?" She sighed and wiped her eyes, careful not to let a tear drop into the quiet water. "Must I sacrifice my own happiness just in order to do right? Is it always so difficult to have a soul? How happy I was without one!" She smiled sadly. "Yet, I have to do more."

She sent for the servants and ordered them to fetch a large stone to stop up the fountain. The men objected, but Undine said mournfully, "It grieves me to add to your burdens, my good friends, but the fountain must be sealed up. Trust me; nothing else will do. It is the only way to avoid great danger."

This was all she had to say. The men, eager to do her a favor, were lifting the huge stone when Bertha ran up.

"Why are you doing that? Stop it immediately!" she called angrily. "Don't you know this water is wonderful for my complexion?" She turned to Undine accusingly. "I won't have it stopped up."

But Undine, instead of yielding as usual, said firmly:

"As mistress of the castle I must do what I consider best." Turning to the men, she said, "Go on with your work."

There was no need to repeat her commands. The servants, glad to please their gentle mistress and to mortify Bertha's pride, hastened to finish their work, and soon the large stone covered the mouth of the well. Undine bent down and with her delicate fingers wrote on its surface. Something very sharp must have been hidden in her hand, for when she walked away the others found strange characters written all over the stone.

When Hugo came home Bertha received him with tearful complaints about Undine's strange lack of consideration for her wishes. But Undine for once stood her ground.

"My lord and master does not judge his meanest vassal without hearing him, much less his wedded wife," she said with gentle dignity. "I'll gladly tell him why I did what I did." She turned to go to her room and Hugo followed her.

"Tell me what it is all about," he asked her, more gently than he had been wont to speak to her recently, and she told him her reason.

"I had to shut the door against my relatives," she said, looking at him with a sad smile. "They want to protect me, they see me weep, they hear Bertha laugh. They notice how your eyes follow Bertha and not me. They cannot know that the joys and griefs of love are so closely linked that tears and laughter live together. A poor, cold life is theirs!" She smiled through her tears into Hugo's face, and her touching beauty overcame his recent reserve. He drew her close and murmured, "My lovely wife," and she went on:

"The well is their only access to us, therefore I stopped it up, and inscribed the stone with characters which cripple their power. Men can remove the stone as easily as ever; my signs have no power over human beings. So you are free to do as Bertha wishes, but she does not know what she asks. The water sprites are very angry with her, and if they had free access here, they might harm her; even you would not be free from danger."

Hugo was touched by a noblemindedness that deprived her of protectors, even when she was reviled by Bertha for doing so. He kissed her fondly and said, "The stone shall remain, and everything shall be done as you want it, my sweetest Undine."

"No harm can come to you now," she said in his arms, "but, Hugo, my dearest heart, Cooleborn is very powerful. Don't scold me, don't make me weep when we are near running water, for there, you see, my relatives have the power to control me. They might think you have insulted one of their race. They would drag me away from you, and I would be doomed to live in their underwater crystal palaces without ever coming back to you again. And if they did send me back, oh, my heart, that would be far worse! If you should break your oath, if you should marry again, then I would have to take your life. Such is our law. Don't forget this, beloved, and spare me, oh, spare me!"

Solemnly he promised to do as she asked of him.

Her purity of heart had recaptured his wavering love. Once more he realized how irrevocably he loved her. Bertha, compared with Undine, seemed coarse and selfish to him. Bertha's world was the world men lived in, day by day, lived their little humdrum lives, one like the other. Bertha's everyday nature was crass compared to Undine's depth of devotion.

Wasn't he the happiest of men to be loved by her? He would make her happy from now on, forever and ever! These were his thoughts, but his foolish heart forgot that grief and guilt are ever present.

For some time after this scene, life was peaceful and quiet in Ringstetten. Bertha sensed how much ground she had lost; she was modest and almost timid. Where could

she go if Undine asked her to leave? Undine bloomed
again in secure possession of her husband's heart; the other
world had no access any more, and peace and security for
all had returned.

Winter went by without any interruptions, and spring
with young green leaves, with blossoms and fragrance, with
white clouds on a deep blue sky began to smile upon the
earth. Their hearts felt light, and, watching the returning
birds of passage, they felt like traveling. Hugo, who had
seen much of the world, enjoyed talking about the glories
of other lands, and soon they were full of plans. A trip
on the Danube particularly appealed to them, and Undine
smilingly joined them. Once Hugo whispered to Undine,
"But might we not get into Cooleborn's power again on
the Danube?"

"Let him come," said she and laughed gaily. "I shall be
with you. He won't dare to attempt any mischief."

The only possible objection to their journey was removed, so they set out, and soon they were sailing along on
the majestic river, full of high spirits and gay humor.

But, contrary to Undine's expectations, the unruly
water sprites began to make their presence felt. At first
they played only sportive tricks, because, whenever they
ruffled the water and raised the wind, Undine repressed
them with a whispered word, making them subside at once.
But soon they would attempt to disturb them once more,
and, again and again, Undine had to subdue them. The
boatsmen they had hired for the trip cast strange looks at
her and muttered to each other, and even their own servants began to be afraid and showed their distrust.

The pleasure of the little party was destroyed.

Hugo said to himself more than once, as he uneasily

watched Undine muttering, waving her hands, wrinkling her brow in her efforts to control the forces of nature who hate control by man, "It is my fault! This is what comes of marrying someone from another world. A son of earth should not marry a wondrous creature of the other world!" Anger welled up in him. "Am I to be fettered and pursued wherever I go by the tricks of my freak relatives?" But he said not a word, thinking of Undine's warnings. He could not help, though, that his heart hardened against her once more. He watched her mysterious behavior with disgust, his eyes were cold, and poor Undine well understood his meaning. Her constant efforts to control the water sprites exhausted her so much that she gave way to her profound fatigue and fell asleep. But no sooner were her eyes closed than the water around the boat appeared to be alive with ghastly monsters. Goblins raised their frightful heads, the sleek bodies of sirens glittered while their shrill laughter evoked the echo of the surrounding cliffs, and the boat was being tossed around in the eddying waters. They all cried out and Undine awoke. Before the light of her clear eyes the host of ghosts vanished. Hugo was so exasperated by these fiendish tricks that he could hardly control himself. But Undine whispered to him beseechingly:

"For heaven's sake, my beloved, be patient now; remember I am in their power."

Hugo kept quiet, but his burning anger showed plainly, and when Undine asked him timidly, "Had we not better give up this foolish journey and go home?" he burst out, "Am I to be kept a prisoner in my castle? And even there I am only safe if the well is sealed! By Heaven, our absurd connection . . ." but Undine softly pressed her white

hand upon his lips before he committed himself entirely. So he held his peace.

Bertha, in the meantime, torn between fear of the goblins and pleasure at seeing Undine in disgrace again with the man they both so ardently loved, had taken off a golden necklace which Hugo had once given her. She held it over the edge of the boat, dreamily watching the golden reflections it shed on the unruly water. Suddenly a large hand reached up from the depths, snatched the trinket away from her, and ducked under the water with it. Bertha screamed aloud and started to weep at the loss of her precious jewel, and Hugo could not contain himself any longer. He jumped up in the frail boat, and challenged everyone —goblin, or king, or siren—to meet his good sword. He raged at the impudence of those who broke into his private life from unapproachable worlds. Bertha's tears were like oil on the flames of his wrath, but still he refrained from accusing Undine.

Undine, in the meantime, kept her hand dipped into the churning water, murmuring incantations. Only occasionally she interrupted her low murmur to beg her husband humbly:

"Dearest love, spare me here on the water. I entreat you, do not destroy us." And so Hugo restrained his tongue.

Finally Undine drew her hand from the water, and showed them a glittering coral necklace, which she offered to the weeping Bertha.

"Take this to replace your lost necklace, my poor child. See, how beautiful it is. I sent for it."

But Hugo darted forward. He snatched the necklace from Undine's hand and hurled it back into the water, roaring furiously:

"So you still communicate with them? You still belong to them? In the name of sorcery, go back to them! And leave us men in peace, witch that you are!"

With eyes aghast, Undine stared at him, then she started to weep.

"What have you done, my dearest! Now I must leave you! Now my life on earth is over forever. Farewell, beloved, farewell!" And in a faint voice she added, "Be true to me. Farewell, beloved, ah, woe is me!" and she slipped out of the boat. Did she mingle with the waters of the Danube? Did she flow away with the waves? Did she sink into the dark-green depths? None could tell. Only the little waves seemed to sob and whisper sadly, and seemed to murmur, "Alas, alas, what have you done, alas, alas, be true to me, alas, alas."

Hugo lay in the boat, choking with grief and remorse, till a merciful swoon brought him release.

Hugo never remembered how he got back to Ringstetten; he was too stunned to think. But the first shock that the unbelievable, the impossible, had happened, wore off, and he was smitten with remorse that he had not heeded Undine's warnings. The intensity of his grief was so overwhelming that it almost filled the void Undine had left. Her image seemed fixed in his soul, now he knew how irrevocably he loved her. What wretched error had his heart committed!

Month after month passed, and nothing seemed to change. But finally he realized that utter loneliness did not reign in the halls and long galleries of Ringstetten after Undine's disappearance, but that Bertha, a gentle and submissive Bertha, was there to share his grief. He regained some interest in life though the joy had gone out of it.

He might have remained a widower, leading a quiet life dedicated to the memory of his lost one, if the fisherman had not arrived one day. The news of Undine's death had reached him.

"Come home with me, daughter," he said sternly to Bertha. "You can't stay here with this knight in his lonely castle."

Bertha tried to hide her despair at the thought of leaving her beloved. But soon her despair turned into trembling anticipation as she recognized that the arrival of her father, although this was certainly not his intention, might help her reach her coveted goal. For with a jolt Hugo had to face the facts.

Well he understood that Bertha could not stay, but he could not bear to be alone—alone with his grief, his remorse, his depression. His desire for Bertha, which had lain dormant under his sorrow and self-accusation, reawakened. He told the fisherman that he wanted to take Bertha as his wedded wife.

The fisherman had many objections. He was not convinced that Undine was really dead. But if, indeed, she had drowned, and her poor dead body was floating down the Danube, or was lying at the bottom of the stream, then Bertha ought to reproach herself for Undine's death. "Ill it becomes you, daughter, to take Undine's place," he rebuked her. But now Hugo was determined to get his way, and the fisherman was very fond of him. "He can't stay a widower all his life," the old man thought, "and nothing will bring Undine back from the deep waters." He also felt sorry for Bertha. She had been abducted as an infant, through no fault of her own, and now did not seem to belong anywhere. So he finally yielded, and gave his consent, and the day for the wedding was settled.

The wedding day arrived and Ringstetten was all decked out for a great feast. Hugo, once he knew his wish to marry Bertha was to be fulfilled, had lapsed into lethargy. Sorrow engulfed him once more, more unbearable than before. Nothing, no pleasure this earth could give, would bring back his extreme happiness with Undine. How he hated himself for losing her! Bertha, who formerly had taken such great pains to humor Hugo's changing moods, was filled with secret joy that she, at long last, was near the fulfillment of her dearest wish. She did not pay much heed to the fact that Hugo was slipping farther and farther away from her, from life, from every prospect of being happy. She did not see that every arrangement for their wedding seemed to increase his feeling of doom; she was happy, and she intended to make a splended wife for Hugo and was sure she could make him happy again.

The wedding at Ringstetten was a remarkable occasion. All was magnificently planned and carried out. The noblest guests, the most famous minstrels, the most renowned musicians, the best wines, exquisite food—in short, a most splendid pageant developed around Hugo. Everybody congratulated him on being wedded to fair Bertha, the court beauty. Bertha at Hugo's side glowed in fresh beauty in her pride at becoming mistress of Ringstetten. Hugo tried to do his best to appear happy, but nothing could penetrate his gloom. Finally, to his secret relief, the feast was over and he could be alone in his chambers.

Bertha had repaired with her bridesmaids to her room. A hectic joy seized her, and a delicious anticipation of the splendid life she was going to lead as Hugo's wife enhanced her beauty. Her maids wished their young mistress joy and happiness, and did not fail to praise her beauty to the skies. But, suddenly, Bertha glanced at the mirror of polished silver and sighed:

"But look at the freckles, just here, over the bridge of my nose!"

They looked and found there was indeed a faint trace of freckles. They called them beauty spots and said they only enhanced her clear skin. But Bertha was not comforted by their flattering remarks and frowned at her fair image.

"Still it is a blemish and I might have cured it so easily!" she remarked with a sigh. "If only the well that supplied me with precious, beautifying water had not been stopped up. I wish I could get just one jugful today!"

"Is that all you desire?" cried a young girl who had

lived only a short time at Ringstetten, and, eager to please her mistress, she slipped from the room.

"Why, she can't be so mad as to have the stone raised tonight!" Bertha called out in pleased surprise. How wonderful it was to have her smallest wish fulfilled so eagerly. As she watched from her window, she saw workmen arrive with their tools. They set to work with large levers and started to heave the heavy stone. But the task was easier than they had expected. Some power from beneath seemed to help them, and soon the huge stone rolled heavily onto the cobblestones of the court.

From the well, slowly and solemnly, arose a column of water—or so they thought as they stepped back in surprise. But then they saw that it was not a waterspout but the figure of a veiled woman, weeping and wringing her hands, who with slow and measured steps began to walk toward the castle. The frightened servants fell back; Bertha at the window stared down at the figure, suddenly seized with a wild fear. Was this indeed Undine who slowly, slowly, proceeded toward the castle entrance? How reluctantly, how unwillingly she moved, as if being dragged to her own execution. Now she had reached the entrance, now the shadowy form entered the castle and nobody in the crowd was able to move hand or foot or utter a sound. In ghastly silence they all stared at the unbelievable sight.

Hugo was alone in his chamber. He had dismissed his pages, after they had helped him to take off his gold-embroidered doublet. The room was lit by only one candle. In despair he looked at his image in a large mirror. There was a soft tap at the door. His heart leaped with a sudden joy. "Undine," he thought, "my dearest heart." But then his gloom returned. "It is only my imagination," he thought bitterly. "The bridal bed awaits me."

"Yes, but it is a cold one," said a faint voice. Slowly the door opened, and in the mirror he saw a shadowy form enter and then softly close the door. His racing heart told him it was Undine. Had she come to bring him death as she had once, long ago, said she would have to do if he married again? But how could she have got into the castle?

"They have opened the mouth of the well," murmured Undine's voice. "Now I have come, and now you must die!"

Terror rose in his heart at the thought of dying so young, so healthy, in possession of everything in life. But did he indeed possess what made life worthwhile? His desperate longing for Undine was stronger than his fear of death. Trembling with fear and love, he approached her to fold the beloved form into his arms. Undine received him in a tender embrace. The veil slipped from her head, and once more he beheld her lovely face, radiant with love. She pressed him close to her heart, his eager mouth found her tender lips. But an icy shudder ran down his spine as he, the ardent lover, received the kiss of death. He felt his heart sink within him, and with a sigh he fell, lifeless, from her arms.

"I have kissed him to death," said the weeping voice of Undine, as her shadowy form passed the petrified pages in the antechamber. Slowly she glided through the long galleries, the magnificent halls thronged with wedding guests. She left the castle, crossed the court, and slipped back into the well, while a deathlike silence smothered the festival clamor of the wedding like a black cover.

Lord Hugo of Ringstetten was the last member of his noble family, and the funeral ceremonies were in accordance with his high rank. He was to be buried in the churchyard which contained the graves of all his forebears. Those of the wedding party who had not fled in terror attended the funeral.

The ceremony in the chapel was over. The pallbearers walked in solemn procession as the heavy oak coffin was borne out into the open. Hugo's coat of arms, his sword and shield were lying on top of the flag-covered coffin. A large crowd, headed by the deeply veiled Bertha, followed the last Lord of Ringstetten to his final resting place, while the mournful tolling of the bells evoked the echo of the valley. The sound of the monks' solemn dirge rose and fell in measured rhythm. Finally they arrived at the open grave.

"Earth to earth, dust to dust, ashes to ashes," the priest's somber voice rang out as he offered up the last prayers. Slowly the coffin was lowered into the grave.

The king's herald stepped forward in dark splendor. He had seized Lord Ringstetten's arms.

"Ringstetten today and never more!" he proclaimed solemnly as he broke the coat of arms, the sword and shield, and tossed the pieces into the open grave. A sigh went through the crowd at the melancholy clamor of the broken weapons, for many had loved the late knight in his youthful splendor.

Then there was only the soft, thumping sound of earth falling over the flowers in the grave, and murmuring and the subdued shuffling of many feet reached Bertha's ears. She turned and saw a veiled woman slowly advancing toward her. A shudder crept over her, as she noticed how everyone shrank back and stepped aside as the white form approached. Was it Undine? Now the veiled stranger had almost reached her. The frightened Bertha mustered up her courage and was about to forbid the stranger to come any nearer, but at that moment the priest raised high his cross, and Bertha and the assembled mourners knelt down to pray in silence.

When they rose from their knees, the veiled woman had gone. Where she had stood, a clear silvery spring now gushed from the earth. The gently murmuring water flowed around the grave till it had almost encircled it. Then it ran farther on through the churchyard into the meadows and fields, through woods and valleys, till its water reached the majestic river.

The brook still murmurs and whispers in gentle mourning, and the villagers of Ringstetten still believe that it is Undine, who at last is forever united with her lover, as she twines her white arms around his grave.

Rain Trudy

*

THEODOR STORM

There had never been such a hot summer as the one a hundred years ago. There was almost no vegetation anywhere. Both tame and wild beasts were lying in the fields, perishing from thirst.

It was midmorning, but the village streets were deserted. The people had fled into their houses; even the village watchdogs were hiding. Only the stout hay farmer was standing complacently in the gateway of his stately house. Sweat beaded his brow as he stood smoking his big meerschaum pipe. With a satisfied smile he was watching the huge wagonload of hay which his farmhands were just driving into the barn.

Years ago he had bought a large expanse of marshy land for a small price. The heat of the last dry years which had parched the grass in his neighbors' fields had filled his

barns with sweet-smelling hay and his strongbox with shining thalers. Now as he stood there he calculated how much
his abundant harvest might net, with prices going up as
they were. "The rest will have nothing," he murmured,
while he shaded his eyes with one hand and looked beyond
the neighboring houses into the distance. "There seems to
be no more rain in the world." Then he went over to the
wagon which was just being unloaded, picked a handful
of hay, brought it up to his blunt nose and smiled cunningly as if he were actually smelling out a few extra
thalers.

At this moment a woman of about fifty entered the
farmstead. She looked pale and ill, and the black silk scarf
she wore emphasized the sad expression on her face.

"Good morning, neighbor," she said, shaking hands
with the hay farmer. "What a scorcher it is again!"

"Let it scorch, Mother Stina, let it scorch!" he answered.
"Just look at that hay! The heat can't do *me* any harm."

"It's all very well for you, hay farmer, you can laugh! But what will become of the rest of us if the heat doesn't let up?"

With his broad thumb the farmer pressed the tobacco down in his pipe. Then he exhaled a couple of mighty puffs of smoke.

"Now you see what happens if one is too smart!" he said. "I always warned your late husband, but he thought he knew better. Why did he get rid of all his marshy lands? Now you're left with land only on the hillsides, where your crops wither and your cattle perish from thirst."

Mother Stina sighed. The stout man adopted a patronizing tone.

"I'm sure you didn't come here just by chance, Mother Stina," he said. "What's bothering you? Go ahead!"

The widow cast down her eyes. "You know very well," was her reply. "I have to pay back those fifty thalers you loaned me by June 24th, and the day is close at hand."

The farmer put his fleshy hand on her shoulder.

"Now don't worry about that, Mother Stina! I don't need the money. I'm not a man who lives from hand to mouth. You can give me your land as security. It is not of the best, that's true, but it will be all right with me. This Saturday you can go to the registrar with me in the city."

The worried woman uttered a sigh of relief. "It means more expense," she murmured. "But I thank you, nevertheless."

The farmer had not taken his small shrewd eyes from her face.

"Well, that takes care of that," he remarked casually. "Since you're here, I'd better tell you something that's been on my mind. Andres, your boy, is going with my daughter."

"Goodness gracious, neighbor! The children grew up together."

"That's true. But if the lad thinks he can marry into my farm, he's reckoning without me."

The gentle woman straightened up and looked at him with eyes that showed a trace of anger. "What fault do you find with my Andres?" she asked.

"Find fault with your boy? Not one in the whole world, Mother Stina, but . . ." His hand glided over the silver buttons of his red waistcoat. "My daughter is my daughter, and the hay farmer's daughter can aim high."

"Don't boast so much, neighbor," the woman replied mildly. "Before the hot years came . . ."

"But they came, and they are here. This year, too, there's no chance that you'll have a harvest. And your farm is getting poorer and poorer."

"You may be right," she sighed. "Rain Trudy must have fallen asleep. But she can be aroused!"

"Rain Trudy?" the farmer asked harshly. "You believe in that nonsense?"

"No nonsense, neighbor," she answered confidently. "My great-grandmother, when she was young, woke Rain Trudy up once. She knew the little verse and recited it quite often. But I've forgotten it long since."

The stout man laughed so hard the silver buttons danced on his fat belly. "Well, Mother Stina, why don't you sit down and try to remember the verse? I trust my barometer, and that has pointed to 'continuously fair' for the last eight weeks."

"A barometer is a dead thing, neighbor. It can't make rain."

"And your Rain Trudy is a notion, a fancy, a mere nothing!"

"I know you are one of those modern unbelievers," Mother Stina replied angrily.

"Modern or old-fashioned," the man answered, "you go and find your Rain Trudy and say your verse. And if you can make rain between now and twenty-four hours, then . . ." He stopped and puffed more fat clouds of smoke.

"What then, neighbor?"

"Then, then . . . hang it! Yes, then your Andres shall have my Maureen!"

At this moment the door of the farmhouse opened and a beautiful slim girl with hazel-brown eyes joined them in the gateway.

"All right, Father," she cried. "That's a bargain!" Turning to an elderly man who was just approaching them from the street, she added, "You heard what he said, Cousin Schulte!"

"Well, well, Maureen," grumbled the hay farmer. "You don't have to call up witnesses against your father! My word is as good as gold." He turned, and he and Schulte entered the house.

Mother Stina and Maureen went across the street into the older woman's house.

"But, child, do you know the verse to wake Rain Trudy?" the widow asked, while she fetched her spinning wheel from the corner.

"I?" asked the girl, turning her head in astonishment.

"I thought maybe you did because you took your father to task so sharply."

"Oh no, I don't know it, Mother. But I thought you might be able to piece it together again. Just search a little in your head. It must be hidden somewhere."

Mother Stina shook her head. "My great-grandmother died when I was little. But I remember well that when something happened to our crops or cattle, she used to say, 'The fire sprite does that to spite us because once I woke up Rain Trudy.' "

"The fire sprite? Who on earth is that?" But without waiting for an answer she ran to the window and cried, "For Heaven's sake, Mother, there's Andres! How worried he looks."

The old woman rose from her spinning wheel.

"Sure enough, child," she answered sadly. "Can't you see what he is carrying on his back? Another one of our sheep has died of thirst."

The young farmer entered the room and put the dead animal on the tiled floor in front of the women.

"There you are," he said grimly, wiping the sweat from his hot brow.

The women looked at him rather than at the dead animal.

"Don't take it to heart so much, Andres," said Maureen. "We are going to rouse Rain Trudy and everything will be all right."

"Rain Trudy," he repeated tonelessly. "Yes, Maureen, if only somebody would wake her up! But it isn't only the poor dead sheep that worries me. Something strange has happened to me."

"Talk about it, son," Mother Stina warned him, "otherwise it might make you sick."

"All right," he replied, "I'll tell you. I was going to look after our sheep and make sure the water I carried to them last night had not evaporated. When I came to the grazing ground, I saw at once that something was wrong. The sheep were gone, and the tub was not there either. I climbed the giant knoll and there were the sheep, on the other side of the hill. They were lying there, panting, their necks stretched out. This poor creature was dead already. The tub was turned over and dry. The sheep couldn't have done it! Somebody must have played a trick on us."

"Son!" his mother interrupted him. "Who would want to harm a poor widow."

"Listen, Mother, there is something more. I stood and looked around, but nobody was in sight. The heat was sweltering in the fields as it has been every day. While I stared in the distance, half furious and half helpless, I heard something like mumbling from the other side of the hill. When I turned around I saw a gnarled manikin in a fire-red coat and a red pointed cap stomping among the heather. I was startled. Where had he come from? He looked so very evil and misshapen. His big red-brown hands were folded on his back and his knobby fingers played in the air like spider legs. I hid behind a bush. The little monster was still moving around. He stooped and pulled out handfuls of dried grass so violently that I thought he would topple over on his big pumpkin head. But he was on his spindly legs again. Crushing the dry herbs in his big hands, he started to laugh so terrifyingly that the half-dead sheep jumped up and raced away in wild flight. The hobgoblin laughed more shrilly. Then he started to jump up and down. I thought the bony little staves under his potbelly would break! It was frightful to behold. His beady black eyes glowed like embers."

Mother Stina touched the girl's hand. "Do you know now who the fire sprite is?" she asked softly. Maureen nodded her head.

"The worst thing about him was his voice," Andres went on. " 'If they knew it, if they only knew it!' he shrilled. 'Those ruffians, those oafs!' And then he sang a strange little ditty with his croaking voice. Again and again he sang it, as if he could not get his fill of it. Wait, I think I can remember it." After a moment Andres started to sing slowly:

> *Haze is the wave,*
> *Dust is the spring,*
> *The woods don't sing.*

The mother stopped her spinning wheel which she had been turning diligently during his tale. She looked at her son with anticipation. "Go on," she said softly.

"I don't seem to know it any more, Mother! It's gone, and I repeated it a hundred times on my way home." But as Mother Stina continued in a wavering voice:

> *In the fields dances the fire sprite!*

he quickly added:

> *Awake! And take care!*
> *Awake! And beware!*
> *Or your mother will fetch you home*
> *Into darkness and night.*

"That's the incantation for Rain Trudy!" cried Mother Stina. "Now, quick! Repeat it! And you, Maureen, listen well so it won't be lost again."

And now mother and son spoke together and without faltering:

> *Haze is the wave,*
> *Dust is the spring,*
> *The woods don't sing.*
> *In the fields dances the fire sprite!*
> *Awake! And take care!*
> *Awake! And beware!*
> *Or your mother will fetch you home*
> *Into darkness and night.*

"All our troubles will be ended now," Maureen cried. "We'll wake up Rain Trudy! Tomorrow all the fields will be green again, and day after tomorrow is our wedding!" Hastily and with shining eyes she told Andres of her father's promise.

"Do you know the way to Rain Trudy's realm?" Mother Stina interrupted her.

"No, Mother, don't you even remember the way?"

"But Maureen! It was my great-grandmother who visited Rain Trudy. And she never told me how to get there."

"Well, Andres," Maureen shook his arm. "Now you say something. You always have good ideas."

"Maybe, I have a good one this time too," he answered slowly. "I have to carry water to my sheep at noon. Maybe I can spy on the goblin again. Since he let the ditty slip out, I might be able to learn the way from him too. His thick head seems to be filled to the brim with these things."

They decided to try his plan since, hard as they tried, they could not think of a better solution.

Soon Andres was on his way to the grazing grounds with a yoke of water pails. From afar he saw the gnome sitting atop the giant knoll. The hobgoblin was stroking his fire-red beard with his fingers. As he combed it bunches of fiery flakes became detached and floated across the fields in the glaring sunshine.

"I'm too late," thought Andres. "I won't learn anything today." He went to the turned-over tub as if he had not seen the gnome. But the goblin addressed him.

"I thought you had come to talk with me," he said with his croaking voice.

Andres returned a few steps. "Why should I?" he replied. "I don't know you."

"But you would like to find the way to Rain Trudy, wouldn't you?"

"Who told you that?"

"My little finger! It's a lot smarter than many a giant's brain."

Andres summoned up his courage and stepped nearer to the little monster on the knoll.

"Your little finger may be very smart," he said. "But I'm sure it doesn't know the way to Rain Trudy. Even the most intelligent men don't know that."

The gnome distended like a toad. With his claw he combed his fire beard a few times, and Andres staggered back from the intense heat. Suddenly, glaring at him with an expression of superior disdain in his evil little eyes, the goblin snarled at Andres, "You are too stupid! Even if I told you that Rain Trudy lives behind the large forest, you still wouldn't know that there is a hollow willow tree where the wood ends."

"I had better play the fool now," Andres thought. "You are right!" he said and opened his mouth wide as if in great astonishment. "Of course, I wouldn't know that."

"And even if I told you about the hollow willow tree, you still wouldn't know that a staircase in that tree leads down to the garden of Rain Trudy."

"How mistaken a man can be!" Andres cried out. "I would have thought one could just enter her garden."

"And even if you found her garden," the gnome said sneeringly, "you still wouldn't know that Rain Trudy can be aroused only by a virgin."

"Is that so? Ah well, that settles it! I guess I'd better give up."

A mischievous smile screwed up the manikin's wide mouth. "Don't you want to pour that water into the tub?" he asked. "Your fine sheep are almost dead from thirst."

"You are right again!" replied the lad and went over to the tub. But as he poured the water into the hot tub, it bubbled up with a hissing sound and vanished in white steam clouds into the air. "It's all right with me," thought Andres. "I'll drive my sheep home and tomorrow I'll take Maureen along with me to find Rain Trudy. Now we know the way, and Maureen will wake her up."

As Andres left with his sheep, the hobgoblin on the hill jumped up from his stone seat. He threw his cap into the air and rolled down the hillside with a neighing laughter. Then he picked himself up and danced like mad on his spider legs, screaming in his rasping voice, "That blockhead! That stupid oaf! He thought he could get the better of me! He doesn't even know that Trudy can be aroused only by the right incantation. Nobody but Eckeneckepen knows the magic verse! And I am Eckeneckepen!"

The evil little creature did not realize that in the morning he himself had given away the magic verse!

The first rays of the morning sun were just touching the sunflowers in her garden, as Maureen opened the shutters and thrust her head into the fresh morning air. The hay farmer who slept in a big alcove in the next room awoke at the slight noise. His snoring stopped abruptly.

"What are you doing, Maureen?" he called in a sleepy voice. "Is something wrong?"

Startled, the girl put her hand to her mouth. She knew very well her father would not let her go if he knew her errand. Quickly she pulled herself together.

"I couldn't sleep, Father," she answered. "It's such a lovely morning, I think I'll help with the haying."

"Well, if you want to. But come home early before it gets too hot. And don't forget my warm beer."

He turned in his bed, the bedstead creaked, and right away the girl heard his familiar, measured snoring. Carefully she opened the door and left the house. "Too bad I had to lie like that," she thought. "The things one does for a sweetheart!" She sighed, but then she smiled.

Andres was waiting for her, dressed in his Sunday best.

"Do you remember the verse?" he called when he saw her.

"Of course, Andres! And do you remember the way?" She laughed up at him, but he only nodded.

"Let's go now," he said.

Just then Mother Stina came from her house. She handed her son a small bottle filled with mead.

"I've kept it all these years. It belonged to my great-grandmother," she said, "and she always held it in high esteem. Take it along; it may do you good along the way."

The young couple walked along the quiet village street, which lay deserted in the cool morning light. Long after the two strong young figures had disappeared, Mother Stina stood in her door, gazing after them.

After they had left the village and had crossed a wide withered heath, Andres and Maureen entered a large wood. Most of the trees were bare, and the ground was covered with dead leaves. Soon it became very hot. The harsh sunlight glared down on them, the changing lights and shades dazzled their eyes. They walked on in silence till Maureen asked, "Andres, do you remember the verse?"

"Of course, Maureen!"

> *Haze is the wave,*
> *Dust is the spring* . . .

And as he hesitated she quickly went on:

> *The woods don't sing.*
> *In the fields dances the fire sprite!*

"Ouch!" she cried out. "That stung! The sun is burning hot!"

"That's true," said Andres, rubbing his cheek. "I felt something sting too!"

At last they came to the end of the forest and now they saw the old willow tree. The mighty trunk was hollow, and the darkness in it seemed to reach far into the depths of the earth. A broken winding staircase took them down into the unknown. Forbidding darkness surrounded them. Yet Maureen breathed easier as they slowly descended. It was cool in the inner earth, and no sound from the surface reached them here.

"When will we come to the end?" Maureen asked after a while.

"I don't know, Maureen."

"Do you think the goblin cheated you?"

"I don't think so, Maureen."

They were silent again as they went down, deeper and deeper. Finally, to their great relief, they saw light—sunlight! But suffocating heat met them as they stepped out into the open air. The scenery was strange and entirely unfamiliar to them. Maureen looked around.

"The sun seems to be the same," she said finally.

"It certainly is not any cooler here than at home!" Andres shrugged his shoulders.

They were standing beside a wide paved dam. An avenue of old willow trees stretched as far as they could see, and they followed the row of trees as if they had been told to do so. On both sides they saw bare and desolate lowlands, stretching to the far horizon. The land was broken up by a maze of channels, grooves, and flat cavities like dried-up rivers and lakes. A dense, reeking haze arose from the rotting rushes and reeds, filling the air with an oppressive mist. The sun was hidden in the milky fog, but the heat was even worse than on earth. Small white flames seemed to leap up before them. More than once Andres thought he saw the fire sprite dance in grotesque jumps and bounds, now on their right side, now on their left side. But when he focused his tired eyes on the spot, there was only the wavering hot air.

The monotonous road seemed to have no end. They walked on and on. They did not speak and their breathing was labored. Suddenly Maureen stopped. She leaned against a willow tree; her eyes were closed.

"I can't go on any more," she murmured. "The air is like fire."

Alarmed, Andres looked into her exhausted face. Then

he remembered the mead bottle. As he unscrewed the cap, a refreshing fragrance, as if thousands of flowerbuds had suddenly burst into blossom, came from the bottle. The girl had hardly lifted it to her lips before the color returned to her cheeks. She opened her eyes.

"Where are we?" she asked. "Why, we must be in a meadow in full bloom."

"No meadow in sight," replied Andres. "But drink a little more. This will refresh you."

She drank and looked around with clear eyes. Then she handed the bottle to Andres. "You take the rest, Andres," she said. "It will do you good."

"That's absolutely delicious, but it's strong stuff!" Andres exclaimed as he drank. "Wish I knew what herbs Great-grandmother used to concoct this drink."

They went on with new strength, talking cheerfully, till the avenue ended in a wide park. Beautiful groups of linden trees, surrounded by flower beds, stood on the lawn. But the grass was scorched, the trees were bare, the flowers had wilted and were lying limply on the ground.

"I think we've reached our goal," said Maureen.

"Yes, this must be Rain Trudy's garden. Now the rest is up to you," replied Andres. "Don't forget your verse, and don't get it mixed up!" He stretched out in the shadow of a huge oak tree, and Maureen went on alone. She crossed the wide lawns and soon he had lost sight of her.

Maureen continued steadfastly in spite of the eerie loneliness of the place. After a while she reached the dry bed of a lake, where the silvery scales of dead fish glistened in the sun. In the middle of its wide expanse stood a tall gray bird, resembling a huge heron. It seemed to be asleep; its head was hidden under a dun-colored wing. There was no other living creature in sight except the motionless, sinister bird. Not even the buzz of a fly interrupted the deep solitude.

Maureen was afraid, but she walked on, fixing her eyes on a group of lofty trees in front of a rocky wall in the near distance. At long last she reached the rocks. Now she stood in an empty sandy basin, which had been formed by a waterfall gushing down the steep cliffs. But now everything was sand and dust.

Quite undaunted, the girl searched for a way among the irregular rocks. A gray mass caught her eye. With a start she recognized that the ashen-gray rigid heap in the middle

of the slope was not a rock formation. Expectantly Maureen climbed the steeply sloping rocks. Now she could see its shape more clearly. A beautiful and stately woman was lying on a ledge of rock. Her eyes were sunk deep into their sockets. Her cheeks were hollow, her long lusterless hair was dusty and full of dried grass and shriveled leaves. Maureen gazed at her in wonderment.

"She must have been very beautiful," she thought. "I wonder if she is Rain Trudy? How pale her lips are." In sudden fear she bent down. "But she is dead! She is not asleep! Oh, it is horrid here, so utterly desolate!" It was true. A deadly nightmare-like silence hovered over the rocks.

But the young girl soon collected her wits. She thought of Andres, and remembered all that was at stake. Kneeling down, she put her red lips to the waxen ear of the sleeper, and, gathering her courage, she recited slowly and clearly:

> Haze is the wave,
> Dust is the spring,
> The woods don't sing.
> In the fields dances the fire sprite!

A low, piteous moaning broke from the pale lips. Maureen said louder and more urgently:

> Awake! And take care!
> Awake! And beware!
> Or your mother will fetch you home
> Into darkness and night!

A gentle wind stirred the trees far below. A low rolling like thunder sounded in the distance. From behind the rocks rose a piercing scream, cutting the still air like the raging howl of a dangerous animal. Maureen looked up.

The woman had risen. She stood erect, her head held high.

"What do you want from me?" she asked sternly.

"You slept so long and so deep, Rain Trudy," answered the girl, still on her knees. "All the plants have withered. Every creature is dying of thirst."

Trudy looked around with dazed eyes as if trying to shake off a heavy dream. Finally she asked in a toneless voice, "The spring does not gush down any more?"

"No, it is dried up."

"Does my bird still circle over the lake?"

"No. It is asleep, standing in the hot sand. There is no lake."

"Woe is me!" moaned Rain Trudy. "It is high time I awakened. Get up and follow me, and bring the jug which is lying at your feet."

Maureen did as she was told, and the two slowly ascended the more gently sloping wooded side of the cliff. Painfully Rain Trudy moved on, yet Maureen thought she noticed a green shimmer where Rain Trudy's foot had trod. Her long gray garment rustled over the dead grassy patches. It sounded like rain, Maureen thought.

"Has it begun to rain already?" she asked her companion.

"Oh no, my child. First I must unlock the well."

"The well? Where is it?" They were emerging from a group of trees.

"There it is," Rain Trudy answered.

Ahead of them loomed an immense building formed of irregular blocks piled up high. It seemed to rise aloft till it touched the sky. The top appeared to melt away in the hazy glare of the sun. The immense walls were pierced by high arched door and window openings. There were no doors, no windows. The two women advanced toward the gray castle till they were stopped by a deep and wide riverbed. A small thread of water trickled through its center. A boat, burst asunder, was lying at the edge.

"Cross the riverbed," said Trudy. "The fire sprite has no power over you. And fill your jug with water; you'll need it later on."

Quickly Maureen walked across the stone-hard caked mud, but suddenly she stood aghast. The hard-packed mud burst open wide. A large reddish-brown fist with gnarled fingers shot out and tried to grab her.

"Courage!" she heard Rain Trudy's voice from the edge. "Close your eyes and go ahead."

Obediently Maureen closed her eyes. She clenched her teeth and walked on, her skin tingling with fear. Presently she felt water touch her foot. She opened her eyes and filled her jug. Swiftly and without seeing any more frightful apparitions, she reached the other side of the river. Now she stood before the castle. Her heart was beating wildly as she entered through one of the open gates. She stood stock-still.

The whole castle seemed to consist of one immense room. Mighty pillars supported the ceiling. Something resembling vast gray spiderwebs were hanging down from its seemingly infinite height. No end could be seen either above, or to the right, the left, or in front. Pillar behind pillar and the dense hazy bunches were all that met Maureen's anxiously searching eye. The floor was thickly covered with bone-dry plants, rushes and reeds, grass and flowers, all completely parched.

Now the girl saw a covered well right in front of her. A golden key glittered at her feet. She stooped to pick it up, but quickly withdrew her hand as she realized the key was not made of red gold but of red fire. Resolutely she emptied her water jug on it. The hissing resounded in the wide empty halls. She picked up the key. It had turned into solid gold. She unlocked the trapdoor of the well and threw it open.

A sweet smell from fresh water rose from the depths. Soon a moist haze filled the vast castle, rising and curling between the pillars. With pleasure Maureen breathed the cool, dewy air. Then a miracle started to take place all around her.

A fresh green hue seemed to ripple over the parched plants. Tender light-green shoots sprang up. The dehydrated plants lifted their heads, filled with new life. Forget-me-nots formed blue patches. Yellow and brown iris flowered, exhaling their tender scent. Dragonflies climbed up the swaying stalks. They stretched and tried their transparent wings, then they were borne aloft and danced over the flowering meadows, glistening like silver sparks. All the time the dewy haze constantly rising from the well continued to fill the air.

Maureen stood enchanted by the transformation from death to life. As she glanced around her eyes opened wide in astonishment.

A woman of exquisite beauty was leaning on the green mossy bank which now surrounded the well. Her silky blonde hair flowed over her gleaming shoulders. She looked at the ceiling and smiled. Maureen looked up too.

What she had mistaken for spiderwebs were really the fine gauze of clouds. Fascinated, she watched how they grew darker and heavier, absorbing the haze still rising from the well. Just then a dark raincloud became detached and sank down slowly. The beautiful woman was enshrouded by the cloud. Her radiant face shone faintly through the gray veil. She clapped her hands. The cloud flowed to the next window opening and drifted out into the open air.

"Well, Maureen," laughed the lovely woman. "Tell me how you like it here now." Her red mouth smiled, her white teeth glistened. She waved to Maureen. "Come and sit down here at my side. Look at the cloud that is just sinking down! Now, clap your hands." Maureen did as she was told. The cloud swam away through a window. "See, how easy it is? You can do it just as well as I."

Admiringly Maureen looked at the fair beauty.

"Who are you? Where do you come from?" she asked timidly.

"But child! Don't be silly!"

The girl regarded her with doubtful eyes and asked hesitantly, "You are not Rain Trudy? Or are you?"

"But who else could I be?"

"Forgive me! But you are so young now, so beautiful and gay."

Trudy was quite still for a moment. "I have to thank you," she exclaimed, clasping the girl to her. "If you hadn't come, the fire sprite would have been master! I would be forced to go back to my mother. Back into darkness!" She shivered. Her white shoulders were hunched as with some deep, inner fear. She added softly, "It is so beautiful, so green on earth!"

But then she smiled again. She stretched out in the luxurious grass, fondling the dewy unfolding flowers.

"Tell me how you got here," she bade Maureen, and the girl related the story of their trials.

"The dam was built by mortals in former times," Rain Trudy informed her young friend. "But that was long, long ago. At that time people would come and visit me. I would give them seeds and seedlings for new plants, and they used to bring flowers and fruits as presents. But it is so long ago. Then they forgot me, and I forgot them. I was so lonely! I must have fallen asleep, and the vicious Eckeneckepen almost gained victory."

Maureen, too, rested peacefully in the swelling green cushions as she listened to Rain Trudy's sweet and bewitching voice.

"Only once, after many years of no visitors, a girl came to see me. You are like her, even your dress has some resemblance to hers." Rain Trudy continued softly. "But that was long ago, too. I gave her some of my meadow mead. That was the last gift a mortal ever received from me."

"That was Andres' great-grandmother!" Maureen informed her eagerly. "It was your mead which saved us today."

Rain Trudy was still thinking of the other young girl. "Does she still have such pretty curly brown hair?" she asked.

"Who?" inquired Maureen, startled.

"Well, Great-grandmother, as you call her. Funny name."

"Oh no! Great-grandmother was stone-old and had wispy white hair," Maureen said. She even felt a little superior to her powerful friend.

"Stone-old?" repeated Rain Trudy. "What is old?" She knew no aging and did not understand. Maureen took great trouble to explain it to her.

"Listen," she said finally, "white, thin hair, and red eyes, and ugly and cranky; that's stone-old."

"Indeed? Now I remember. There were some women like that among my visitors." Curiously she looked into Maureen's sweet face. "Will you be old and cranky too one day?" she asked.

"I guess so," replied the girl, a little crestfallen. "That's the way with us."

"That's too bad," Rain Trudy said, full of regret. "But you must send Great-grandmother to me. I liked her! I'll make her young and fair again."

Maureen shook her head. "She has been dead and buried a long, long time," she explained. "Buried in the dark earth."

"Poor Great-grandmother," Rain Trudy sighed. Then they were silent, comfortably stretched out among the flowers.

Suddenly Rain Trudy sat up. "But, Maureen! Look what we did!" she cried. "We forgot to make rain! Now, quick!" She laughed. "We are nearly buried in clouds."

Maureen looked around. "Why, I can hardly see you."

"Just clap your hands. But be careful! Don't tear a cloud or you might drown here."

They both started to clap their hands, very softly at first. The clouds started to shift. Soon they crowded at the openings and then they drifted outside, one by one. After a little while the air was clear. Maureen saw again the mighty pillars, the flowers at their feet, the endlessly stretching green flower-studded grounds. Sitting up, Maureen looked out of the window. Fat, dark clouds crowded in the sky. The sun was hidden. A few more moments, then the downpour started. She heard the welcome rush of the rain, the rustling and sighing of the trees and bushes in Rain Trudy's garden.

"It is raining!" the girl said fervently.

Suddenly a wild scream rent the air. Maureen jumped up and ran to a window. Dense white steam clouds pushed their way through the fissures of the parched riverbed. Hissing and gurgling, ear-piercing screeching, and splashing mingled in a deafening din. But soon the agonized screams were muffled by the gurgling, gushing waters. The steam clouds rose up high, clustering together as they sank down and hid the river.

Frightened and trembling Rain Trudy clung to the young mortal. "Now they are drowning the fire sprite," she whispered. "Listen, how he fights!"

They held each other till the terrifying uproar abated. Finally all was quiet, and they heard only the gentle murmur of rain. Rain Trudy loosened her tight grip from Maureen's shoulder, smiling with relief. Then she stooped, closed the trapdoor of the well, and locked it.

Maureen kissed her white hand. "I thank you! Oh, I thank you so much! You saved us all from starvation." In a hesitant voice she added, "I have to go home now."

"Go home so soon? Can't you stay a little longer in the rain country?"

Maureen blushed. "My sweetheart is waiting for me, so I'd better go now. He'll be wet through." They both laughed.

"All right, my child," Rain Trudy sighed a little. "And tell your people they should not forget me again. Then I will remember them too and send rain in time. Now come, I'll show you a shorter way back."

How everything had changed in that short time!

Luscious green, multicolored flowers grew wherever they looked. Birds were singing, insects buzzing, the sweetest fragrance filled the air. The dry river was a swift-flowing stream now. The boat, mended by magic, was waiting for them and gently rocked them across. On the other side of the river they crossed the wide park. Soon they ought to be near the place where Andres was waiting.

Yes, there he was, sleeping under the tall oak tree. Maureen turned to tell Rain Trudy he was there, but then she hesitated. Suddenly she felt ugly and coarse in her simple dress beside Rain Trudy with her queenly bearing. "That won't do!" she thought. "It is better that he doesn't see her."

She said politely, "A thousand thanks for escorting me so far. Now I can find my way alone."

"But I want to meet your sweetheart."

"Don't trouble yourself. He's just a lad like any other, good enough for a peasant girl like me."

Rain Trudy looked at her with keen, searching eyes. "You are very pretty yourself, you little goose." She raised a cautioning finger. "But are you sure you are the best-looking girl in your village?"

Scarlet red with embarrassment, Maureen cast down her eyes, but Rain Trudy smiled at her again.

"All right, we will part here," she said kindly. "Now, listen to me. You can go home by a shorter way. Since all the springs are flowing again, there is water enough to travel through the lowlands. Take the little boat which you will find at the willow-tree dam. It will take you home safely." She embraced Maureen and kissed her. "Farewell, my precious little friend."

Rain Trudy turned and walked away under the dripping

trees across the green lawn. She started to sing, a sweet and monotonous melody. Maureen stared after her, listening to the soothing sound of the rain. Did she still hear the tranquil voice of Rain Trudy, or was it only the gentle murmuring of the rain? She strained her ears to catch Rain Trudy's entrancing voice. Then she realized it was only the lulling ripple of the water that she heard, sweet and monotonous.

She walked toward the group of trees where Andres was standing now. "What are you looking at?" she asked, as she came nearer.

"Goodness alive!" Andres replied in a hushed voice. "Who was that beautiful woman?"

The girl grabbed his arm and turned him around to her. "You'd better not look at her! That was Rain Trudy, she's not for you!"

"Indeed? Well, Maureen, I'd already noticed that you awakened her!" He laughed and looked tenderly in her flushed face. "Never have I seen such growing and blossoming as today. But let's go home now, your father must redeem his promise."

They found the boat, and it carried them quickly through the maze of rivers and canals in the lowlands. It kept on raining, a gentle, penetrating, fertile rain. Soon the landscape became familiar.

"Look, Maureen," Andres pointed to the right, "that's my wheat field, way over there."

"How green it is!" Maureen clapped her hands with pleasure. "But look at my father's meadows. They are flooded! All the hay is afloat."

Andres took her hand. "It's all right, Maureen," he said kindly. "I think it is not too high a price. The harvest from my fields will balance the loss."

Their waterway had turned out to be the little brook which ran through their home village. At the big linden tree in the middle of the village they finally halted their boat and alighted. Hand in hand they walked along the street, cheered by everybody. Mother Stina had obviously been talking about their daring endeavor.

"It's raining!" the children called and jumped into the largest puddles.

"It's raining!" Cousin Schulte said, cheerfully waving his hand as they strode past his house.

"Well, well! It's raining!" The hay farmer grinned. He was standing in his gateway, smoking his big meerschaum pipe. "You gave me quite a tale this morning, daughter! But it's all right now. Come in, come in, you two! Andres is a good, honest lad, I agree with Cousin Schulte. Maybe it will rain now for three years, and his land may do better than mine." He laughed and slapped Andres' shoulder. "Lowland and hilly land ought to be together anyhow, as I've always said. Come on now. Let's go to Mother Stina and settle everything."

Several weeks had passed. Rain and sunshine had alternated in due course. The contents of the last heavy harvest wagon, decorated with colorful streamers and gay flower wreaths, was safely stored away.

It was a beautiful, sunny day. A bridal procession was approaching the white village church. Andres and Maureen, decked out in wedding garments, led the way. The entire village population was following. Already they could hear the organ playing as a little cloud obscured the sun for a minute. A few raindrops fell and glistened like jewels in Maureen's bridal crown.

"That means splendid good luck!" everybody called out joyfully.

"That was Rain Trudy's congratulations," whispered the bridegroom, and pressed Maureen's hand.

The sun was shining again. The wedding party entered the church. The organ was silent, and the priest gave them his blessings for a long and happy life together.

The Cold Heart

*

WILHELM HAUFF

A long time ago there lived in the Black Forest a widow
named Frau Barbara Munk. Her husband had been a charcoal burner, and after his death her sixteen-year-old son
Peter followed the same trade. At first Peter did not mind
sitting all week at the smoldering kiln. Nor did it bother
him when, blackened and sooty and avoided by everybody,
he had to travel to the neighboring towns and sell his
charcoal. But a charcoal burner has a lot of time for brooding. Day after day Peter sat alone at his kiln in the deep
stillness of the gloomy fir woods, and his heart was filled
with a vague longing. Something bothered him, something
annoyed him, but he could not put his finger on it.

Finally he knew what made him so unhappy—it was his
trade. "To be a dirty, lonesome charcoal burner—that's a
poor life," he thought. "How well esteemed are the glass-

workers, the watchmakers, even the musicians on Sunday evening. But when I, Peter Munk, scrubbed and dressed up in my father's best jerkin with the silver buttons and with brand-new red stockings, go to the village fair, and somebody walks behind me and thinks, 'Who on earth is that nice slender fellow?' and he admires my red stockings and my swinging gait, that's fine. But when the man overtakes me, then he thinks, 'Ah well, it's only Coal Peter.' " Poor Peter's heart felt like breaking. "It's no good," he thought.

He brooded about the lumbermen who lived in the other valleys of the Black Forest. They were bold and strong men. They felled and lopped the firs, logged them down to the rivers, and floated them through the Nagold and the Neckar into the Rhine. They were well known all along the Rhine and sold their timber wherever it was wanted. Their longest beams they saved for the Mynheers in The Netherlands, because the shipbuilders there paid big money for the tremendous firs from the Black Forest. They were a fearless and hard-working lot. It was their joy to drift down the majestic river Rhine and see the wide world; it was their sorrow to walk home again.

On Sundays they would visit the glassworker valleys, and Peter Munk would stare at them in envy. They were splendidly dressed in dark-colored linen jackets, and over their snowy shirts they wore green, embroidered braces of a hand's width. They sported black leather breeches and the largest boots imaginable. They carried pounds and pounds of silver as buttons, buckles, and heavy watch chains, and Peter always thought they must be the happiest people on earth! They watched the dancing couples haughtily, and cursed in Dutch and smoked clay pipes an ell

long, just like the most distinguished Mynheers. Peter would look at them in bewilderment, and finally he would slink moodily home to his hut. He had seen them gamble away more money in one evening than poor Father Munk had earned in a whole year. "This can't go on," Peter thought one day. "If I don't get ahead soon, I'm liable to commit suicide."

It was the day after a carnival. Peter had joined the merrymakers but nobody had even noticed him. "If only I could be as rich as Fat Ezechiel, or as daring and strong as the Long Shlurker, or as renowned as the King of the Dancers. They all spend gulden as other people spend pennies. How on earth did they get so rich?" Thus he had often wondered when he sat alone in the woods, eating his heart out in envy. He forgot that nobody liked them, for the three were as hard as nails. In spite of all their money, they were possessed by an inhuman greed. But everybody knows how these things are: though the three were hated for their avarice, they were also highly respected for their riches. Who else could spend gulden as they could, as if gold grew on fir trees?

This was the way Peter's thoughts ran while he sat and stared at the sooty, slowly smoldering kiln in front of him. He considered all kinds of ways to earn plenty of money, but none of them pleased him. He even thought about the old folk tales: of how people in olden times had become fabulously rich with the help of the forest sprites, Dutch Michael and the Little Glassman.

When his father was still alive, they often had company in the evening, and the good people loved to talk about rich folks and how they had acquired their wealth. Often he had heard of the Little Glassman who had helped many a man in need. He could almost remember the verse which one had to recite to conjure up the gnome. It started:

> Treasure-keeper in forest and wold,
> Many hundred years are you old.
> Thine is all land where fir trees grow . . .

But, hard as he tried, he could not recall the last line.

"I ought to ask among the old folks, somebody might know the verse," he thought. But he was ashamed to reveal his inner thoughts. He was also fairly sure that no one would remember it any more—there were so few rich people in the Black Forest. Why had his father and his friends not tried to improve their luck? Once he made his mother talk about the manikin, but she did not remember the last line either.

"It's too bad, Peter, but the last line has slipped my mind," Frau Munk said regretfully. "The Little Glassman shows himself only to Sunday children, so you might have a chance. You were born on a Sunday at noontime! But, of course, one also has to know how to call up the little man. It's no use, my son."

But Peter was quite beside himself with longing to undertake the adventure, now that he knew he was a Sunday child. "It ought to be enough that I was born under a lucky star and know most of the verses. I'm sure I can invoke him," he thought.

The next time he sold all his charcoal, he did not build a new kiln but dressed in his Sunday best. He put on his peaked Sunday hat, took his five-foot-long blackthorn staff, and said goodbye to his mother.

"I'll go down to the city today and see the conscription officer," he told her. "I want to make sure he realizes that I am an only son and that you depend on me."

"You are a good and thoughtful boy," Frau Munk said and looked proudly at her good-looking son. "That's right, you have to make sure they don't put you on the draft lists."

But Peter did not go to the city. He took the road to the Little Glassman's abode on the summit of the rolling Black Forest Mountains. He knew well that people said it was not safe here, which was the reason none of these trees were ever felled. The most magnificent firs grew here, but people avoided the spot. Lumbermen who had dared to work in these woods had met with bad accidents. Trees had tumbled down unexpectedly and injured or even killed the workmen. No raftsman would ever accept a log from the Little Glassman's fir knoll, because a raft which contained one was bound to sink. There was no village, not even a hut for miles and miles. No axes rang, no saws droned, no dogs barked. It was a long and lonely climb.

Finally Peter reached the summit and stood under a fir of tremendous girth. A Dutch Mynheer would have paid hundreds of gulden for that tree! It was very dark under the deep-hanging, thickly needled boughs. There was no sound but Peter's own step. No bird sang, no animal stirred. A shiver of eeriness and awe chilled Peter's heart. "This must be the place," he thought. "I'm sure the little man lives here." He took off his broad-brimmed Sunday hat, cleared his throat, and bowed deeply to the fir tree.

"I wish you a pleasant evening, Mr. Glassman," he said in a trembling voice. But nothing happened. It was as quiet as before.

"Guess I have to recite the verse," he thought and stammered:

> Treasure-keeper in forest and wold,
> Many hundred years are you old.
> Thine is all land where fir trees grow . . .

His heart pounded for he saw a strange, very small figure appear from behind the fir tree. He was dressed like the glassmakers in Peter's village. He wore a little black jerkin, enormous closely pleated plus fours, red stockings, a peaked hat with a very wide brim—Peter saw it all quite clearly, even the pale clever little face. But alas! Just as quick as the gnome had made his appearance, he had vanished again!

"Mr. Glassman!" Peter called after a minute of deep silence. "Please, don't make a fool of me!" He waited awhile. "If you think I didn't see you, sir, you are mistaken. I saw you very well behind your tree."

Still no answer, but Peter thought he heard a low, hoarse

chuckle. Finally his impatience became greater than his fear.

"Wait, you little lad," he called out, "I'll catch you soon enough." With that he rushed behind the fir. But there was no treasure-keeper of the green forests, only a dainty little squirrel which ran up a tree. Peter Munk shook his head. He understood that he had nearly succeeded with his conjuration. If he only knew the missing rhyme, he might be able to entice the gnome to stay and talk with him. He racked his brain but he found no rhyme.

The squirrel sat now on one of the lowest branches, licking its paws and looking at Peter with clever eyes. Peter did not know whether it was encouraging or teasing him. He was almost afraid to be alone with the little creature. For a moment it seemed to have a human head and to wear a peaked hat. When he looked closer, it had a squirrel's head again but now it sported red stockings and tiny black shoes. A coldness trickled down his spine. "There's some deviltry about it," he thought and shivered.

He beat a retreat, leaving much more hurriedly than he had come. The darkness of the fir thicket around him seemed to increase. The stillness became so overpowering that he started to run and did not stop till he heard dogs barking and saw smoke rising from a hut. He caught his breath and walked on. When he came nearer he realized that in his blind fear he had headed in the wrong direction. People were not wearing the glassworker's garb as in his home valley but the lumberman's garments. They were woodcutters; an old man, his son, and his large family. Peter was heartily welcomed. He was offered a cool drink of cider, and for dinner they had a large mountain cock, best of all Black Forest dishes.

After dinner the good housewife and her daughters sat down to ply their distaffs by the dim light of a chip of resinous pinewood. The boys were busy carving spoons and forks from well-seasoned wood. It was very cozy in the hut, but outside a storm raged. One could hear the howling of the strong winds. The trees sighed and creaked as they bent under the force of the gale. Sometimes they heard a tree crash down and heard the shotlike sound when the large branches snapped. The boys would have liked to run into the forest to admire the gruesome spectacle, but their grandfather forbade it with firm words.

"I wouldn't advise anybody to leave the safety of the hut tonight. Heaven only knows, he might never come back." He added meaningfully, "Dutch Michael is felling trees for a new raft tonight."

The boys had often heard of Dutch Michael, but now they asked Grandfather to tell the old tales again, and Peter joined in their request.

"What, you don't know about Dutch Michael? You

must surely live far from this part of the forest! Dutch Michael is the Master of our woods. I'll tell you all I know about him."

He lighted his brier pipe, and after a few puffs he started his tale.

"More than a hundred years ago, or so my grandfather told me, there were no people on this earth as humble and as honest as the Black Foresters. Times have changed, I know; there's too much money around now. Folks swear and drink and dance on Sundays—it's a shame! And I have often said so: it's all Dutch Michael's fault.

"Well, about a hundred years ago a rich timber merchant lived here. Many lumbermen worked for him, and he traded his timber far downstream. His work was blessed, for he was a good and pious man. One evening a stranger came to his door and asked for work. He was the tallest and strongest man the merchant ever had laid eyes on, and he took the young giant into his service gladly. Long Michael worked just as his master had expected him to. When they felled trees, he worked as hard as three. When they logged wood and six men strained at one end, he easily carried the other end. After half a year he approached his master and said:

" 'I have felled and lopped and hewed and logged enough trees. Now I want to see where my trees go. I would like to become a raftsman.'

" 'You are a good worker, Mike, and I'll not stand in your way,' the master said. 'You are certainly a marvelous woodcutter, but it takes skill to be a good raftsman. However, you may try it just once.'

"The raft they were going to float down the river had eight joints, and they had used nice large timber for it.

But what happened? On the last evening Long Michael
carried eight enormous beams down to the river, and nobody knew where he could have felled such tremendous
trees. But Long Michael carried them on his broad shoulders as if they were mere sticks. The merchant was delighted when he saw these logs and figured out the large
profit he would obtain for them. But Michael laughed
scornfully.

" 'No, sir, these are mine. You think I would ride on
those splinters?'

"He roped the eight logs together and tied them to the
raft as a ninth joint. Then he brought forth a pair of raftsman's boots, the like of which nobody had ever seen. My
grandfather assured me they weighed at least a hundred
pounds and were five feet high.

"Well, they started on their trip downstream. The other
raftsmen had grumbled; they were sure Michael's heavy
logs would slow up the trip and they would make no progress. But it was quite the opposite! As soon as they had
left the small Nabod and got into the Neckar, the raft
speeded up and they sailed cheerfully down the river. The
Neckar is a meandering river, and usually it took a lot
of hard work to keep the clumsy raft clear of the rocky
shores and to prevent the float from running aground on a
sand bank. This time they had no difficulties. Michael in
his enormous boots jumped into the water at troublesome
places. He pushed here, he pulled there till the ungainly
craft was all straightened out again. Smoothly they glided
past all the dangerous spots. But when there was a straight
run ahead, you should have seen Long Michael! Two strides
and one leap and he was on the first joint.

" 'Take in your poles!' he shouted in his thunderous

voice. He pushed his beam into the gravel, a little pressure —and like an arrow the raft flew straight ahead. Villages and towns seemed to rush past them. It was a trip to everybody's liking. In half of the usual time they were in Koeln, where they used to sell the timber. How they cheered Long Mike! But he said cunningly:

" 'You don't know what's good for you! You think the Koelner merchants use all that timber for themselves? Oh no! They buy it from you at a cheap sum, and then they sell it to the Mynheers in Rotterdam for double the price. Let's go to Holland and do a little business of our own. What we make beyond the usual price will be our own profit.'

"They all were content. Some simply wished to see far-away, sumptuous Holland; the others to make a lot of money. Soon they were in Rotterdam where they got four times the usual price for their logs. The Mynheers paid heavily and even gladly for the enormous logs of the ninth joint, which would make splendid masts for sailing ships.

"Long Michael divided the money. One-fourth he put aside for the master, the other three-fourths he distributed among the men.

"Well, they all went on a long spree. Those simple, hard-working Black Foresters mixed with drunken sailors and other wild rabble. They drank heavily, they ate their fill, they gambled and cursed—and Dutch Michael laughed. They thought Holland was paradise on earth, and Dutch Michael, as they called him from then on, was their king and master.

"It took a long time before the timber merchants at home learned about the double-crossing dealings of their rafts-men. Gambling, cursing, and drinking have steadily infiltrated the quiet woodlands since then, and it is true that all these bad things go back to Dutch Michael's days. Dutch Michael disappeared and nobody knows what became of him. But he is not dead, I assure you. For a hundred years he has carried on his mischief in our woods. People say he has helped many a man to become rich, but at the price of his soul! This much is sure: on a night like this, Dutch Michael is afoot. He fells the tallest firs and gives them to his followers. The Mynheers still pay high prices for mast beams from the Black Forest. If they only knew that every ship which has a single plank of Dutch Michael's wood in her rigging is doomed! That's why we hear so much about shipwrecks. As soon as Dutch Michael fells another tree here on a stormy night, one of those ships springs a leak, and she sinks with every man and mouse.

"Well, that's the tale of Dutch Michael as I heard it from my grandfather. It's true, he is able to make you rich, but for what a price! I wouldn't like to be in Fat Ezechiel's shoes or in the Long Shlurker's either. The King of the Dancers, they say, is also one of his followers."

The storm had abated, and the family withdrew. They gave Peter a sack filled with leaves as a pillow. He stretched out on the bench by the side of the enormous green tiled stove and fell asleep.

Never had he had such wild dreams as on that night! Now he saw the gigantic Dutch Michael offering him a bag full of gulden. The goblin shook it, the gold tinkled enticingly, and Dutch Michael laughed triumphantly and murmured:

I can give you gold
As much as you choose!
You have nothing to lose.
Why don't you get hold
Of my gold—my gold?"

Then he saw the Little Glassman sitting astride a huge
green bottle, chuckling hoarsely:

"Rhyme, Peter! Rhyme. Can't you find a rhyme for
'grow'? Simpleton! And you a Sunday child! Rhyme, simple
Peter, Rhyme!"

Peter moaned and groaned in his sleep as he tried to
find a rhyme. He had never tried his hand at making
verses before, and his efforts in his dream were in vain. But
when he woke up in the morning and stretched, and
yawned, and rubbed his eyes, the dream came back to him.
He thought, "Well, I ought to be able to find a rhyme. It
can't be too hard." But, try as he would, he could not find
a word that rhymed with "grow." As he was sitting there,
torturing his brain for a word ending with "ow," he heard
three wanderers who were singing loudly and lustily:

My sweetheart sits in her garden
Where roses and lilies grow,
And when I pass and wave my hat
Her sweetest smile she'll show.

It struck him like lightning. To make sure that he had
heard right, he jumped up from the bench, rushed from
the house, and ran after them.

"Stop, my friend," he called out and grabbed one of the
men by the sleeve. "What were you singing just now?"

"Are you crazy? Let go!" The Black Forester tried to

shake off Peter's hand. "Can't I sing whatever I want, you fool?"

"Oh, please, tell me what you were singing!" Peter was quite beside himself and held on tight. The other two joined in the fray with a will, and Peter got a good beating before he let go. The boys laughed.

"That serves you right! Next time let harmless people sing what they want, you crackpot!"

"I sure will remember that," poor Peter sighed as he picked himself up from the ground. "But now you may just as well tell me: what *did* you sing?"

How they guffawed and teased him. But one of them took pity on him and repeated the ditty, till Peter knew it by heart. Chuckling and laughing, he then joined his fellows, and they went singing on their way.

"Well, well, well!" Peter rubbed his elbows and dusted his knees. " 'Show' rhymes with 'grow'; I should have thought of that myself. All right, soon I'll have the manikin at my beck and call!"

He went back into the hut, said goodbye to his hosts, took his hat and staff, and started on his way home. He went slowly and thoughtfully for he had to make up a whole line now. It still was hard work for him. Finally he had it! He jumped with joy and hastened his steps.

From behind a cluster of dark trees a man suddenly came toward him on the narrow woodpath. He was the tallest man Peter had ever seen, and as a walking stick he carried a mast in his fist. Peter's heart sank. "That's Dutch Michael," he thought and shuddered.

The huge man was silent as he walked at his side. Peter stole a glance at him. The man was not old but not young either; his face was deeply lined. He wore a linen jacket, and Peter recognized the enormous boots, well drawn up over the black leather breeches.

"Peter Munk, what are you doing here?" the king of the woods finally asked in a deep, rumbling voice.

"Good morning, *landsmann*." Peter tried to hide how scared he was. "I'm on my way home."

"Peter Munk." The giant gave him a piercing glance. "Your way home does not lead through this part of the woods."

"Oh well, it's a hot day," Peter ventured. "I thought I would enjoy the shadowy path here better than the sunny road down there."

"You're lying, Coal Peter!" Dutch Michael thundered. "Don't lie to me or I'll brain you with my little stick!" Then he added more quietly, "Do you think I didn't see you when you went begging to the Little One? It was stupid of you to ask the Little Glassman for help. That runt is greedy and doesn't like to give. When he does give, people don't have a chance to enjoy their lives. It was your good luck that you didn't remember the whole silly verse."

They walked on in silence, Peter's head whirling from all he had heard. After a while Dutch Michael started again.

"I feel sorry for you, Peter. A good-looking, quick-witted fellow like you, having to spend his life as a charcoal burner. When others throw around their gulden, you can hardly spend a few pennies. It's a wretched life you are leading."

"It's true, sir, it's kind of miserable."

"Well, I wouldn't mind helping you as I have helped others in their need. Tell me, how many hundred gulden would you want for a start?"

Dutch Michael jingled the coins in his huge pocket. They sounded just as they had in Peter's dream, and his heart fluttered anxiously. He grew hot and cold at these enticing words. But Dutch Michael did not look as if he were a man to give something for nothing. The warning words of the old man came into Peter's mind and, gripped by an irresistible fear, he stammered:

"A thousand thanks, sir. But—I don't want to have any dealings with you. . . . I know who you are!" With that he took to his heels as fast as he could. But Dutch Michael kept up with him, murmuring threateningly:

"You'll regret this, Coal Peter! It's written on your brow, I see it in your eyes, you'll be mine one day! Now stop and let's talk it over. We are already at my border."

When Peter heard that and saw a small brook just ahead of him, he raced on in the hope of crossing the border in time. Dutch Michael started to run too, swearing and threatening as he lumbered on. Peter with a last desperate effort reached the brook and jumped across just as the giant raised his pole to crush him. But the pole splintered in the air as if Dutch Michael with his enormous strength had struck an invisible wall. A large piece of wood fell down at Peter's feet.

Triumphantly he picked it up to hurl it back at the furious giant, but with horror he felt the piece of wood come alive in his hand. He saw he was gripping a monstrous snake which was baring its fangs and preparing to strike at him. He tried to throw it away, but the snake entwined itself around his arm. The flat, three-cornered ugly head swayed nearer and nearer, and he cried out in agony. An enormous mountain cock rushed to the rescue. The big bird pounced upon the snake with its strong beak, tore it away from Peter, and flew off with the helplessly struggling and coiling reptile. Peter fell down in a swoon, and dimly he heard Dutch Michael continue to roar and rave. Helplessly the giant had to look on from beyond the little brook, and see the snake defeated by a power stronger than his own.

After a while Peter picked himself up. Exhausted and trembling, he went on his way, but doggedly he kept on. The path became steeper, the scenery wilder, and soon he reached the enormous old fir tree atop the mountain. Just as yesterday he bowed politely to the invisible Little Glassman and haltingly recited:

> *Treasure-keeper in forest and wold*
> *Many hundred years are you old,*
> *Thine is all land where fir trees grow,*
> *Only to Sunday children you do yourself show.*

"Well, it's a bit uneven, but since it's you, Peter Munk, I'll let it pass for a verse," Peter heard an amused low voice saying. Quite astonished, Peter looked around. A tiny old man in a black jerkin, red stockings, and a black peaked hat was sitting under another big fir tree, smoking his pipe. He had a friendly, finely cut face with a short white beard as delicate as a spider's web. His pipe was made from blue glass, and the baffled Peter realized that the garments, shoes, and hat of the manikin were also made from colored glass. But the glass was as pliable as if it were still hot. It clung to him like cloth when the little man moved.

"So you met that ruffian, that Dutch Michael," said the Little Glassman and coughed delicately. "He certainly frightened you. As for his magic stick, he'll never see it again."

"Yes, Sir Treasurer," Peter answered with a respectful bow, "I was good and scared! I guess you were the mountain cock who killed the snake—a thousand thanks! I have come to ask your advice," he went on determinedly, while the little man looked at him with keen and appraising eyes. "I'm so poorly off, sir. A charcoal burner has no future to look forward to and since I'm young I thought I ought to try to better my condition. When I think how far other people get in a short time! Just take Fat Ezechiel, or the King of the Dancers. They seem to be rolling in wealth."

"Peter Munk," the little man said sternly and exhaled deeply. "Peter, you'd better not mention them! What good will it do them if they appear to be happy now? Later on they'll be much worse off! Don't underestimate your trade. Your father and your grandfather were upstanding, God-fearing men. I hope it isn't just laziness that leads you to me."

Peter felt the blood rush to his face at the manikin's stern words. He was a little scared but he tried to defend his ideas.

"No, Sir Treasurer of the Black Forest," he answered humbly, "I know well: 'Idleness is the root of all evil.' But you cannot blame me if I like other trades better. Charcoal burning is such a despised occupation. Glassmakers, watchmakers, raftsmen are held in much higher esteem."

" 'Pride goeth before a fall,' " the Lord of the Black Forest answered dryly. "Human beings are a strange lot. Very rarely is there one who is content with his trade. I bet if you were a glassmaker, you would want to become a timber merchant. And if you were a timber merchant, you would aspire to the chief ranger's office! But it's all right with me. Promise to work hard and lead a good life, and I'll help you. It's my habit to grant three wishes to a Sunday child who knows how to find me. The first two wishes are free. The third one I can decline if it is too foolish. Now wish for something, my boy! But, Peter, remember: something good and useful!"

"Huzza, hei! You are the most wonderful Little Glassman, and rightly they call you Treasure-keeper of the Black Forest! Well, if I can have my heart's desire—my first wish shall be that I can dance better than the King of the Dancers, and that I always have as much money in my pockets as Fat Ezechiel!"

"You fool!" the little man cried angrily. "What a stupid wish that is! You ought to be ashamed of yourself for depriving yourself of your good luck this way. What good will it do you and your poor mother if you are a good dancer? What good will money do you if according to your wish you have it only for wasting time in an inn? You'll starve all week long and be worse off than you are now." Angrily he puffed away on his glass pipe. "Well, you have another wish coming. But try and wish for something more sensible."

Peter scratched his ears, and after a while he said hesitantly:

"All right, I'll wish for the best and richest glassworks in the whole Black Forest, with everything that goes with it and the money to run it."

"Nothing else, Peter?" the Little Glassman asked quite concernedly. "Peter, don't you know of anything else to wish for?"

"Well, you might add a horse and a carriage . . ."

"Oh, you stupid fool, you idiot!" the little man called out. Angrily he hurled his blue pipe at the big fir tree so that it was smashed to bits. "Horses? A carriage? Common sense, you should have wished for! Good common sense and knowledge, you should have wished for, not for a horse and a carriage! Now, don't look so downcast, we'll see that you make out all right. On the whole your second wish was sensible. A good glass factory will support its owner nicely. Only you should have asked for the knowledge and sense to know how to manage a factory. Horses and a carriage could have been acquired easily."

"But, Sir Treasurer," Peter replied in a dejected tone. "I have another wish coming. I could wish for common sense if you really think that I need it that urgently."

"Nothing doing, my boy! You'll be in trouble soon enough with your crazy first wish. And you'll be glad to know there might be help for you." He pulled a small leather pouch from his pocket and handed it to Peter while he talked. "Go home now. Here are two thousand gulden, and don't come back begging for more money or I'll have to hang you from my tallest fir tree! That's how I've dealt with mortals ever since I lived in this forest. Now listen to me. Three days ago Old Winkfritz, who owned the large glassworks in your valley, died. Go there and bid for the works, an honest bid as is the custom. Now you be good and work hard." The little man gave Peter an appraising glance. "I'll come around once in a while and help you out with some advice, since you were too stupid to ask for good sense, but your first wish was very bad. You be careful now that you don't pick up too much trouble with drinking and gambling and all kinds of foolishness. 'Emperor of the Dancers,' my foot!" He chuckled angrily. "Peter, Peter!

Anybody hanging out in a pub all the time is asking for trouble." He pulled a shiny new glass pipe from his pocket, filled it with dry moss, and put the pipe into his toothless little mouth. Then he extracted a large magnifying glass from the other pocket and went over to a sunny spot. With the magnifying glass he lit his pipe and inhaled with obvious pleasure. A pleasant aroma of the best Dutch tobacco filled the air. In a friendly manner the little man shook hands with Peter.

"Now run along, my boy, and try to make out all right," he said, smiling at him. Then he disappeared in the tobacco clouds which drifted and curled, and soon hid the Little Glassman.

Peter rushed home, as proud and happy as a king. His mother had spent an anxious day. She was afraid they had drafted poor Peter right away and he would never come home and take care of her. Joyfully he told her he had met a friend who had lent him a large sum, and that now he was going to be a rich glass manufacturer. Frau Barbara Munk had lived all her life in their humble abode, and she was as used to sooty and blackened men as a miller's wife is used to her husband's floury face. But when she learned about Peter's astonishing good luck, she preened and carried on.

"You certainly deserve a break, Peter! And I have been a good mother and wife all my life! Of course, now, as the mother of a rich glass manufacturer, I will sit in the front row in church on Sundays. I will have to be quite choosy about my friends, since now I'll be so much higher up on the social ladder, and Dick's and Tom's and Harry's wives will have to greet me first! This certainly is a lucky day for us!" And she hustled and bustled around in the kitchen to prepare the best meal she had to offer.

Peter soon came to terms with the heirs of the glassworks. He kept on all the glassworkers who knew their trade well, and he let them make glass day and night. In the beginning he enjoyed his new occupation wholeheartedly. With his hands in his pockets he strutted through the factory; looking here, looking there; saying this, saying that; and his glassblowers were much amused since he did not know the least little bit what he was talking about. He was fascinated by the many-colored pliable warm mass from which his workers blew such extraordinary things. He loved to form little figures with his hands—men and beasts, and little ornaments.

But after a while he became bored with work he did not understand, and he came to the factory for only a few hours a day. Soon it was only every other day and then it was only once a week, and his workmen did as they pleased.

The main reason for his negligence was that he was quite intoxicated by the excitement he derived from his Sunday visits in the Sun, the village inn. Full of expectations he went to the inn the Sunday after his visit to the Little Glassman. And who was the first one he saw but the King of the Dancers, skipping nimbly. Fat Ezechiel sat at a table with the largest stein imaginable and gambled for gulden. Peter searched his pockets. Fat Ezechiel must be well heeled for Peter's pockets were crammed with gold and silver coins. When the dance was finished Peter and his girl, the prettiest wench on the floor, hazel-eyed and curly-haired, joined the dancers.

It was marvelous! When the King of the Dancers took a jump three feet high, Peter jumped four feet. When the other executed extraordinary and elegant steps, Peter's feet tapped and slid and glided so gracefully, he leaped and pranced and capered in such intricate patterns, that the on-lookers burst into wild applause. Peter was as proud as a king! And when people saw how he threw gulden at the musicians at each round, when they heard that he had bought Old Winkfritz' glassworks, then there was no end to their marveling and conjecturing. Had he unearthed a golden treasure while working in the forest? Had he in-herited the money? It did not matter. Everybody paid the highest respect to Peter Munk.

Peter was beside himself with pride and joy. With open hands he gave to the poor; he remembered so well how depressing it is to be poverty-stricken. He was lord and master in the inn, and graciously he accepted his new nickname "Emperor of the Dancers." He certainly was not "Coal Peter" any more! He was well liked in the inn, for it did not bother him when he lost large sums, and mostly he lost to Fat Ezechiel. It was exactly as he had wished: he always had as much money as the fat man in his pockets.

But his pleasure in this new life did not last very long, for soon he became used to extravagant gambling and rich living. He attracted quite a following of rabble, and the better elements withdrew from him. Before long he was not the "Emperor of the Dancers," but "Gambling Peter," for he—what a disgrace—played on every workday!

By and by his glass factory started to go downhill. He had manufactured a vast amount of glass but he lacked the knowledge where to sell it. In the end he was forced to sell it for half the usual price in order to be able to pay his workers.

One evening on his way home from the Sun, he felt very depressed about his failure. He had been drinking heavily to cheer up, but it had not helped. Suddenly he felt he was not alone, and looking around he saw the Little Glassman at his side.

"There you are! Why did you come? Do you want to gloat over my misery?" Peter cried in a violent fit of rage. "How happy I was when I was only a poor charcoal burner; now I have nothing but troubles and worries! What good is my glass factory to me or my horse and carriage? The bailiff might come any day to assess and mortgage my property. He even might put me in jail for my debts! It's all your fault!"

"Is that the way you see it?" the Little Glassman answered sternly. "Is that your gratitude? Peter, Peter, do you blame your failure on me? Didn't I tell you to wish carefully? Knowledge, my boy, common sense is what you need."

"What for! Common sense indeed!" Peter called out angrily. "I'm just as smart as anybody and I'll show it to you right away, Little Glassman!" He lurched at the manikin and grabbed his collar. He shook him madly. "Now I've got you, Treasure-keeper! And this is my third wish and you better grant it to me right away: I wish for two hundred thousand gulden and a splendid house and . . . oh, ouch! OUCH!" He screamed and jerked his hand away. The gnome had transformed himself into molten glass. Peter's hand was badly burned, and the Little Glassman had disappeared.

For a couple of days his swollen hand reminded him of his folly and ingratitude, and he was ashamed of himself.

But then he became hardened again and thought, "Let them sell the glassworks and all I own, what do I care! I still have Fat Ezechiel and as long as he has money I'll not be lacking for anything."

Right, Peter, but if Fat Ezechiel has no money? And that was exactly what happened one day, and it was a very strange piece of arithmetic!

All seemed as usual the next time Peter drove to the Sun. His friends, crowding at the windows, made their malicious remarks about him. "Look, who's coming, our Gambling Peter!" "Well, well," said the second, "the Emperor of the Dancers! The rich glass manufacturer." But a third one shook his head. "What do you mean by 'rich'? Somebody told me the bailiff will pay him a little visit quite soon. He is in debt up to his ears!" "No wonder," said the first one, "Gambling Peter will have gambled away his last penny pretty soon. Mark my words!"

Peter, unaware of the biting comments about him, had entered.

"Good morning, everybody," he cried cheerfully. "Innkeeper, is Fat Ezechiel here?"

"Come here, Peter. Come and sit down," a rumbling basso answered. "We're already quite busy in here with a little game."

Peter's hand slipped into his pocket: the fat man had provided well, Peter's pockets were heavy with money. He joined the gamblers and they played. He won and lost and lost and won, and they kept the dice rolling till darkness fell. Some men left for home, but there was still a group. By candlelight they went on gambling till two men got up, yawning and stretching.

"Well, we'd better leave, it's getting pretty late." They gathered in their spoils and were gone.

"I won't stop! Don't you leave, Ezechiel!" cried Peter Munk. "Let's go on with the game."

"All right, just let me count my money," answered the fat man. "And then we'll play for five gulden a point. Everything else is chickenfeed."

He counted and saw he had exactly a hundred gulden, and Peter did not have to bother counting; he knew he had the same amount. They played, but Fat Ezechiel lost and lost. His luck had turned and he swore viciously about Peter's lucky streak. Finally he put five gulden on the table and said:

"This is my last piece of money, and if I lose it I won't stop. You have to lend me some of your winnings, Peter."

"Gladly, and as much as you want," Peter answered cheerfully.

The fat man cast the dice.

"Fifteen points!" he called.

"Eighteen!" Peter cried triumphantly, but a deep, well-known voice murmured:

"All right, fellow! That was your last throw!"

The startled Peter turned around. Dutch Michael towered behind him and grinned maliciously. But neither Fat Ezechiel nor the innkeeper saw the forest sprite.

"You lucky dog," the fat man laughed hoarsely. "Now lend me ten gulden as you promised."

Peter put his hand into his pocket; why, it was empty! Hastily he rummaged through all his pockets, there was not a single copper! Only then he remembered his foolish wish: "Always as much money as Fat Ezechiel has." And that was exactly what he had, NOTHING!

The innkeeper and Fat Ezechiel had looked with rising astonishment at Peter's antics. First they did not believe their own eyes. They turned his coat and trouser pockets inside out—nothing, absolutely nothing!

"Where is the money? Did you hex it away? The devil is your blood brother, it seems!"

"A sorcerer! God help us!" cried the innkeeper. "To-morrow morning I'll report you in town, and then you'll see where you'll end up!"

Furiously they assaulted him, and the stunned Peter got a severe thrashing before they threw him out—bloody and beaten up, and with torn clothes.

It was very dark when Peter crept home, but he could see clearly a tall dark figure at his side, and hear the familiar voice:

"That was the end, Peter Munk, of your splendid life! Didn't I tell you before you would have only trouble if you dealt with the Little One? But I feel sorry for you and I'm still willing to help you. You know where to find me. Come tomorrow, come and let me help you."

Peter did not answer. He was deeply frightened and ran all the way home.

Next morning the bailiff paid Peter an unwanted visit in his glassworks. After a cold "Good morning," he presented Peter with a long list of his debtors.

"Can you pay?" he asked gruffly. "Just say 'yes' or 'no.' I don't have much time, and it's a three-hour trip to the jail."

Peter admitted that he had no money. Gloomily he looked on as the bailiff and his helpers started to assess house and factory, stable and barn, garden and fields, horse and carriage. And while they were listing the value of Peter's earthly possessions he thought, "The Little One caused me only trouble. I'd better get help now from the Tall One. It isn't far to Dutch Michael's realm."

Unnoticed, he sneaked away. Then he started to run as fast as he could till he had reached Dutch Michael's haunt. Still out of breath, he started to call:

"Dutch Michael! Come and help me, Dutch Michael!"

And there stood the gigantic raftsman right before him.

"Hello, Peter, there you are! I knew it!" Dutch Michael laughed thunderously. "Were they going to skin you alive and sell your skin to your debtors? Now take it easy, I'll gladly help you. You shouldn't have dealt with that little stinker, that troublemaker, that hypocrite! He gives like a miser and not freely as I am wont to do. Now, come this way to my house," he said and turned into the dark woods. "We'll soon come to terms."

"Come to terms?" thought Peter. "What on earth can he want from me? Maybe I have to serve him for a while."

Without a word he followed Dutch Michael along the steep path which soon ended at a dark, deep ravine. Nimbly Dutch Michael leaped down the rocky walls as if they were smooth marble steps. On his arrival at the bottom of the pit, Dutch Michael suddenly stretched and stretched till he was as tall as a steeple. He held up his hand—it was as big as a table! Peter heard his rumbling voice, deep like a mourning bell:

"Step on my hand and get hold of a finger, then you won't fall."

Peter trembled like a quaking aspen but he did as he was told. He stepped over to the gigantic hand and held on tight to the giant's thumb. He was taken down rapidly. To his astonishment it grew brighter and brighter, the deeper he traveled. There was a house at the bottom, such as any rich peasant in the Black Forest might own.

Dutch Michael had assumed his usual stature, and they went into the house. The living room was not distinguished in any way from other people's living rooms except by its lonely appearance. There was the same cuckoo clock, the same immense tile stove, the sturdy table, and the wide bench made of larchwood. The same crockery, the same tin jugs and earthen mugs stood on the shelves around the wainscoted walls as in any other peasant's home.

Dutch Michael bade Peter sit down and brought out an immense jug of wine and tumblers. He poured the heady red wine and started to talk. He told Peter about the pleasures in life, he spoke of strange countries, beautiful cities and rivers, till Peter's heart was filled with a great longing to see the wide world, and he said so to his host.

"I see. Just now you feel like a daring fellow. But are you not really quite a fainthearted lad?" Dutch Michael replied, looking at him with a sly grin. "How upset you were about today's injuries to your precious honor! How your heart beat when they called you a scoundrel! Tell me, did you feel it in your head when they said you were a cheater, a dirty swindler? Did your stomach hurt when the bailiff came to chase you away from house and homestead? Tell me, where did it hurt?"

"In my heart," Peter answered, and pressed his hand on his anxiously throbbing heart.

"You threw hundreds of gulden away to beggars! Did it help you any? They wished you God's blessings and good health. Are you more healthy for their wishes? For half of what you squandered you could have had the best doctors. Blessings! Well, I call it quite a blessing to be turned out of house and home." Dutch Michael leaned over the table and asked leeringly, "But tell me what made your hand slip into your pocket as soon as a beggar stretched out his hand? Your heart it was! Only your heart! Neither your eyes nor your tongue, neither your arms nor your legs, only your heart made you act that way. As the saying goes, 'You took it to heart!' "

"But what can I do about it? Even if I try to suppress it, it still beats and throbs and pulsates till it hurts me."

"Of course," the other agreed with horrid laughter. "You can't help that, you poor dolt. But give it to me, that stupid, throbbing thing, and you'll see how easy life will be."

"My heart?" Peter cried out, horrified. "But I could die on the spot. No, never! Never!"

"Certainly, if one of your doctors undertook to cut your heart out, then you would die. But it's different with me. Come and have a look, and you'll be convinced."

He arose and led Peter to a small chamber. As Peter crossed the threshold, his heart contracted painfully. He paid no attention to it, what he saw was so weird and unexpected.

A collection of glass jars filled with a transparent liquid were standing on several shelves. Each glass contained a slowly pulsating heart. The jars were labeled and there were names written on each one; Peter full of curiosity read them. There was the name of the bailiff who had just assessed his property, the heart of Fat Ezechiel, of the

King of the Dancers, of the chief ranger. There were six hearts from corn dealers, eight from recruiting officers, three from pawnbrokers—in short, it was a collection of the most respected hearts for twenty miles around.

"Look, Peter, all these people have left behind life's anxieties and unrest," he heard Dutch Michael's deep voice saying. "None of these hearts beats excitedly or is troubled by anything. And their former owners feel much better since ridding themselves of such a restless guest."

"But what on earth do they have instead of a heart?" Peter asked. His head spun from all he had seen and heard.

"This." Dutch Michael opened a drawer and showed Peter—a heart of stone!

"What? A heart of marble?" Peter cried out and shuddered. "But that must feel cold, sir, cold in the breast."

"Yes, it's pleasantly cool. Why should a heart be warm? In winter a good hard drink warms better than a warm heart. In summer when it is hot and humid, well, you wouldn't believe how such a heart cools you. And, as I said before, neither fear nor anguish, neither foolish pity nor any other stupid emotion bothers such a heart."

"And that is all you have to give?" Peter said in disgust. "I hoped for money and you offer me a stone."

"Well, I think a hundred thousand gulden ought to be enough for a start. If you lend it out cleverly, you'll soon be a millionaire."

"A hundred thousand?" the poor charcoal burner called out merrily. "Don't throb so violently in my breast, we'll soon be done with each other! All right, Michael, give me the stone and the money, and you can take that restless thing out of its casing."

"I knew you would be a sensible fellow," Dutch Michael said with a friendly smile. "Now come, we'll have a drink on the bargain and then I'll give you the money."

They went back to the living room and drank, and drank some more, till Peter fell into a deep sleep.

Coal Peter awoke to the merry tunes of a bugle. He was sitting in a beautiful carriage and they rolled along a smooth road. In the far distance, as he leaned out of the window, he saw the blue mountain range of the Black Forest. First he could hardly believe that it was poor Peter Munk who was driving in such state through the country and in such an elegant vehicle. But then he remembered everything that had happened the day before and he soon gave up meditating and called out:

"I am Coal Peter! That's sure, and nobody else!"

He was astonished that he did not feel sad at leaving his home country for the first time in his life. He thought of his mother, but it did not worry him that he had left her penniless and without saying goodbye. "Ah well, what does it matter? Tears and sighing, longing and anguish come from the heart, that's sure. And mine, thanks to Dutch Michael, is a cold stone."

He pressed his hand to his breast. It was quiet there, nothing stirred. "Let's hope he was as reliable with the money as with that stupid thing." That was all he thought. He searched his pockets and the carriage till he found a valise containing many thousand gulden. "Now I have what I wanted." He leaned back comfortably. The postillion gave forth with another gay tune, and Peter was on his way into the wide world.

For two years Peter Munk traveled.

He glanced out of his carriage as he drove. He looked to the right, he looked to the left. He saw the shingle of the inn when they stopped. He asked to be shown the most extraordinary sights and beauties of each city, but he could not enjoy anything. No lovely landscape, no picture, no music, no marvelous building made an impression on his heart of stone. His eyes and ears were deadened to beauty. Nothing was left but the pleasure of eating, and drinking, and sleeping. And thus he lived. Without purpose he traveled all over the world. He ate for enjoyment, he slept from boredom.

Sometimes he remembered how happy he had been as a young boy, how he had laughed at every little joke. He could not laugh. When others laughed, he smiled politely, but his heart knew no joy.

Finally he decided to go home.

When he saw the blue mountain range; when he traveled through the dark forests, when he heard the familiar dialect, saw the well-known garments, he felt his blood rush quicker through his veins. He touched his breast. He was sure his heart was beating again and would make him laugh and cry at the same time. How could he be so foolish! He had a heart of stone, and stones are dead and know neither laughter nor tears.

His first errand was to visit Dutch Michael who received him cordially.

"Michael," Peter said dejectedly, "I have traveled and I have seen all there is to see. It is all nonsense, and I am bored. By the way that stone in my breast certainly protects me from many things. I'm never angry or sad, but I never enjoy anything. I feel I'm only half alive. Could you not make that stone move just a little? Or still better give me back my old heart! I got so used to it during my younger years, I miss it now. And even though it sometimes made me do foolish things, it was a good and cheerful heart."

The forest sprite laughed grimly.

"When you are dead, Peter Munk," he answered, "then you shall have back your soft and movable heart. Then you will feel what is coming your way: sorrow or joy. But on earth it will never be yours again." Peter looked at him with tired eyes, and Dutch Michael went on, "Listen to me, Peter. You traveled, but it was all useless because you had no aim. You were lazy. That's why you were bored and now you blame it on your heart. Settle down here. Build a house, marry, and have a family. Let your money work. You won't be so bored when you have something to do."

Peter recognized how right Dutch Michael was. He received another hundred thousand gulden and they parted as friends.

Soon everybody in the Black Forest knew Peter Munk was back and was richer than ever.

And it was as it always has been and always will be. They welcomed the rich man. They shook his hand, praised his horse, inquired about his travels, and soon he was gambling again with Fat Ezechiel—the rich and highly esteemed Herr Munk. He was not a glass manufacturer any more. Now he dealt in grain and loaned money at a high rate of interest. After a while half of the Black Forest people were indebted to him. Now he was a good friend of the bailiff's. If some poor devil did not pay a debt the

very day it was due, the bailiff came to chase people from their homes, and nobody was troubled as to what became of them.

At first Peter was pestered to some extent by these unfortunates. They gathered before his house and begged for mercy. But he bought two big dogs which he set on the beggars, and soon that "caterwauling," as he called it, had stopped. Then there was only "that old woman" who was bothersome: his mother who had become very poor. He had come home an extremely rich man, but he did not take care of her. She would come once in a while, old and feeble as she was, and wait outside the house. She did not dare to enter after he once had her turned away. His stone-cold heart was not moved by her pale, well-known face, her outstretched hands, her frail figure. Sulkily he took half a gulden from his pocket and sent it to her by a servant. He heard her trembling voice when she gave her thanks and wished God's blessings upon him. He heard her cough as hesitantly she left his door. He did not give it another thought. Just the thought that he had thrown away some good money bothered him a little.

After a while Peter decided to marry. He was well aware that every father in the Black Forest would be more than pleased to have his daughter marry rich Peter Munk. But Peter was choosy. He wanted to be the envy of all in this matter, just as in money matters. He wanted the fairest maiden in the Black Forest. He went here and there. He inquired and went to all festivals, but there was always something amiss. Finally he heard about Fair Lisbeth, the most beautiful and most virtuous of all fair maidens. Her father was a poor woodchopper, but Peter did not mind that and went to see her.

He rode to their hut in the deep woods, and her father was very honored by the visit of the rich gentleman. He was both astonished and pleased to hear that Herr Peter Munk wanted to become his son-in-law, and did not hesitate to grab his good luck. Surely, his poverty and worries would all be ended now, and he gave his consent without asking Lisbeth. The good, docile child became Frau Peter Munk without any argument.

Fair Lisbeth was not as happy as she had hoped she would be. She thought she was a good housekeeper but she never pleased Peter with anything she did. She felt pity for poor people. Since her husband was such a rich man, she thought it no sin to give a penny here and there to a beggar.

One day Peter noticed this and scolded her with rough words.

"What? You squander my money by throwing it to beggars! Did you bring anything into our marriage that makes you think you have the right to give away things? Don't let me catch you again or you'll feel my hand."

Fair Lisbeth cried bitterly over her husband's hard heart. Often she wished she were home in her father's poor hut. From then on, when she was sitting on the bench before their house, and a beggar stretched out his hand and murmured his plea, she would close her eyes so as not to see his misery. She would clench her hands so they could not slip into her pocket and extract a penny. So it happened that Fair Lisbeth was reputed in the whole Forest as being even more miserly than Peter.

One day Lisbeth was sitting on her bench with her spinning wheel, humming a tune. It was a lovely day. Peter was out horseback riding, and her heart was not as heavy as usual. She saw a little old man approaching. He was burdened with a heavy sack, and she heard him panting from afar. "He shouldn't carry such a heavy load, that poor old man," Lisbeth thought, full of sympathy. The little old man came nearer, stumbling and gasping. Just as he had reached her house he collapsed under his heavy load.

"For the sake of the Lord, please, give me a drink of water," he groaned. "I can't go on any more."

"You shouldn't overdo at your age," Lisbeth said, getting up from the bench.

"I have to earn a living as a porter," he replied. "A rich woman like you doesn't know how bitter poverty is. Let me have some water, please."

Lisbeth went into the house. She filled a mug with water, but then she changed her mind. She took a cup from a shelf, filled it with wine, put a piece of bread on top of it, and took it to the old man. He looked at her. Tears gathered in his old eyes. He drank and then he said:

"I am very old, and I have seen much. But not often have I met with people who know how to give as gracefully as you. But you'll be rewarded for your goodness."

"She shall have her reward right away!" a terrible voice cried out. As they turned in fright, they saw Peter, purple with rage.

"My best wine you pour to beggars, my own cup you put to their lips. Wait! Here's your reward!"

The horrified Lisbeth begged his forgiveness but his stone-cold heart knew no pity. With the handle of his ebony whip he struck her fair brow so hard that she sank lifeless into the old man's arms. When Peter saw what he had done, he seemed to repent his rash deed. He stooped to see whether she was still alive, but the old man said, and well Peter knew that voice:

"Don't trouble yourself, Peter Munk! She was the fairest and loveliest flower in the Black Forest, but you trampled on her. She will never bloom again!"

Peter's face had turned an ashen color. But he answered coldly:

"Ah! It's you, Sir Treasurer? Well, what is done is done. I guess it was bound to happen. I hope you won't report me as a murderer."

"You wretched creature!" replied the Little Glassman. "What good would it do if I sent your mortal body to the gallows? You have to fear another, a harsher judgment. You sold your soul to the devil!"

"And if I sold my heart," Peter cried out in agony, "if I sold my heart, nobody but you and your deceptive treasures are to blame for it! You led me to disaster, you mischievous spirit! *You* drove me to the other one! Yours is the whole responsibility!"

He had hardly finished when he saw the Little Glassman grow and grow till a gigantic, menacing figure towered over him, eyes aflame, his mouth a terrifying fire-spitting cavern. Peter fell on his knees. His stone heart could not prevent him from shaking like an aspen. Vulture's talons gripped Peter by his neck. Like dry leaves tossed about by a whirlwind, Peter was shaken violently. Then he was dashed to the ground, and he thought every bone was broken.

"Earthborn creature!" The voice was like rolling thunder. "I could break you to pieces if I wanted to for you offended the Lord of the Black Forest! But for the sake of your dead wife, who fed and refreshed me, I'll give you eight days' grace. If you don't repent and renounce your evil ways in that time, I will return and smash your very bones, and you shall die in your sins!"

In the evening neighbors found rich Peter Munk lying on the ground. They turned him over and searched for his breath, but for a long time their efforts were in vain. They bathed his face, and finally Peter moaned. He opened his eyes and looked around in a dazed way.

"Where is my wife?" he asked, but nobody had seen her. He thanked his neighbors for their kindness. Then he crept into his house and searched for Lisbeth. She was nowhere; not in the cellar, not in the attic, nowhere. And then he remembered. He had strange thoughts as he moved restlessly through the house. He did not grieve; cold was the heart in his breast. But as he brooded over Fair Lisbeth's death, he thought about his own end. One day he would die, steeped in sin, laden with the tears of the poor, the misery of thousands, the curses of those he had chased with his dogs. He would be charged with the mute desperation of his old mother and with the blood of Lisbeth, the good, the fair! How could he account for her if her father should come and ask, "Where is my daughter, your wife?" How should he answer Another One? He thought long-forgotten thoughts about Him Who owns forests and mountains, rivers and lakes, and the lives of all men!

Peter was tormented in his dreams. Every so often he awoke for he thought he heard a sweet voice whispering:

"Peter, get a warmer heart!"

Next day he went to the inn seeking diversion, and there he met Fat Ezechiel. He sat down beside the fat man. They talked about the weather, about war and taxes, and finally about death. How quickly one or the other of their friends had passed away!

"What do you think of death, Ezechiel? What will happen hereafter?"

"Well, the body will be buried, and the soul will either ascend to heaven or descend to hell—that all depends."

"And the heart, will that be buried too?" Peter waited anxiously for the answer.

"Sure thing, that will be buried too."

"But if a man no longer has a heart?"

Ezechiel looked at him in subdued and terrible fury.

"What do you mean? Do you want to tease me? You mean I have no heart?"

"Oh, heart enough, but as cold as a stone," replied Peter.

Ezechiel glared at him. He turned around to see if they were alone. Then he said:

"How do you know that? Could it be that your own heart, too, is not beating any more?"

"It does not beat any more, at least not in my breast," Peter answered quietly. "But tell me since you know now what I mean: how will it go with our hearts?"

"Why bother, friend?" The fat man laughed carelessly. "We have our share on earth and that's enough. That is the best thing about our cold hearts. We know no fear, even when thinking that kind of thought."

"That's true. But sometimes one does think about it. Now, of course, I know no fear. But I remember well how scared of hell I was when I was an innocent little child."

"Well, we won't be too well off, naturally," Ezechiel said. "I asked a teacher about it, and he said that every man's heart will be weighed after he has died to find out how heavily he has sinned. The light ones will rise, but the heavy ones will sink down. I can imagine our stones will be quite weighty."

"You're right, Ezechiel. What's the use of talking about it. But, you know, sometimes I think it is most disquieting that my heart is so dead and unconcerned when I think such thoughts."

Next night he heard Lisbeth's voice again, whispering into his ear:

"Peter, get a warmer heart."

He remembered it distinctly when he awoke, and thought about it all day. He did not repent that he had killed her. But when he told his servants, "My wife is traveling for a while," he thought, "I wonder where she has gone."

Six days had passed, and always he heard her voice in his sleep, and always he thought of the Lord of the Forest and his terrifying threat. The seventh morning he said to himself on arising:

"All right, I'll try to get a warmer heart. That cold stone in my breast makes life dull and dreary anyhow."

He saddled his horse and rode into the forest, up to the summit where the Little Glassman lived. When he was near the top of the mountain, he dismounted, tied his horse to a tree, and climbed the last stretch. Soon he reached the well-known huge fir tree. He took off his hat, bowed, and said in a low voice:

> *Treasure-keeper in forest and wold,*
> *Many hundred years are you old.*
> *Thine is all land where fir trees grow,*
> *Only to Sunday children you do yourself show.*

The Little Glassman appeared at once; he was not friendly and congenial as usual but depressed and sad. He wore a coat of black glass, and a long strip of crape streamed from his hat. Peter knew well for whom he was mourning.

"What do you want, Peter Munk?" he asked him in a hollow voice.

"I still have my third wish free, Sir Treasurer," Peter answered and did not lift his eyes.

"Are hearts of stone able to wish for anything?" the gnome replied. "You got everything you desired in your evil mind. I will not fulfill any wish of yours."

"But you promised me three wishes, and the third one is still left."

"I may deny it if it is a foolish wish. But, all right, I promised it. Tell me your wish."

"Give me back my living heart," Peter said.

"Did I make that bargain with you?" the little man replied bitterly. "Am I Dutch Michael who gives wealth and stone hearts? You have to go to him if you want your old heart back."

"He'll never give it back to me," Peter said sorrowfully.

There was silence for a little while, then the Little Glassman said in a gentler voice:

"I feel sorry for you, even if you don't deserve it. Your wish is not foolish, and I cannot deny you my help. Listen, you cannot retrieve your heart by force but maybe by a trick. It might not even be very difficult, for Michael is just a simpleton, in spite of thinking he is very smart. Now you go to him right away and do as I bid you to do." He told Peter in detail what he should do. Then he gave him a cross of clear glass. "He cannot take your life, and he has to let you go if you hold up this cross and pray. Now, good luck, my boy! And come back here after you get your heart back."

Every word the Little Glassman had said was imprinted on Peter's mind. Thankfully he received the glass cross. Then without hesitating he went his way to Dutch Michael's dwelling.

Three times he called him, then the giant stood before him.

"So you killed your wife!" Dutch Michael said and laughed uproariously. "I would have done the same. She squandered your good money. But you'll have to leave the country for a while. There will be some commotion when people find out that she disappeared. I guess you need more money now."

"You're right," Peter said, "and this time I need a lot. It's a long way to America."

They went to the giant's house, and Michael opened his coffer and took out many rolls of gold. While they were counting, Peter remarked casually:

"You are a nice fellow, Michael, but you pulled my leg. You lied to me when you said you had my heart, and I had only a stone in my breast."

"But, Peter, that's the way it is." Dutch Michael was very astonished. "Tell me, do you feel your heart? Isn't it cold like ice? Do you know grief? Do you repent anything?"

"You have only stopped my heart in my breast. Fat Ezechiel says the same. You lied to us. You are not the man to do a risky thing like that and tear out a living heart. You would be a magician if you could do that."

"But I assure you," Dutch Michael said sulkily, "you and Ezechiel and all those rich people who took my money have stone hearts and I keep their proper hearts here in my jars."

"What a liar you are!" Peter laughed. "You can tell that to other people but not to me. While I was traveling I saw such ruses by the dozen. Those hearts in your jars are made of wax. You are a rich fellow—that I'll admit—but you are surely no sorcerer."

Angrily the giant threw open the door to the chamber.

"Come in and see for yourself. Read the labels and look! This one here is Peter Munk's heart! Can you read that? Can you see how it trembles?"

"It's only wax." Peter shrugged his shoulders. "No real heart acts like that thing there, and my heart is in my breast. Oh no, *you* can't work miracles!"

"I'll prove it to you," the other called out in hot anger. "You shall feel that THIS is your heart."

He opened Peter's jerkin, removed the stone from his breast, and showed it to Peter. Then he took the trembling thing from the jar, breathed on it, and carefully put it in its place. Peter felt it throb, and a wave of happiness surged through him.

"How do you feel now?" Dutch Michael asked and smiled proudly.

"Really, you were right! I feel the difference," Peter answered. He felt his heart beat anxiously, and surreptitiously he took the cross from his pocket. "I wouldn't have believed that you could do that."

"See? I was right! I *can* work miracles, and you'll have to admit it. But come on now, I'll put the stone back into your breast."

"Oh no, Dutch Michael, never again that stone! This time I got the better of you." Stepping back, Peter held the cross up high and started to pray.

Dutch Michael started to tremble when he saw the cross. He shrank and shrank, he staggered around till he fell to the ground, writhing as if in pain, moaning and gasping as if in agony. All the hearts in the jars throbbed wildly and beat so loud that it sounded like in a watchmaker's shop. Peter shuddered. He became frightened and ran. He rushed out of the house and in blind haste he scaled the steep rocky walls. He heard Dutch Michael scramble to his feet, cursing and raving and setting about to pursue him. Peter ran for his life. A terrible thunderstorm was brewing. Then lightning struck to his left and to his right, trees crashed down in his path, the thunder roared—but he reached the Little Glassman's realm unharmed.

Peter's heart beat joyfully, only *because* it did beat! But ere long a cold wave of desperation seized him: he saw his life as it had been. He thought of Fair Lisbeth whom he had murdered in cold-blooded avarice. He remembered the curses of the poor. Ah, he was the scum of the earth, and crying bitterly he finally reached the Little Glassman's fir tree.

The Treasurer of the Black Forest sat under the tree smoking his pipe and looking much more cheerful.

"Why do you weep, Coal Peter?" he asked. "Could you not get your heart back? Do you still have a stone in your breast?"

"Oh, sir, I never wept when I had that heart of stone!" sighed Peter. "But you know yourself how I have lived and now my heart will break."

"Peter, you did much wrong," the little man said earnestly. "Greed and laziness wrecked your life till your heart had turned into a stone and knew neither joy nor grief, neither pity nor sympathy. But if I were sure that you feel truly sorry, I still might be able to do something for you."

"I don't want anything," Peter said, hanging his head dejectedly. "I'm done for. I'll never be happy again. Lisbeth is dead, and my mother will never forgive me. Take my life, Sir Treasurer, and my sufferings will be ended."

"All right. If that is your sincere wish, I have my ax right here."

Quietly the little man took his pipe from his mouth,

knocked the ashes out, and put it in his pocket. Then he got up and went behind the big fir tree.

Peter sat down in the soft green grass. He wept because his life held nothing further for him and would be over so soon. Patiently he waited for the end. Soon he heard soft steps and thought, "Now he is coming with his ax."

"Turn around, Peter Munk," said the Little Glassman. Peter turned around.

There stood Lisbeth and his mother!

He jumped up.

"Lisbeth! You are alive! Oh, Lisbeth, I'm so happy!" he cried. "Mother, Lisbeth, can you two forgive me?"

"They have forgiven you," said the Little Glassman. "Go home now to your father's hut and be a charcoal burner as before. And if you are industrious and honest, you'll be appreciated for your own self, and your neighbors will like you better than if you had tons of gold."

Heartily the Little Glassman shook hands with them, and he smiled kindly as Peter happily thanked him. They went home through the forest, a lighthearted, united family.

Lightning had struck Peter's rich house. It had burned to the ground with all he owned, but Peter did not mind. He headed for his father's hut. But how astonished they were to see how it had changed. Where the humble hut had stood, there was now a beautiful peasant's house with a deep-drawn thatched roof. Broad balconies went all around the spacious house. Red geraniums bloomed in the wide flower boxes on the railings of the balconies. The sturdy beams of the structure were a warm brown, but the walls of the house shone in a creamy white. Everything in the house was good and simple and plentiful.

"How lovely it is!" cried Lisbeth. "I like it much better than the big house with all those servants." And Peter wholeheartedly agreed.

They lived a contented life. Peter became a hard-working, well-respected man, and soon he had acquired a modest fortune. He was well esteemed in the whole Forest.

Peter Munk visited the Little Glassman once more, and that was after the birth of his first son. He went to the well-known spot and recited the little verse, but the manikin did not show himself even though Peter called:

"I don't want anything, sir! I only came to invite you to be godfather to my first-born son."

There was no answer. The wind stirred in the tree and three fir cones fell down before Peter's feet. He picked them up and said:

"I'll take them home and keep them as a souvenir. And again I thank you, sir, for all you did for me."

At home Peter took off his Sunday jerkin, and his mother turned the pockets inside out to brush and clean them before putting the Sunday garment away. Three rolls of money fell from the pockets.

That was the gift of the Little Glassman for Little Peter.

They lived happily forever after.

Even when Peter was an old man, he still continued to say:

"It is better to be content with less than to have all the money in the world and have A COLD HEART!"

The Peasant and His Son

*

EDUARD MÖRIKE

One morning while they were getting up, Peter said to his wife in astonishment, "Look, Eve, at all the bruises I have! Why, my whole body is black and blue! And I haven't even been in a fight!"

"Oh, Peter," she wailed, "I'm sure you have beaten that poor horse Hansel again till he is half lame. I heard it more than a hundred times from my grandpa: if anybody mistreats an animal, be it ox, or ass, or horse, they'll send black spots to the tormenter in the night, and he'll wake up bruised himself. Now, it has happened to you!"

But Peter mumbled, "If only it doesn't mean something worse." He kept quiet, thinking the spots might announce his death.

He was calm and peaceable for a couple of days, and the whole household benefited. But as soon as his skin healed again, he became the same grim Peter, with a hot head and a fierce tongue. Hansel had an especially bad time, and was forced to go hungry as well. Sometimes, in his stable, when all his bones ached from being worked too hard, he would say to himself, "I wish a thief would come and steal me. How gladly I would carry him away!"

Now the peasant had a kindhearted son, named Frieder, who did the poor creature all kinds of favors. If the stable door opened a little more softly than usual, Hansel at once turned his tired head to see if it were Frieder, smuggling his breakfast or supper bread to him.

One day, the boy entered the stable and stopped in amazement. On Hansel's back sat a beautiful angel in a silver-bright frock, with a wreath of meadow flowers on her fair hair. With her white hands she smoothed Hansel's bumps and bruises. The angel looked at Frieder and said:

> *Good Hansel will have a splendid life*
> *When he carries the king's wife.*
> *Poor Frieder, with a stick in his hand,*
> *The goats of the village he must tend!*
> *But what a rich man he will be*
> *When he shakes the black walnut tree!*

With that, the angel disappeared. The boy shivered, and quickly slipped out the door. But as he thought over the words that he had heard, he became sad. "Alas! Goat herder of the village!" he thought. "That's a poor, lazy life. I wouldn't earn the salt in the soup for my poor mother. And nuts? Where from? There are no nut trees in my father's garden. And even if I could gather whole sacks of nuts, as the angel promised, they wouldn't feed anybody. I know what I'll do if I really have to tend goats,

I'll gather twigs and learn how to make brooms. That will bring a little money at least."

All day he had such thoughts, even in school, and sat there like a dreamer.

"How much is six times six?" the teacher asked in arithmetic. "Wake up, Frieder! What are you thinking about today? Answer my question!"

The startled boy did not know whether to say, "Broomsticks," or, "Thirty-six"; for, really, both answers were right. Therefore he said, "Broomsticks."

There was such uproarious laughter that all the windows rattled. And for a long time they had a saying in that school for a boy lost in thought, "He has broomsticks in his head."

That night Frieder could not sleep. Once he thought something strange was going on in the farmyard, and sat up in bed and looked out of the window. Imagine! Light shone from the stable, and Hansel came out, the angel riding on his back. Hansel stepped as lightly as if the earth were made of cotton. In that first moment, Frieder almost cried out aloud, but right away he thought, "But that's Hansel's good luck!" He lay down quietly and wept silently into his pillow because Hansel was gone now and would never come back.

As the angel and Hansel went down the open road, the worn-out nag saw his shadow in the bright moonlight. He thought, "Alas! I'm all skin and bones. No queen will ever ride me!" The angel said nothing. Soon she took a dirt road to the left, and after a while they came to a beautiful pasture where golden flowers grew. It was a magic

meadow, invisible to ordinary folks, and at daybreak it would draw back into the near-by forest where nobody could find it. But when a good child of poor folk came along with a cow or a goat, the angel would let them see the pasture. Marvelous fodder grew there and many strange herbs, which made the cattle thrive almost miraculously.

Here the angel alighted, saying, "Graze, Hansel!" Then she ran to the brook and disappeared. It was just as if a star had flashed across the sky.

As for Hansel, he grazed on and on. As he grew full, he felt almost sorry, the tender grass was so rich and milky. At last he felt tired and stretched out near a hill where beech trees grew, and rested for four hours. Suddenly a bugle woke him. It was broad daylight, and the sun shone bright and clear. He jumped up, saw his shadow on the green turf, and said, astonished, "Oho! What a spruce fellow I am! Smooth and trim and polished!" It was true, his hide shone like silk.

The king of the country had been hunting in that vicinity for some days, and was just now emerging from the woods with his followers.

"Oh! Look, look!" he cried out. "What a handsome charger! See how he exercises his proud limbs, leaping and bounding!"

Talking thus, he came nearer with his courtiers. They all marveled over the horse, and affectionately patted his neck.

Said the king, "Ride, hunter, ride into the village, and ask if the steed is for sale. Tell them it would have a good master."

The hunter rode a piebald mare, and Hansel took to her at once. Willingly he trotted back into the hamlet, where soon the curious peasants stuck their heads out their windows.

"Listen, you people! Who owns this fine bay horse?" the hunter called out, riding through the lanes.

"That's not my horse,"—"Not mine!"—"That one doesn't belong here," he was answered from all sides.

"Look, Frieder, that's a Hungarian thoroughbred," said Peter. "Wish he were mine."

Finally the blacksmith assured the hunter that no one owned such a fine horse for at least six miles around.

The hunter, followed by Hansel, rode back to the king. "The horse has no owner," he reported.

"We'll keep it then," said the king, and the kingly suite rode on.

Meanwhile, Peter thought it about time to feed his beasts and, yawning, he pushed open the stable door. Well! The ruffian opened his eyes wide when he saw Hansel's empty stall. For a long time he stood dumbfounded, all his senses benumbed. Then he flew into a rage.

"Confound it!" he cried. "That strange horse must have been my Hansel! What evil trick kept me from recognizing him?"

Peter almost tore his hair out, but what could he do? The horse was gone. His two small oxen were to be pitied, for the brute took his rage out on them in the next few days, and they had to work for three. Blows, beatings, and hunger were bad enough, but what made their lives unbearable was their longing for Hansel. They grieved for him, and were so set against Peter that they did everything in the most contrary way.

Finally Peter said to his wife, "There is no getting around it, the oxen are bewitched too!" They agreed to sell the pair to the butcher for a ridiculously small sum, and the two little oxen were slaughtered in the city.

But then what happened? One night when everybody was asleep, there was a knock at Peter's shutters.

Cried he, "Who's there?"

Two deep bass voices answered:

> Brindle and Brownie—moo, moo!
> Cold and hungry, we have come,
> To get our fodder. Give us some! Moo, Mooo!

A cold shiver ran down Peter's spine. He nudged his wife, "You get up, Eve!"

"Not I!" she answered. "They want their fodder from you!"

No longer bold, Peter got up, trembling. He threw down some hay, and when they were finished with it they went away.

New misfortunes came, blow after blow.

Peter brought home two oxen the next market day. But soon it became obvious that no cattle would stay in the stable no matter how they were treated; both oxen and the cow fell ill, and Peter gave them away at a loss. Peter ran to a hexen-layer (that means an arch villain!) and readily paid him a thaler. The hexen-layer gave him a powder to fumigate the stable at high noon. Peter fumigated, indeed so deftly that he set the straw on fire. Soon the red cock flapped his wings on the roof, as the saying goes—yes, stable and barn went up in flames, and the fire brigade could barely save the farmhouse.

Peter, Peter, what is to become of you?

Next night, there was a knock at the shutters again. "Who's there?"

Brindle and Brownie—moo, mooo!
Cold and hungry, wet with rain,
We want hay. Feed us again!—Moo! MOOO!

In desperation Peter jumped out of bed, wrung his hands, and cried out, "Good Heavens! Must I feed the dead? Soon I'll have nothing for the living!"

Then the beasts took pity on him. They went away and never came back.

Peter should have mended his cruel ways now, but, instead of trying to repair his faults, he went to the inn to forget his misery in merry company. The more his wife scolded and lamented, the less he liked it at home. He ran into debt, and soon house and farm had to be sold. Now he had to work by the day, and his poor wife had to spin other people's thread. And Frieder? He sat outside the village; with a stick in his hand he tended the goats and made brooms to sell.

Three years had passed in this way, and then again the king came hunting the wild boar, and his queen came too. Since it was winter and very cold, the royal party did not eat their meal in the open air, as is usual on hunting days. Instead, the king's cooks prepared dinner at the Griffin Inn, and the gay company feasted in the upper hall, while the fiddlers struck up merry tunes. The common folk stood in the streets and listened. After the grand dinner the horses were trotted out again. As the queen's horse was being reined, a young goatherd in the front row boldly called to the stableboy, "That's my father's horse, I'd like you to know!"

Everybody laughed aloud, but the proud bay neighed merrily three times and rubbed his head on Frieder's shoulder. The queen, who was at the window, was highly astonished when she heard and saw this, and told her husband at once. The king sent for the goatherd, and Frieder entered the hall, humble but quite plucky. He was barefooted but his cheeks were as red as roses, and he was a nice-looking boy with laughing eyes.

Said the king, "You claim the handsome horse in the yard is your father's, do you?"

"With all due respect, Sire, I do; for it is true."

"Can you prove that, lad?"

"Sire, I can, if you'll permit me. I heard the stableboy boast that the horse lets nobody mount but the queen who owns him. Let me try it. You'll see, he'll keep still for me, and he'll come if I call him Hansel, for that's his name. If I can mount him, then you'll know I told the truth."

The king was silent for a little while, then he said to his courtiers, "Have three good men of the community brought before me. Let us hear what they have to say about this."

The three men came and were questioned about the horse, but their opinion was not in Frieder's favor. Then the boy himself started to tell the story of the angel, simply and truthfully: how she had led Hansel away, how she had recently appeared to him and shown him the invisible meadow which had made Hansel so handsome.

Of course, the listeners were very much surprised by this tale. Some looked amused, but the queen said, "Certainly, he is a God-fearing boy. Truth is written on his face."

The king himself seemed well inclined toward the lad, but since he was in a high good humor, he said, "He still must take the test."

He called Frieder to a side window that looked upon a wide, flat lawn. In the middle stood a nut tree, some hundred feet from the inn. Snow lay everywhere, for it was December.

"Do you see the large meadow there?" asked the king.

"Well, why shouldn't he," murmured the king's jester, "though it is a really invisible meadow, for it is all snowed under!"

The courtiers laughed, but the king said to the boy, "Don't pay any attention to him. Look, you may ride Hansel. Use the nut tree as a center and mark off a circle in the snow. If all goes well, all the ground inside the circle is yours."

The courtiers were delighted, thinking it would be a good joke. But Frieder was so confident, he grinned from ear to ear.

The stableboy took off the queen's golden saddle, and led Hansel out. All the people cheered, and Hansel neighed lustily as Frieder mounted in one great leap. Slowly he rode to the meadow, halted, and with his eyes measured the distance around the tree. Then he let Hansel trot, canter, and finally made him gallop full speed. He rode like the wind, and it was a pleasure to see how well and easily the lad sat the horse. He was not foolish, but made the circle as wide as possible, yet he made the ends meet as precisely as if it were done by rule and compass.

Frieder was greeted with great cheering as he leaped down and kissed Hansel. The king at the window beckoned to him to come into the upper hall.

"You acquitted yourself very nicely," he said to the boy. "The meadow is yours! But I cannot give Hansel back to you since I have presented him to my queen. You shall not lose anything by that," he added, and gave the boy a purse well lined with ducats.

Frieder was delighted, especially when the queen said, "You must come to town each year and call on me in the castle, and pay Hansel a visit."

"Oh, I'll do that!" Frieder cried eagerly. "And at harvest time I'll bring you a little sack of fresh nuts from the tree."

"That would be fine," replied the queen with a smile, and then they parted.

Frieder ran home through the gay, lustily shouting

crowd. From afar Peter, his father, had watched the ride, and now he made a vow in his heart. I need not tell what that vow was. Hansel and Frieder had helped him to get a new start in the world, and he became a worthy and well-esteemed man, even a rich man; and his son became still richer.

Since that time nobody in that village has ever again mistreated an animal.

The Man Who Lost
His Shadow

*

ADELBERT VON CHAMISSO

One rainy September morning in 1813, Leopold, my valet,
was standing in the door of my house. A stranger
approached him.

"Is this the house of Baron Chamisso?" he asked.

At the affirmative answer, he handed Leopold a bundle
of papers. "Give this to your master," he said and turned
to leave. "No, thank you. It is not necessary that I see
him." And he was on his way.

I was leisurely sipping my breakfast chocolate when
Leopold came in with a startled face and a rather thick
sheaf of papers. I glanced at the signature and jumped up.

"Where is he? Where is Peter Schlemihl?" I called excitedly. But he was gone.

Leopold tried to describe the stranger. "He looked— Excuse me, sir, but your friend looked very quaint indeed!

He wore a very worn-out black cassock, and a specimen box was slung over his shoulder. His boots were very large and old, and, imagine, he wore felt slippers over them!"

I shook my head. Then I started to read the life story of my long-lost boyhood friend, Peter Schlemihl.

Here is the story, one of the strangest ever told, as Peter Schlemihl wrote it down in the Libyan Desert and sent it to me, his old friend, to do with as I pleased.

After a long and rather strenuous voyage, we reached the harbor of a small North German town. As soon as we had unloaded, I gathered together my few belongings. Pushing my way through the milling crowd, I looked for the nearest, cheapest hostelry, where I asked for a room. The boots gave me an appraising glance and took me upstairs to the garret. Next I inquired for directions to the house of Mr. Thomas John, the man who, as I hoped, would help me realize my modest ambitions.

It was still early. I took time to dress carefully in a clean ruffled shirt and my best black coat. It had been re-modeled but still looked quite all right, or so I thought.

As soon as I was ready, I started out, following the long street till I reached an impressive mansion of white and red marble. "Here it is," I thought. I dusted my shoes, straightened my neckerchief, and, with a throbbing heart, I rang the bell. The door opened. An imposing butler an-nounced me, and I was asked to come to the garden where Mr. John was entertaining. I recognized him at once; he was a man who exuded great self-complacency. He received me graciously, as a rich man receives a poor devil who comes to ask him a favor.

"Ah, from my dear brother," he exclaimed, as he took

my letter of introduction. "It's a long time since I heard from him. He is well? . . . Yes, there!" He turned to his guests. With the letter he pointed to a near-by hill. "That's where I'll have my new house erected." Carelessly he broke the seal, but continued with his dissertation on riches.

"One should have at least a million," he said. "Otherwise, forgive this hard judgment, one is just a poor wretch."

"Oh, how true!" I answered feelingly.

He must have liked that, for he smiled at me and said, "Stay here, good friend. Maybe I'll find a little time for you later on."

He pocketed the unread letter and turned to his guests. They all climbed the rosebush-clad hill, and I trailed behind without bothering anybody. Nobody paid any attention to me. I felt as if my poverty had rendered me invisible to these rich and carefree people. They all were very gay; they laughed and flirted, and I clenched my teeth.

We had reached the top of the hill when one of the young ladies caused quite a commotion. A thorn had pricked her finger, a drop of blood flowed. She and all the others were quite concerned and called for court plaster. A quiet, gaunt, elderly gentleman put his hand into the tight breast pocket of his old-fashioned dark-gray coat and produced a plaster. With a respectful bow he handed it to the young lady. She received it without thanks. Her scratch was attended to, and we all turned to the marvelous view.

It was an imposing sight indeed. In the near distance the majestic ocean glittered across the fair country. A bright speck appeared on the horizon.

"A telescope! I need a telescope!" Mr. John called impatiently. "That must be one of my ships!"

Before the servants could fetch one, the thin man in gray handed a telescope to Mr. John. I looked at the man and wondered idly in which pocket of his tight-fitting taffeta coat he could have carried such a bulky object. The telescope went from hand to hand but not back to its owner.

Refreshments were served, rare fruits from the Orient. Mr. John addressed me a second time. "Eat, my good friend," he said patronizingly. "I'm sure they did not serve such fruit on your ship." I bowed, but he did not see it. He had already turned to the others.

"We should have a Turkish carpet to stretch out on," one of the young dandies called out jokingly. He had hardly finished saying this when I saw the gray gentleman eagerly trying to pull the desired object from his pocket. The servants came to help him. They assisted in unfolding a large, costly, gold-threaded Turkish carpet. Soon the gay company was seated on it as if it were the most natural thing in the world. In confusion I looked at the man, his pockets, the carpet. At least twenty feet long and ten feet wide it was! I rubbed my eyes. How extraordinary it was, and nobody took any notice of it.

It was getting quite warm. One of the young ladies laughingly asked the gray man, whom nobody had addressed as yet, "Don't you have a tent in your pocket? The sun is bothering us."

He answered with a deep and humble bow, as if a great and unexpected honor had been bestowed upon him. He put his hand into his pocket. Heavy brocade fabric, poles, strings, iron implements; in short, everything necessary for a splendid pleasure tent emerged from his pocket. The young gentlemen helped to erect it. It covered the whole length of the Turkish carpet, and still nobody seemed to think it strange.

I was disturbed, horrified indeed. But imagine how I felt when the gray man, at the next careless wish, produced three horses! Three beautiful large riding horses, with saddles and bridles. Imagine, for Heaven's sake! Imagine, three live riding horses from the same little pocket from which a court plaster, a telescope, a twenty-foot carpet, and a tent had already come forth! I would never have believed it had I not seen it with my own eyes!

The man, humble and embarrassed as he seemed to be, became sinister to me. I could not bear the sight of him, yet I could not take my eyes from him. I decided to visit Mr. John next morning to try my luck. Maybe I would even muster enough courage to inquire about the frightening stranger.

Unobserved, I left the gay company on the hill. I was just crossing a wide sunny lawn when, to my secret terror, I noticed that the gray man was following me. Soon he had caught up with me.

He took off his hat and bowed lower than anybody had ever bowed to me. No doubt, he was going to speak with me. I stared at him, hypnotized like a bird by a snake. He seemed to be very embarrassed. He did not lift his eyes but he bowed several times, and I returned his politeness quite shakily. Finally he addressed me in a low and timid voice.

"Will you please excuse my taking the liberty of bothering you with a request, sir?" he said. "Would you kindly allow me . . ."

"For goodness' sake, sir!" I interrupted him, startled. "What on earth could I do for a man like you, a man who . . ." I stopped, discomfited.

After a brief silence he started again.

"In the short time in which I had the pleasure of enjoying your presence, sir, I admired . . . Oh, sir, excuse my saying so, but I deeply admired the remarkable, the beautiful shadow you throw! Would there be a chance of my buying your shadow?"

He was silent, and my thoughts raced. He must be crazy, I thought. Therefore I answered kindly, "But, my good friend, you have a nice shadow yourself. Is that not enough? And, besides that, how on earth should I go about . . ." But he interrupted me.

"Never mind, sir, that would be my problem. Please do consider the bargain seriously. I have several little treasures in my pockets, sir, among which you may choose. There is the genuine springwort, for example. Or an alraun, a hatching penny, a bottle imp; but that, I trust, is not what you want. But there is Fortunatus' wishing hat, as good as new; Fortunatus' lucky purse . . ."

Fortunatus' lucky purse! I forgot my fear. Giddily I thought of the tempting shimmer of gold ducats.

"Would you kindly inspect and test the bag, sir?"

He took from his pocket a medium-sized sturdy leather pouch fastened with two strong leather thongs, and handed it over to me. I trembled and took it.

I pulled out ten ducats, another ten, ten more, and more. I would be rich! Now people would take notice of me! What did I need with a shadow?

I offered him my hand.

"Agreed! That's a bargain! You can have my shadow for this purse!"

We shook hands, and the deal was on. The gray man knelt down. With admirable dexterity he lifted my shadow, from head to foot, up from the grass. He rolled it, folded it neatly, and put it in his pocket. He got up, then bowed again and retreated behind the bushes. I thought I heard low, fiendish laughter, but paid no attention to it. My hand clutched the bag. The ground all around me was bright with the sun, but I did not care.

When I had recovered from my shock, I hurried to leave the garden. But first I filled my pockets with gold, tied the strings of the pouch around my neck, and hid it under my clothing. Then I took the road to town.

Suddenly I heard someone calling me. "Young man! Hey, young man!"

I turned around and saw an old woman.

"Be careful!" She raised a cautioning finger. "Be careful, you have lost your shadow!"

"Thanks, Grandma," I called and threw her a piece of gold for her well-meant warning.

At the gate I was asked quite sternly by the guard, "Where did you leave your shadow, sir?" and some women called out, "Goodness gracious! That poor man has no shadow!"

I was annoyed and carefully avoided the sunlit side of the street. But it did not always work. I had to cross Broad Street in full sunlight, just after school had closed and all the little rascals were running home. They spied at once what was the matter with me. A hunchbacked brat betrayed me with shrill laughter. In no time I was surrounded by a troop of boys, taunting, laughing, deriding me, flinging mud at me. I threw some gold in front of them to get rid of them and jumped into a carriage.

I was quite shaken when I reached the inn, and I bade the driver go and fetch my modest bundle. I paid him handsomely and asked him to drive me to the best hotel in the city. It faced north. I rented a whole suite where I would not have to fear the sun. As soon as I was alone, I locked the door.

I wanted to see gold, and plenty of it! Was it not the substitute for all I had lost? I already knew I would have to pay dearly for my riches. I opened Fortunatus' lucky pouch. In a frenzy which grew and grew in me as I touched the glistening metal, I extracted gold—gold—gold, and ever more gold. I threw it on the floor, I trampled on it. My poor heart enjoyed the enticing tinkle. Intoxicated by the sound and the shimmer, I could not stop till I waded in ducats. A golden bed for me! I threw myself on it, I was rolling in wealth, wasn't I? I played with the shimmering, clinking mass as if it were sand, I wallowed in it, I burrowed deep down into it.

Thus I spent the day, the evening; I did not eat or drink, I did not open my door. I fondled the gold, I embraced it till, exhausted, I fell asleep on it.

I awoke in the small hours of a pale morning, aching all over from my hard bed of gold. I was hungry, thirsty, and worn out. Full of disgust, I pushed the gold aside. What should I do with it? It could not just lie there; it was too much, too much!

Moodily I tried to conjure it back into the lucky purse, but that did not work. Finally I had to pick it up, carry it to a big closet, and hide it there. I had to work hard to get rid of the unwanted treasure, and I hated it already. I kept only a few handfuls in my pockets, then I rested wearily in a chair till morning came and I could send for the landlord.

I gave him my orders, and I asked for a reliable servant. He recommended Bendel, whom I liked on first sight. Tailors and bootmakers came, and I was busy all day. I bought horses and carriages, also precious stones and elaborate jewelry to get rid of some of the gold. But these purchases hardly diminished it.

Time passed and I became calmer. But I did not dare to leave the house. One moonlit evening I decided to venture forth, for I could not stay in the house forever. Wrapped in my redingote, I sneaked from the inn like a criminal, keeping in the friendly shadows of the houses. It took a long time till I mustered up enough courage to brave the moonlight. Oh God! It was the same! Wherever I went, fear followed the man without a shadow, or horror, or scorn, or worse than all: pity, pity! I cannot bear thinking of it, I cannot endure to recall how I crept home, a trembling, a defeated man.

I stood in my dark room and looked out into the quiet street, washed by moonlight. I pressed my hot brow against the windowpane to cool my reeling brain. What had I done? I could not understand what went on in people's minds when they noticed that I had lost that unnecessary, that ridiculous appendage, my shadow. Why was I rejected as if I were Cain?

"This is beyond reason," I thought. "How can I define my loss? Why is a shadow so important? Such a mere nothingness!"

With unseeing eyes I stared up at the silver disk. "Other people have dealt with the devil before me. They are the more respected for it if they became as rich and independent as I am now. Where is the difference?"

Then it struck me like a blow.

"It shows that I have dealt with the devil! It is blazingly manifest that I have stepped beyond human boundaries. Society will not tolerate a man who has excluded himself from the common fate of toil and strife. Oh, loneliness! Unbearable for the outcast! I want to live with people, I long for their respect, I crave recognition and appreciation. I know I did it more for that than for the stupid money."

Restlessly I paced my rooms, but my racing thoughts could not be appeased.

"I trampled on the unwritten laws of mankind. Now I have to shun the sun which exposes my guilt. *That* is the sign of Cain, *that* is what frightens people away from me." Deeply exhausted, I leaned against the wall. "I must undo what I have done, I must find the gray man, cancel our bargain. I don't want gold, I want *people!*"

Next morning I asked my faithful Bendel to go and look for the man in the gray coat. I described him in detail, and told him all the strange happenings in Mr. John's garden. I did not give away my secret, though. I asked Bendel to inquire everywhere and find out who the gray man was. I gave him as many ducats as he could carry.

"Spend it all, spend more if you want," I said. "My peace of mind depends on finding that man. Do find him for me."

Bendel came home late and sad. Nobody remembered the man or his strange deeds, not even Mr. John. The carpet, the tent, the riding horses—everything had been in Mr. John's possession long since. I was the victim of a strange delusion. I listened without comment, then I dismissed him. He hesitated.

"There is one thing more," he said. "This morning when I set out, I met a man and he said to me, 'Tell Mr. Schlemihl he will not find me here. But in a year and a day I'll take the liberty of paying him a visit and suggest a business transaction which he, in all probability, will gladly accept.' I asked his name, but he said you would know anyhow who he was."

Full of misgivings, I asked Bendel to describe the stranger; it was the gray man.

"You wretched fellow!" I cried out bitterly. "That was the man you were sent to find."

Bendel was desperate. "Why did I not recognize him? Fool that I was! Now I have betrayed my good master!"

He was so upset and frightened that I had to console him. Well I recognized the workings of a sinister power. I knew I could not blame poor Bendel. I sent him out again to the harbor, though I had very little hope. He came home discouraged.

The gray man had disappeared, had vanished like a shadow.

What good was my gold? What good are wings to a man in chains? They only make him suffer doubly.

I was lying on my treasure like Fafnir, the dragon, removed from human help, starved for companionship. I did not have the courage to leave the house, afraid of scorn and pity. I envied the last of my servants. He had his shadow, he could walk in the sun.

I made a last try. I sent to the most famous painter of the town. I received him like a king, gave him handsome presents, praised his art.

Then I asked my question. "Could you, Professor, paint a shadow for a person?"

"You mean a cast shadow?"

"That is what I mean."

"But how can anybody lose his shadow?"

"A friend of mine lost his shadow in Russia," I lied brazenly. "It was so extraordinarily cold that the shadow froze to the ground and broke off."

"How strange, indeed," said the maestro. "But the shadow I could paint would be liable to be lost at the slightest movement. Especially with a person so careless as to lose his own shadow." He got up and gave me a piercing look. "Your friend should avoid the sun, that is the best advice I can give him."

He left, and I sat there, my face buried in my hands. Bendel found me thus and I, seeing his pitying glance, could not resist.

"Bendel," I cried, "you alone seem to share my grief. Do not leave me as anybody else would do who knew my horrid secret. Bendel, I am rich, and free, and open-handed, but, oh, God in Heaven, I have no shadow!"

"No shadow?" the lad cried out in consternation. "How dreadful that I was born to serve a master without a shadow." He was silent, his face twisted in fright.

"Bendel," I groaned, "now you know my secret. You can go and betray me to the world."

I saw the struggle in his honest face. Then he fell on his knees, and grasped my hands. Tears ran down his cheeks.

"I'll never leave you! I'll not care what people say or think. I'll take care of you, I'll lend you my own shadow,

I'll help you all I can. And if I cannot help you, at least I'll be at your side."

I embraced him with deep gratitude. I knew he was not doing it for the gold.

My life changed somewhat for the better, Bendel kept his word. He was everywhere, foreseeing every danger. When sudden exposure threatened me, he quickly covered me with his own shadow for he was taller and stouter than I was. So I dared to get about.

I became acquainted with people of society and, being so fabulously rich, I was well received. I had to assume many queer foibles, oddities, and moods but, since the truth was well hidden, I enjoyed everybody's respect. I waited more quietly now for the return of the gray man. "It's done now," I thought. "I might just as well take the good along with the evil."

One evening, I had invited guests to my country home. After an opulent meal, I took a walk in the spacious garden with Fanny, a very fair lady. She seemed to be quite impressed by my wit and eccentric habits. She had taken my arm and we were crossing a wide lawn. Blushingly she lowered her glance at one of my rather daring compliments. Suddenly the moon broke through the clouds, and she saw only her own shadow before us! She started with fright and looked at me in alarm, then she glanced down again. Terror distorted her face in such a queer way that I nearly burst out laughing. But well I knew what this meant for me, and an icy chill ran down my spine. She fainted, and I fled. I rushed past my startled guests, threw myself into the next carriage, and drove back to town. Unfortunately

I had left Bendel home this time. One word to him was enough. He hurried to hire a post chaise for me. I took only one servant with me, Rascal, a cunning rogue. But he was smart and useful, and he knew nothing of tonight's incident. Bendel stayed behind to put things in order. He reached me the next day, and we continued our hurried trip through the country till we reached the mountains. But only after days of hurried traveling through the mountains could I be persuaded to rest. I decided to settle down in a small resort.

I had sent Bendel in advance to buy and furnish a suitable house. He spent money lavishly and talked mysteriously about the rich gentleman who was his master. As soon as everything was in order, he came to fetch me.

About a mile from the little town, our carriage was stopped by a gay crowd in festival attire. We halted. Music, the salutes of guns, and the tolling of bells were heard; people cheered and threw their caps into the air. White-dressed maidens advanced, the most beautiful of them came blushingly forward. She carried a wreath of laurel and roses on a velvet cushion and whispered something about majesty and veneration and love. I thought an angel had descended from heaven. The choir sang a song about a good king and the happiness of his people; I did not know what to make of it. I sat in my carriage, like one transfixed, looking at the lovely girl, but I did not dare to approach her. The sun shone brightly. I could not, I must not move. What I would have given for a shadow then!

Finally Bendel came to my rescue. He jumped from the high seat of the carriage. I called him to me and handed him a jeweled spray. Bendel thanked everybody for the unexpected honor which his master could not and would not accept. There must be an error, he said, but he took the laurel wreath and put the diamond spray in its place. Then he waved the cheering people aside. At full gallop we entered the flower-bedecked town.

The carriage stopped at my house, and I hastened through the crowd which was waiting for me. There was more cheering, and I had a rain of ducats thrown among them. In the evening the town was illuminated. I still did not know for whom I had been taken. I sent Rascal out as a scout, he came home, laughing, and told me people thought I was the king, traveling incognito. It was very funny the way he told it, how he had even strengthened people in their error by dark hints and ambiguous reproofs. I scolded him, but I laughed and was flattered, nevertheless.

Next evening I gave a banquet under the shadowy trees before my house. My gold had made everything possible at such short notice. The whole town was invited; it was a splendid festival. People called me "Count Peter." I laughed, but let it go at that and was Count Peter from then on.

Late in the evening the beautiful girl who had greeted the "king" so touchingly appeared with her parents. Timidly she followed her father, the chief ranger. In her golden hair she wore the jeweled spray from me, but she did not seem to know how very beautiful she was.

My heart went to her as swift as a bird. She sat at my side, we danced together. I was happy, I was in heaven!

Next morning Bendel disclosed he was sure Rascal had embezzled sacks of gold. "I don't care," I replied and laughed. "Let the scoundrel enjoy his loot. I love to give, why not to him too?" No more was said about it. Rascal stayed, the first of my servants. But Bendel was my friend, my confidant.

I continued to live in that pleasant little town, spent money with open hands, and people admired me greatly. But my dreary heart could not forget. I used every possible caution to hide my secret. As long as the sun was shining, I stayed in my rooms which nobody but Bendel was ever allowed to enter. "The count is working in his study," people said. But in the evenings under the trees, or in my splendidly candlelit rooms—Bendel had worked out a careful scheme that allowed no shadows anywhere—I gave gay parties. I went out on cloudy days, but always with Bendel as protector. Soon I took only one walk, to the chief ranger's home.

Only there, only in Minna's gentle presence, I felt free from sin, and my soul was at peace. How I loved her, the pure, the innocent! But as soon as I was alone, I fell into brooding. My secret seemed to me more ghastly than ever. I should have fled then, I should have avoided Minna and not involved her. But I could not tear myself away.

Once I told her, "I am not the man you think I am. I'm only a rich man, but utterly wretched. A curse is upon me!"

Her tears welled up because I was unhappy. But she only thought I was some prince banned from his home country. There was no conception of any possible guilt of mine in her innocent heart.

Then again I said, "Minna, the last day in May will decide my fate. If it does not change, then I will die. I cannot bear to make you unhappy, and yet I cannot live without you."

She smiled at me in heavenly trust. "My only wish is for you to be happy. But if you are luckless, let me share your fate."

"Minna, Minna! Take back those words, you don't know what you are saying. You don't know my misery, or do you? . . . Do you?"

She took my hand. "I love you, Peter. I'll never forsake you . . ."

Her father entered, and I told him that I wanted to marry his daughter but had to wait till June when I must make some grave decisions. I don't have to say that he was overjoyed.

Time crawled. My heart felt the burden of my secret ever harder to bear. Sometimes I found Minna in tears, though she tried to smile at me. My soul was steeped in darkness; only her parents remained completely delighted.

Finally the last day of May came, the day I expected the gray man. I had taken precautions and had filled some boxes with gold. How I hoped I would get rid of the unlucky "lucky purse."

I sat and waited for midnight to come, though I doubted that he would be that punctual. The clock struck twelve. I sat there, my eyes glued to the clock. I counted the seconds, the minutes—nothing happened. It struck one, struck two. The leaden hours dragged by. Nothing happened. The first light of morning dawned and found me shivering and waiting. Nothing. Noon—afternoon—evening. The hands of the big clock moved relentlessly, my hopes wilted. Eleven o'clock in the evening it was now, and he had not appeared. I counted the minutes, the seconds, they were like dagger wounds. The first stroke of the twelfth hour: he must, he must come now or never! The last stroke of twelve o'clock died away: he had not come!

Tomorrow, shadowless forever, I would propose to Minna. I sank back in despair.

I was awakened early by a quarrel just outside my door. I listened. Bendel was forbidding Rascal to enter my bedroom. I heard Rascal's impudent voice. "You have no right to allow or forbid me anything, stupid," he sneered. "I'll enter our fine master's rooms whenever I choose." I heard struggling and shuffling, and jumped from my bed.

"Rascal, you scoundrel! What's the matter with you?"

He looked at me coldly. "If you please, Count Peter, I only want to ask most respectfully that you show me your shadow. The sun is now shining very brightly in the garden."

I was thunderstruck. Then I pulled myself together. "How dare a servant . . ."

He interrupted me impudently. "A servant might be so honorable that he would not be willing to serve a shadowless man. I ask for my dismissal."

I had to come down a peg. "But, Rascal, what an extraordinary idea . . ."

Again he interrupted me. "People say you have no shadow. Either you show me your shadow, or dismiss me at once."

I tried my last resort—money, the great pacifier. But it had lost its power. Rascal flung the purse of ducats at my feet.

"I won't accept anything from a shadowless man!" He turned his back on me and, whistling a merry tune, he left my room. I stood in stunned despair.

Finally I pulled myself together and went to the ranger's garden. I felt like a man with leprosy. Wasn't I just as banished from human company as he was?

In the shadowy arbor where we used to meet, Minna was sitting, pale and beautiful. Her father, a letter in his hand, came toward me; her mother did not lift her eyes when I entered.

"Do you, my dear sir," he asked with suppressed fury, "know one Peter Schlemihl?"

I was silent. He waited, till finally I said, "And if I myself were that man?"

"The man who lost his shadow!" he stormed.

Minna, in an attempt to be brave, cried out, "I have known for a long time that he has no shadow." She threw her arms around her mother's neck and sobbed bitterly.

"And you dared to intrude here! You, an outcast!" her father accused me savagely. "You sneaked in and stole my child's heart. See, how she suffers." Minna's sobbing pulled at my heartstrings.

"Well, a shadow is only a shadow," I said, deliberately frivolous. "It does not hurt to live without one." How well I knew how it hurt to be scared of each ray of sun, to live in darkness like a bat! I saw the fury work in his face, and rushed on, "You place too much importance on a mere trifle."

"Trifle!" he exploded. "How did you lose it? Confess, which devilish tricks . . ."

"Oh, it was nothing, just a mishap," I lied shamelessly. "A boorish fellow stepped so clumsily on the delicate little thing that he tore a large hole in it. I'll have it repaired. Don't worry, I expected to have it back by yesterday."

"All right. I'll give you three days' time," he replied icily. "If you come back with a well-fitted shadow, you will be welcome. But the fourth day Minna shall marry another man. She is my only child, I have to take care of her. There are better men than you who want to marry her."

I turned to my weeping betrothed. "Minna, my only beloved," I said tenderly, and waited in vain for a response.

I tried it again. "Minna, listen to me. You know me well enough . . ." But the terrible sobbing only grew more violent. She clung more tightly to her mother, who signaled me to withdraw.

I staggered away. Why, oh why, had the gray man not come yesterday? I wandered through the silent woods. Why, oh why, in my greed had I severed my natural ties to mankind? Was there another man as lonely as I? How unique I was, different from any living or dead thing. A tree, a stone casts its shadow on the ground!

I sat on a boulder on a sunny slope. The sun, so long feared and avoided, beat down on me. My pale hands felt gratefully the life-giving warmth. My fingers tried childish silhouettes; they could not shape those "Chinese shadows on the wall." Even that innocent little pleasure was denied to me. Poor, shadowless fingers.

A fiendish laughter interrupted me. I sprang to my feet: there stood the gray man!

"Well, my friend." He slapped my shoulders and laughed as I flinched at his touch. "Well, you couldn't bide your time. Today is our appointed date. A year and a day, I said."

I stared at him. I counted. Indeed, I had been mistaken, today was the day!

"Nothing is lost yet," he said comfortably. "We'll do our little business transaction right away. Then you'll go back with your well-fitted shadow, as befits a bridegroom, hah, hah!" he snickered. Oh, how I hated him! "And fair Minna is yours. They'll be delighted, and you can tell them the whole thing was just a joke. And Rascal, that scoundrel, who betrayed you and wants to marry Minna, is mine. His account is full anyhow. I'll take him on myself. Nothing to worry about."

My heart leaped with joy. Eagerly I pulled out the "lucky purse." But the gray man stepped back.

"No thanks, Count Peter. You can keep that as a souvenir." I looked flabbergasted, and he continued, "I want only one small thing from you. Please sign this paper here, and your shadow is yours again." He presented a parchment, and I read the words:

I hereby bequeath my soul to the holder
of this document after my soul's natural
separation from my body.

I stared at the parchment. The gray man had a pen in his hand. With it he caught a drop of blood from my hand, where I had scratched it in my senseless rush through bushes and thorns. He handed me the pen.

"Who are you?" I finally managed to whisper.

"What does it matter?" he replied lightly. "Guess I'm just a poor devil trying to do favors to his friends, that's all. Now, sign here, right-hand corner. Right here."

I looked at his bony finger with its long, curved nail, I shook my head.

"Excuse me, sir. I will not sign that document."

"You won't sign it? Why not?"

"It seems to me rather frivolous to sell my soul for a shadow."

"What!" He shook with laughter. "Frivolous, indeed! May I ask what you can do with a soul? Have you ever seen one? But your shadow is something substantial. It will help you to obtain all you wish for: bride, and honor, and riches. How can you hesitate?"

The temptation seemed irresistible. How cleverly he had managed his timing, how well he knew my heartbreak! But I could not, I would not sell my soul!

Turning to that fiendish creature, I said coldly, "Sir, I sold my shadow to you for this very wonderful purse, and I sorely regretted it. If you are willing to exchange your purse for my shadow . . ." He shook his head firmly. "Very well. I'm not willing to sell anything else to you." And I turned my back on him.

"Too bad we can't do any business today." He burst into his sneering laugh. "I'm rather sure I'll see you soon, that you'll come begging for your shadow." Then he added, as if in afterthought, "By the way. Allow me to show you what good care I take of the things I buy. Have a look at your shadow."

To my deep horror he took my shadow from his pocket, shook it out, and spread it on the sunny ground. My poor shadow adhered to the soles of his feet. It had to follow his every movement, his slightest bend as he strutted before me with two shadows! One at his right side and one at his left! My heart nearly broke as I looked at my shadow after so many months, saw it obey such a wicked master.

Contemptuously the gray man smiled at me, then—that devil!—he walked away from me between the two shadows.

I don't remember how I spent the next days. I have a vague memory of mad fleeing, desperate rushing through the dense forest, of wild fruit I ate, spring water I drank. It does not matter what I did, but I remember how I suffered.

One stroke of the pen—and the nightmare would be ended: Minna mine, my honor restored. Could I leave her, poor innocent meek child, who had known no harm till she met me? Could I leave her to that brute, that rascal? My heart turned over in me, flames of jealousy devoured me. If only she had answered, if she had given me but a glance—but she had turned away. She was a submissive girl, unable to take the side of an outcast. How could she endure to live with a man condemned to hell? If I signed my soul away for her, I would suffer the pains of hell on earth. All I had heard of hell came back to me. Oh, merciless conflict!

Could she bear to be the cause of my torment and of my eternal perishing? "Oh, Minna, Minna!" I groaned. "It was easy to say, 'I'll share your misery.' It was easy to say for one who knew no despair, knew only protection and love." My heart longed for my golden-white angel, my tame dove, my unspoiled flower—but my mind knew I had lost her.

I could not sell my soul, not even for her.

After five days I went home in the evening, a quiet, tired man. I heard people talk of the splendid marriage of Minna to that fabulously rich man, Mr. Rascal. So it was all over. My heart fluttered, but I was too worn out for much emotion.

My house was a shocking sight. Every window was broken, books and furniture were strewn over the garden. What had happened? Where was Bendel? He was sitting quietly in my little antechamber, waiting for my return. We were both glad to see each other unharmed. He was shocked to see that my hair had turned white in these few days, and I was only two and twenty!

He told me how under Rascal's leadership the mob had stormed the house of the "sorcerer," the shadowless man, stealing and despoiling whatever they could. The servants had fled. Only he had stayed, but he had been powerless against the howling mob. The police came after everything was over and issued an expulsion order for me. It seemed, Rascal had known my secret from the beginning. He had bidden his time, stealing an immense fortune. Now he thought the right moment had come.

Quietly I listened to Bendel's furious and excited report.

"Bendel, my friend," I said to him, "I alone am to blame for this situation. The shadowless man has to accept his fate, but I do not want to involve anybody else in my misfortune. Loneliness is my lot in life; I have been my own undoing! I will leave you, and you may keep what is left of my riches."

Bendel was heartbroken. He pleaded with me to take him with me, but I remained firm. In the early morning hours I mounted my horse, took one last look into Bendel's honest face, and off I went. I did not care which road my horse chose. I had no aim. I no longer had any purpose on earth, no wish, no hope.

I was riding through a long, meandering valley when I overtook a wanderer. He asked if he might put his bundle on my horse's back, since we were going the same way. I agreed, and he thanked me very civilly. He was a pleasant man, and I half listened to his agreeable talk. A rosy shimmer heralded the day. I looked up. The pitiless light of a radiant dawn stole over the countryside. I was terrified. Light meant shadows, and I was not alone. I glanced down at my companion and was dumbfounded; he was nobody else but the gray man! He smiled mockingly at my dismay.

"Why shouldn't we share each other's company for a while? We can always part," he said, before I could utter a word. "I see you are scared of the rising sun. May I lend you your shadow for the time being? All I ask is that you tolerate me for a while." I was silent, turning things over in my mind, and he continued, "I know you don't like me, and that's too bad. But I'll be quite useful for you. And, you'll see, the devil is not quite as black as he is painted."

The sun had risen, the road was not lonely any more, and I, in spite of inner forebodings, accepted his offer. With a cunning smile, he unfolded my shadow, shook it a little to straighten it out, and put it on the horse's shadow. With greedy eyes I looked at my shadow, borrowed from my enemy. It felt strange to be inconspicuous again. We passed a group of peasants, who greeted me politely, envying the rich man on horseback.

Light-footed my companion walked on, whistling a merry tune. He was on foot—I was on horseback. The temptation was too great. At a crossroads I put spurs to my horse and galloped away, but I did not kidnap my shadow! Looking back, I saw it at the crossroads, waiting for me to return. Quite ashamed, I had to retrace my steps. My enemy smirked at me, put my obedient shadow back into its position on my horse, and told me the shadow would adhere to me only if I acquired it rightfully.

"I hold you by your shadow." He showed his white and pointed teeth as he smiled his hateful smile. "You cannot escape."

We continued our journey. I traveled with all possible comfort. I was rich. With my borrowed shadow I could move umhampered by sun or moonlight. I was well received wherever I went—it was all dust and ashes in my mouth! My companion was always pleasant and entertaining, annoying me only by his absolute confidence that one day I would redeem my shadow. He knew how I hated and feared him. But he was convinced I could not do without him or the ease of life that was mine so suddenly.

I felt sure in my heart that not for all the riches on earth would I sell my soul to the devil, after having refused to sacrifice my eternal soul for my love. Yet I did not know how it all would end.

Weeks passed, and nothing changed.

One day we sat in the mountains, near a bottomless pit. I sat with my head in my hands, listening to the beguiling words of the Great Enchanter. He spoke about the marvelous deeds I would be able to do with the gold at my disposal, the pleasurable life I would lead once I was rid of him. I felt he was right.

Suddenly it struck me that I could not hold out much longer. I had to end this, one way or the other.

"You seem to forget, my dear sir, that I permitted your presence only under certain conditions," I started my struggle for freedom. "I reserved the right to absolute freedom. I do not want to be annoyed by your talk."

"If you want me to, I'll pack up."

His threat was quite familiar to me. I was silent, he started to roll up my shadow. I clenched my teeth. I felt faint, but I remained mute. A long silence followed. He was the first to break it.

"You hate me bitterly, I know it. I even understand it. We must part, that is obvious. Now, for the last time, I advise you to redeem your shadow."

I offered him the purse.

"No, Peter Schlemihl, not for that price."

"All right," I said firmly. "We will part. The world is wide enough for the two of us."

"As you wish, sir." He bowed and said cunningly, "Before I leave you, let me inform you how you can call me

back, if you should feel too lonely without your shadow."
I was silent but could not help but listen anxiously. "If
you change your mind, just shake the pouch. The tinkle
of gold will immediately attract me. You hold me by my
gold—I hold you by your shadow—we should be insepara-
ble." He bowed again. "Your humble servant will always be
at your disposal and fulfill your every wish. But your
shadow, dear friend, your shadow is yours only in return
for your soul."

I looked at him. My mind was clear and cool. "I cannot
fight him with his own weapons," I thought. "One day I
shall fall into his pit if I don't part from him and his
property." A memory stirred in my heart.

"Do you have a signature from Mr. John?" I asked
quickly.

"That was hardly necessary." He hesitated. Then he
pulled a struggling something out of his pocket. He held
Mr. John in his fingers, a small, distorted figure, babbling
in a horrible voice—faint, and feeble, and horribly human
—"Judged by God's righteousness, condemned by God's
righteousness . . ."

I stood petrified. Then I hurled Fortunatus' lucky purse
into the abyss.

"Get Thee behind me, Satan!" I cried. "And never come
back to me."

He rose from his seat, silent and sinister, a grim and
fearful power to behold. Then he vanished from my sight.

I sat there, without a shadow and without money, but a
heavy load was taken off my heart. I was almost happy as
I searched my pockets and counted my money. I had only
a few coins left. I laughed; it did not matter. It was noon,

I had to wait till sundown. I stretched out on the ground and slept peacefully.

When I awoke, it was morning again. But I did not mind that the sun shone brightly. I decided to take a shadowy road through the mountains and, without looking back, I started on my journey. In the woods I met an old peasant. We walked together for a while; he was a good and sensible man and I enjoyed his simple companionship. But soon our road crossed a stream and we had to pass the shadowless bridge. Anxiously I let him go first. He turned in the middle of the bridge for some well-meant warning and stopped short.

"How is it possible, sir? You have no shadow."

"Yes, isn't it too bad?" I sighed. "I was very sick and lost my hair, my nails, my shadow. Look, my good man, my hair grew back white, and that at my age! My nails are still very short, but my shadow hasn't even started to grow."

"Well, well! That's bad. No shadow." Sorrowfully he shook his head. "That must have been a bad disease you had." He looked at me with pity, but was silent from then on. At the next side road he left me.

My happiness was gone, but I walked on, keeping to the darkest parts of the woods. Sometimes I had to wait for hours before I dared to cross a sunlit valley, and only after sunset would I take refuge in a village inn. My money was running out, I had to earn a living. I resolved to become a miner and work in the perpetual darkness of the earth. I trudged on patiently, but my boots gave out on me. They had been made for "Count Peter," not for a homeless wanderer.

This was a serious problem and when, on a rainy day, I came to a village on market day, I looked around for boots. Soon I found a sturdy pair, and the blond-haired boy who took care of the stand charged very little. As soon as I was beyond the village, I sat down at the roadside, pulled off my old shoes, and put on the new boots. They felt good on my feet, and I got up and walked on. I had not paid much attention to my surroundings, but after a few steps I felt queer. Somehow I must have left the dark pine wood, for I trod on stony ground. I looked up. I was in a rocky, mountainous region. There were no trees, only shrubbery grew between the naked rocks. I strode on. The air changed, it was piercingly cold, the stillness of death reigned. The icy sheets of hardpacked snow stretched endlessly wherever I looked, a dark-red sun just dipped behind the horizon, the cold was unbearable. I did not know what was happening to me! The benumbing frost forced me to hasten my steps. I heard the pounding of a faraway ocean; a few steps and I stood at the edge of a sea covered with floating ice. A school of seals jumped bellowing into the dark flood. I followed the coast. First I saw naked rock, then steppes, then birch trees, pine woods, fields. I walked a few more minutes. The heat was oppressive. I gazed around and saw that I stood amid well-tended rice fields. I sat down under a mulberry tree and glanced at my watch: only fifteen minutes had passed since I left that little German village!—I must be dreaming. I closed my eyes and heard strange sibilant words in an unknown tongue, two Chinese men in flowing silk robes stood before me, bowing politely. I jumped up and stepped back, they disappeared . . . I was in a jungle now. Monkeys swung in the vines, a tiger roared. I took a step to inspect a magnificent flower whose like I had never seen. Everything had changed again.

Now I pulled myself together, with slow, measured steps I walked. Behold! A marvelous panorama unfolded before my unbelieving eyes. Fields, mountains, rolling plains, steppes, deserts . . . Was it possible? There was no doubt: I wore seven-league boots!

I knelt down and thanked God.

Suddenly I had a purpose, a future again. I saw it all clearly with my mind's eyes. I still would have to live outside the human community, but now I had work. With my magic boots I would roam the earth, map the unexplored parts of our globe, collect and describe unknown plants, watch animal life, explore the North Pole, the South Pole, Tibet. I could go where no human foot had ever trod.

With kingly pleasure I took possession of my vast dominion.

I strode through Europe, how small it was! I crossed the frozen Arctic Ocean, and over Spitzbergen and Greenland I reached the American continent. I followed the ranges of mountains through both Americas. Carefully and slowly I stepped from peak to peak. Sometimes fire-spitting volcanos, sometimes snow-covered summits were my foothold. Breathing was often difficult as I wandered in these tremendous heights, but I followed my way to its end. At Cape Horn I reached the limits of my world, and I retraced my steps till I arrived at the other end. There I crossed the Bering Straits, jumping over to Asia and following her meandering coast. I had a look at the Soenda Islands. Alas! Australia was out of my reach. I returned to the mainlands and after stepping across the plateau of Tibet, I reached Persia, Mesopotamia, and the frightening deserts of the peninsula of Sinai. At dusk I was in Africa, admiring the pyramids. In the desert near the hundred-gated Thebes I noticed the caves where Christian hermits of old had dwelt. I chose a dry and airy one for my dwelling. I needed a place to come home to from my expeditions, a place to store my collections, to write my notes.

I needed only a few implements. Sextants, physical instruments, books, reams of paper, and, last but not least, some pairs of slippers. My magic boots carried me too rapidly, but when I put felt slippers over them I slowed down to a normal pace and had time to examine and to study. Whenever I got into dangerous situations, when wild beasts or men frightened me, I threw off my felt slippers and just stepped out of reach.

I lived on tropical fruit and eggs, especially those of the ostrich. As money for my few needs I used ivory which I picked up in inner Africa. I could take only the smaller tusks, it is weighty "money." As a small compensation for my lack of companionship, I had Figaro, my poodle, who lived in the cave with me and greeted me with joyful barking when I came home—he did not care whether I had a shadow or not.

Once I had an adventure that was almost fatal. I was in Spitzbergen, gathering lichen and algae, when suddenly a polar bear attacked me from behind a huge boulder. I threw off my felt slippers to step over to the next island and did not notice that one slipper was frozen to my boots. I must have put the slippers on when my boots were wet. Enough, it did not come off and, trying to get a foothold on the other island, I fell into the icy water. I was paralyzed with the cold, and only by the greatest effort was I able to save my life. As soon as I had firm ground under my feet and had gotten rid of that unlucky slipper, I rushed as fast as I could to the Libyan Desert to dry in the sun. But the difference in temperature was so great, I got a terrific headache. To cool my aching head, I staggered north. But it was too late, I had caught a severe cold, a violent fever burned in my veins. Restless and half fainting, I tried to find relief and ran from east to west, from north to south. Sometimes it was night, sometimes it was day, sometimes winter, sometimes summer—I don't know how long I stumbled with quick, faltering steps around the globe. With my last conscious effort I finally reached my cave. I must have been lying in a raging fever for a long time, but slowly I recovered. After a while I was able to take up my studies again, but I had to avoid the northern regions for a whole year.

And thus I live. In my studies and in the miracles of nature, I find compensation for all I lost. My boots don't wear out as I first feared, but my strength is failing. I am consoled by the thought that I have not wasted God's gift which he so graciously bestowed upon me, though in my youth, I fooled around with the devil's toys.

As far as my seven-league boots carry me I have explored the earth. My *Historia stirpium plantarum utriusque orbis* is my contribution to man's timeless efforts to reconnoiter our globe.

Here ends my story.

On a cloudy day I will take these papers to you, my friend Chamisso, that you may do with them what you think right.

Here is what I learned in heartfelt agony:

If you want to live in the human community, you first have to honor and appreciate what may seem mere shadows, and then all the other things which can be weighed and measured.

If you want to live only for yourself, my friend, then you need no advice.

The New Melusine

*

JOHANN WOLFGANG VON GOETHE

I was a roguish and lighthearted young fellow in those days. I had acquired the habit on my travels, when I entered an inn, of looking around first for the innkeeper's wife or the cook, and wheedling myself into her favor. That—I had found out—could be very helpful in reducing my bill.

I was just about to enter the mailcoach inn of a little town one evening when a splendid double-seated coach, drawn by four horses, came clanking and clashing to a stop at the entrance. I turned around and saw a very fair lady sitting in it all by herself, without a lady's maid or servant. I hurried to open the coach door for her, and asked if there was anything I could do for her. She had a beautiful figure, but her lovely face showed a trace of sadness.

"Oh, thank you for your kindness," she said in a gentle

voice. "I would be very obliged if you would take the box from the seat and carry it upstairs. But I beg of you to handle it very carefully and don't shake or upset it."

Gingerly I took the box; she shut the coach door, and we walked upstairs together. She told the servants she was going to stay overnight. I put the box on a table and, since she seemed to want to be alone, I took my leave, kissing her hand with great warmth.

"Would you be so good as to order dinner for me as well as yourself?" she said, and with the greatest pleasure I delivered the message, giving a cold shoulder to landlord, landlady, and cook. Impatiently I waited for her, and soon she came down into the dining room. Dinner was served, and I enjoyed the good food and even more so my pleasant companion. She seemed to grow fairer and fairer by the minute! We were finished all too soon, but I hesitated to leave her; I tried all kinds of subtle tricks to impress her, but in vain. A certain dignity kept me within bounds and, half against my will, I said good night quite soon.

I spent a restless night, dreaming of her, and was up early to ask if she had ordered her horses; but she had not, and I went cheerfully into the garden. She stood at the window of her room. I rushed up to her and started to declare my ardent devotion.

"If you really want to devote your time to me, I'll be very happy," she said, and somehow her lovely and aloof smile put a check on my too daring behavior. "Hear my terms. I came to visit a friend and to stay with her a few days, but I want my carriage and the box to proceed on their way. Could you manage that for me? You have only to lift the box into the carriage and out, sit down at its side, and watch over it so that it does not come to any harm.

At the inn you are to rent an extra room for it and just put it on a table. You are not allowed to sit or sleep there, and you have to keep the room locked at all times. Here is a master key which opens and locks all doors and has the peculiar property that nobody can open the door but you."

I looked at her and felt very strange in my heart, but I said, "I promise to follow your instructions with the greatest care, if I only can hope to meet you again. You have to seal this bargain with a kiss," I added.

She kissed me, and from that moment on I was entirely enthralled by her.

We then discussed the direction I was to go, and where I should meet her again. She handed me a purse of ducats and seemed to be moved when she said goodbye. I was already confused as to what I was doing or ought to do. She sent me downstairs, then, to order the horses, and when I came back the door was locked. I tried the key, the door sprang open but the room was empty; only the box stood on the table where I had put it.

The coach was waiting for me. I carried the box down and took my seat in the comfortable carriage.

"Where is the lady?" asked the innkeeper's wife, and a child answered, "She went into town."

Casually I greeted the people watching me depart, and bade the coachman drive on. I felt very superior in my carriage; last night I had arrived here with dusty boots.

Now I had time and opportunity to count my money, to look at the mysterious box, and to think the whole adventure over; but I came to no conclusion. I drove straight ahead till I arrived in the town where I was to wait for my fair, mysterious friend. I followed her orders to the letter, and enjoyed my leisurely life in the inn.

Soon I became bored. I was not used to living all by myself. But I found company enough in coffee houses and other public meeting places, once I started looking for it. I lived high and spent money carelessly, and soon my ducats dwindled away. Ere long I spent my last piece of gold in an evening of hectic gambling. Very upset, I returned to my room. I was in great distress, all my money was gone and I had run up quite a bill, since I was taken for a man of means. I also felt apprehensive as to how and when I would meet my fair friend again. I longed for her fervently and felt I could not live without her and her money.

I paced up and down in my room, talking to myself, cursing my folly, tearing my hair—in short, I was very ill-behaved. Suddenly I heard rustling in the next room where the box was kept, and then somebody knocked at the connecting door. I groped for my master key, but the door sprang open and there stood my fair lady! I rushed to her to kiss her hands; hardly daring to lift my eyes to her face, I confessed my fault.

"It is pardonable," was her gentle reply, "only your happiness and mine will be postponed. You have to drive on into the wide world again for a while before we shall meet again. Here is gold, and more than enough, but do try to husband it. You got into trouble by drinking and gambling; now I beg of you to beware of wine and women. I am hoping for a happier meeting in the near future."

She stepped back into the other room, the door closed. I knocked, I begged her to open the door, but she did not answer.

Next morning when I asked for the bill, the waiter grinned at me. "Now at last we know why you keep your door so artfully locked that our master key can't open it," he said. "We thought you were safeguarding precious wares and jewels, but I just met your treasure when she came downstairs. Well, such a treasure is worth keeping safe."

I did not answer but paid my bill, took the box, and stepped into my carriage to go on with my strange journey. I had the best intentions of heeding the warnings of my mysterious friend, but as soon as I settled down in the next big city, I became acquainted with certain charming ladies. All my splendid resolutions were forgotten. I lavished gifts on them, I squandered my money and never thought of my purse. Great was my astonishment and my pleasure when, after a couple of weeks of reckless spending, I noticed that my purse was still as round and pleasantly plump as ever. To make sure of this impression I sat down and counted the ducats, and then I went back to my pleasurable way of life. There were excursions by land and by water, there was dancing, and singing, and all kinds of entertainments, and the money flew. But alas! Soon I noticed that my purse had become lean, and limp, and finally it was empty. My cursed counting had obviously done away with the money's pleasant property of being uncountable. What should I do? I felt I could not back out of all my pleasant obligations, and soon I was at the end of my means.

I cursed my situation, in my heart I scolded my fair lady who had led me into temptation; I was very annoyed that she did not come to my rescue at once. Scornfully I renounced all my duties toward her and decided to break open the box, for I was sure it contained precious jewelry. I was resolved to do this, but postponed the undertaking till night and went to a banquet to which I had been invited. We all were swaggering young blades, and we got into high key with wine and music, dancing and talking. I became jealous over one of the charming ladies; soon I had words with her escort, we quarreled, and I drew my rapier. I was carried home, bleeding from several deep wounds.

The surgeon came and tended my injuries and left me in the care of a manservant. It was deep in the night— and the man had fallen asleep—when the door of the side room opened. My fair friend came in and sat down by me on my bed. She asked how I felt, but I did not answer, I was faint and sullen. She talked gently with me, rubbing my forehead with a certain balm. Right away I felt so much better that I had strength enough to scold her. I blamed everything on her, on my longing for her, my boredom as I was kept waiting for her next appearance. I became more and more vehement and finally I swore if she would not marry me, I would do away with myself! She hesitated to answer, and in my rage I tore off the bandages, determined to bleed to death. But behold! My wounds were healed, my skin was smooth and whole, and my sweet friend was in my arms.

We were the happiest pair in the world. Soon we sat together in the coach, the box on the opposite seat, and we traveled, happy and gay, from land to land. I thought she would never leave me again.

But one morning she was not there, and, sullenly, I went on alone. I had not pondered much about this adventure; I expected a quite natural explanation would come forth some day. But something happened which threw me into anxiety, even fear.

I had become so restless that I traveled day and night.

One dark night the lamp in the coach went out, and I slept for a while. When I awoke, I saw a pale shimmer of light on the side of the coach. I found out it came from the box which seemed to have cracked in the hot, dry weather. At once I thought of the jewels which, I felt sure, were in the box. Maybe a large carbuncle was shedding this mysterious light.

I crouched on my seat and bent, straining till my eye was in close contact with the crack. How astonished I was to look into a brightly lit room, well and even luxuriously furnished. It was as if I peeped into a royal chamber through a hole in the ceiling. A fire was burning in the grate, an easy chair stood in front of it. I held my breath as I continued to watch. A tiny woman, a book in her hands, entered the room. She was my wife! I recognized her at once, though her figure was extremely contracted. She sat down in the chair and started to read, after having trimmed the burning logs with the daintiest of fire tongs.

After a while I had to move a little to ease my cramped body, and when I put my eye to the crack again, the light had disappeared, and I looked into empty darkness.

I was astonished, even afraid. I pondered on the strange sight, but could find no solution of the mystery. Finally I fell asleep, and in the morning I thought it must have been a dream, produced by my longing for her. But I felt uneasy and handled the box with the greatest care whenever I had to touch it. I did not know whether I hoped for her reappearance in human size or if I dreaded it, but I felt estranged from her, as if I had found out something base about her.

After a while, my beloved entered my room in the evening. She wore a white dress and appeared taller than I remembered her. All the old stories came to my mind about melusines, nixies, and goblins who increase in length at dusk. She rushed into my arms, but I felt uncomfortable and she drew back at once.

"Your reception shows what I already know," she said sadly. "You have seen me since I last left you. Now you know the condition in which I exist at certain times. Our happiness is disrupted, it may even be destroyed. I must leave you and don't know if I'll ever see you again."

Her sweet presence, her gentle charm at once dispelled the memory of that dreamlike vision. I embraced her. Lovingly I assured her that seeing her had been pure coincidence and did everything to reassure her and myself.

"Search your heart, my beloved," she said anxiously, "and find out if this discovery has not hurt your love. Do you think you can forget that I have two forms? My smallness may cause your love to diminish!"

She was more beautiful than ever, and I thought, "Is it really such a misfortune to have a wife who sometimes turns into a midget and has to be carried around in a box? It would be far worse if she should change into a giantess and put *me* into that box!" All my cheerfulness returned. I could not let her go, not for anything in the whole wide world!

"Dear heart," I replied, "let it rest, we are still the same. How could the daintiest picture I ever saw leave a bad impression on me? I promise I'll take extremely good care of the box if you want to use it again. And maybe all this is just a trick, just some sleight of hand? Maybe you are only teasing and trying me? But you shall see how well I'll behave from now on."

"It is more serious than that," my fair one answered, "but I'm well content if you can take it so lightly. And everything may turn out all right, yet. I'll trust in you, and I am going to do everything that is in my power to bring about a happy ending. But you must give me your solemn promise never to reproach me! And I also beg of you, beware of wine and your hasty temper more than ever."

I promised what she asked of me, I would have promised anything, but she herself finished our serious talk, and everything seemed to be the same as before.

We remained in the large city where we happened to be, and soon we had many friends and led a gay life. My wife was well liked by everybody, she had great charm and also a certain dignity. She was very gifted, she played the lute splendidly and sang very beautifully to it; all social events were crowned by her talent.

I must admit I never cared for music, and my beloved,

realizing this, never tried to entertain me with music when we were alone. But she enjoyed singing in company, and always attracted quite a crowd of admirers.

Against my will my love had diminished after that fateful discovery, though even to myself I did not admit it. I became jealous. I think I loved my beautiful wife less than before, since she seemed to have something to hide. One evening I could not contain myself any more, and my long-subdued anger broke forth, bringing us great misery.

We were in merry company. I laughed and talked gaily with my two charming neighbors at table and was not sparing of my wine. Some music lovers induced my wife to play the lute, and soon everybody sang, solo or in chorus. I fell into an ugly mood. The music lovers seemed too forward, and all that gay singing annoyed me. There is an evil nature in anger; once it has taken hold secretly, it continues to seethe. I became more spiteful by the minute, especially when my wife started to sing to her lute, and those confounded music lovers begged for silence. Why! Was it even forbidden to talk? And how that music pained me, almost like a toothache! It is not astonishing that finally a small flash drew sparks.

Greatly applauded, the fair singer finished her song and looked at me lovingly. But I was enraged and gulped down my goblet of wine and refilled it. She cautioned me, smiling, with a raised forefinger, "Don't forget that that is wine," she said in an undertone.

"Water is for nixies and the like," I cried rudely.

She turned to my neighbors. "Crown the goblet with charm," she said gently. "Maybe it won't be emptied so often."

"You shouldn't take that," a bystander whispered into my ear. "To be chided like that!"

"What does the pixie want of me?" I asked in a fit of temper and spilled the wine as I put down the goblet fiercely.

"Much has been spilled here," my most beautiful one said softly. She struck the chords as she turned to the company and sang. I was ashamed, for I realized I had made a bad mistake. For the first time ever I was moved by her voice as she sang a farewell song. Love, hurt love, was bidding farewell to anger and willfulness.

We went home in silence and I expected trouble. But she was as gentle and impish as ever, and I felt I was the happiest man on earth.

In the morning I said to her, "You sang such a touching farewell song last night. Now, please sing for me; sing a pretty and cheerful song of welcome that will make us feel as if we were meeting for the first time."

"That I cannot do, my friend," she answered earnestly. "My song last night was truly a farewell song for I must leave you. Your insult had very grave consequences for the two of us. You flung away your good fortune, and as for me, I have to give up my dearest wishes."

I entreated her to explain her words.

"I can easily do that, for my staying with you has come to an end," she replied sadly. "Believe me, I would have preferred to tell my story much, much later." She sighed, and then she began her astounding tale.

"The tiny form in which you saw me is my proper and natural size, for I am a descendant of King Eckwald, the famous and glorious prince of the dwarfs. Our people are still as busy and hard-working as in the oldest times. Formerly they made magic swords and impenetrable shields, magic hoods and invisible chains, but nowadays they mostly fashion ornaments and articles of convenience. Our silversmiths and jewelers surpass by far all artists on earth. You'd be surprised if you saw our workshops and warehouses.

"So far so good, but there is a peculiar feature about dwarfs and especially about the royal family, which threatens our existence." She fell silent.

"What is that?" I inquired impatiently, and she took up her tale again.

"It is well known that God, after having created the world, and after the earth was dry and the mountains stood mighty and splendid, made the dwarfs. He wanted the Little People to live in His mountains so that there would be beings endowed with reason to admire and praise His miracles in the inner earth. That, as I say, is well known. It also is common knowledge that later on the Little People rebelled and ventured to conquer the earth. God then made dragons to drive the dwarfs back into their mountains.

"The dragons, after having defeated the Little People, settled in the mountainous caves and cliffs which are the dwarf folk's realm. Dragons are very fierce creatures, always spitting fire and committing all kinds of atrocities, and soon the dwarfs were in dire straits. They turned to the Lord and prayed, humbly and fervently, that He should destroy the unclean dragons. God in His wisdom did not want to destroy His creatures, the dragons; but, in order to help the dwarfs in their plight, He created the giants who slew the dragons, and greatly lessened their number.

"After having dealt with the dragons, the giants, too, became insolent and committed many a vile deed, especially against the dwarfs, till the Little People again cried to the Lord. And God lent them His ear again and created the knights, who fought dragons and giants alike, and lived in peace with the dwarfs. And forever after knights and dwarfs were allies against dragons and giants.

"You can see, my friend, that ours is the oldest race on earth, which of course is a great honor, but also has a severe drawback.

"Nothing is immortal in this world. All that has once been great must become small, and will diminish and dwindle away. The Little People, too, are subject to this law, and since we were the first to come, we are the first to decrease. We grow constantly smaller, and the royal family, being the purest race, suffers most. Our sages therefore decided, long ago, that from time to time a royal princess is to be sent out into the world to marry an honorable knight and thus to renew King Eckwald's family."

Doubtfully I looked at my wife as quite simply she told her story. Was what she was telling me a hoax? I had not the slightest doubt about her own dainty lineage, but that she should have singled out me as her knight filled me with distrust. I knew myself too well to assume my ancestors had come into the world by an immediate act of creation!

I concealed both my astonishment and my doubts, and asked her good-naturedly, "But, my dear child, tell me how did you acquire this tall and stately figure? For I know few women who can compete with you!"

"That you will learn now," replied my fair lady.

"Since times of old," she went on, "it has been the

custom in the royal council of the Little People to postpone extraordinary steps as long as possible, and I think that is wise and natural. They might have delayed a long time sending a princess out into the world once again, if something dreadful had not happened. My little brother, born after me, turned out to be so exceedingly small that the nurse actually lost him out of his diapers! Nobody knows what has become of him! This has never happened before and the alarmed sages decided to send me out to marry a mortal."

"They decided!" I cried. "That's all very well! It's easy to make a decision. But how did your sages manage to endow a midget with such a divine figure?"

"It has been done before," she answered. "In the royal treasure house lay a monstrous gold ring, at least that is how it seemed to me when I first saw it. It is the same ring I'm wearing now on my finger. Before I was sent away, everything was explained to me, and I was told in detail what I had to do.

"A replica of my parent's favorite summer palace was made. It was a stately building with side wings, and equipped with all one could wish for. It stood at the entrance of a large rocky cave, a lovely sight indeed. On the appointed day the whole court moved there, and my parents followed with me. The army paraded, and twenty-four priests, not without great trouble, carried the magic ring on a splendid litter. It was placed on the threshold of the new palace, and after many ceremonies I stepped forward and placed my hand on the ring. I started to grow immediately; in a few moments I had reached my present size, and then I put the ring on my finger.

"The side wings of the new palace retreated into the

main building, the portals, doors, and windows closed, and instead of the palace there stood the box which you know so well. I stooped and picked it up and went away. It was a marvelous feeling to be so big and strong. Still a dwarf, compared with trees and mountains, I was a giant to grass and herbs and above all to ants which have been our enemies of old.

"Later on I'll tell you about my adventures before I found you. I tried many others, but you seemed to me the only one worthy to renew the race of the glorious Eckwald."

My head was in a whirl with her tale. I asked all kinds of questions, but all I learned was that my wife had to return to her parents after being so grievously insulted by me. I felt very sad, but she hoped she would get permission to come back to me soon. But now she had to go home, otherwise all kinds of troubles would arise, the purse would soon fail and other disasters befall us. When I heard that we would soon be out of money, I fell silent. I shrugged my shoulders, and she seemed to understand me.

We packed our things and left, and drove away to the mountains. The box stood in its usual place, opposite our seats; certainly, it bore no resemblance to a palace! Finally we reached the mountains, halted, and alighted. My wife took the lead and I followed with the box. A rather steep and narrow path took us to a small green valley, crossed by a clear brook. She pointed to a low knoll in the meadow and told me to put the box down there.

"Farewell," she then said mournfully. "You will easily find your way back. Do not forget me—I hope to see you again."

She was so captivating as she stood there, in the setting

of green pasture, brook, and mountains—who could have been so bereft of feelings as to let her go? I came forward to clasp her in my arms, but she pushed me away, threatening me with grave danger if I did not leave her at once.

"Is there no way for me to stay with you?" I exclaimed in great anguish. "No possible way you can keep me beside you?"

She was moved by my grief.

"There is indeed a way we can stay together," she admitted but hesitated to go on. Nobody was happier than I! But only with great difficulty could I persuade her to come out with it.

"If you were willing to become a dwarf as I am, then you could live in our realm as a member of the royal family," she finally declared.

I was not very pleased with this proposal, but I just could not tear myself away from her. I had become used to miracles since I had known her and, always ready to act on the spur of the moment, I said, "All right, my dear, you may do with me as you please."

She told me to extend the little finger of my right hand. She placed hers against mine, and with her left hand she gently pulled the golden ring from her finger and let it slide over to my finger. As soon as this was done, I felt an excruciating pain, the ring contracted and tortured me horribly.

I cried out aloud and involuntarily grabbed for her, but she had disappeared. I cannot explain how I felt. I can only tell how, all of a sudden, I found myself in a forest of tall grass stalks, and there was my wife too! I embraced and kissed her, unbelievably happy to see her again after

such a short but strange separation. The little pair was as happy as the large one had been.

It was very difficult to climb the hill, because for us the meadow had turned into an almost impenetrable wood, but at last we arrived at a clearing, and there I saw a large regular block which I soon recognized as the little box.

"Knock at the door with your ring, my friend," said my beloved. "You'll see a miracle happen."

I did as I was told, and imagine! the plain box unfolded into a maze of colonnades, pillars, side wings, doors, and windows. In no time there stood a complete palace; my sweet companion took my hand and we entered it together. I recognized at once the large sitting room with fireplace and easy chair, where my wife had been sitting that night which seemed to be so very long ago. I lifted my eyes, and saw in the dome the crack through which I had peered down.

I'm not going to describe the palace in detail, it is enough to say that everything was exquisite and tasteful and very spacious. Soon I heard martial music from afar,

and my wife sprang joyfully to her feet, announcing the arrival of her royal father. We went to the entrance door and watched a magnificent procession emerge from a big rocky cave. Soldiers, courtiers, servants, all in gorgeous attire—it was a splendid sight! Amidst a gold-glistening crowd the king finally approached. His loving daughter rushed to greet him, clasping my hand and pulling me along with her. We knelt down before the tiny majesty, and very graciously he raised me to my feet. I noticed as I stood in front of him that in this miniature world I was, even in my present size, by far the tallest man. Together we entered the palace, and in the presence of the entire court the king expressed his pleasure at my joining the Little People. He welcomed me as his son-in-law, and to-morrow was to be the wedding day, according to the laws of the Little People who do not recognize human ties.

All of a sudden I was terrified! I felt horrible as he talked about marriage, for it made me aware of the permanence of my dwarfish existence.

A great festival was held to welcome us; but I cannot remember anything about it for I paid no heed to any of it. The daintiest food, the most precious wines held no pleasure for me. I kept thinking what I could do, but there was not much choice left. When night fell I decided to steal away and to conceal myself somewhere. I found a chink in a rocky wall near the entrance of the big cave where we celebrated, and I crept into the crack, hiding as best I could. I tried to remove the hapless ring from my finger but that was impossible. The more I pulled, the tighter it became, causing me violent pain which subsided at once as soon as I stopped pulling.

Early next morning I woke up—I had slept very well in

spite of my cramped position—and was just going to look around for a way out, when it started to rain, or so I thought. Sand and grit in large quantities poured down on me through grass, leaves, and flowers. I looked up, and was horrified when suddenly everything around me seemed to come alive. A huge army of ants fell on me! They attacked me from all sides. I fought valiantly enough, but they pinched and nipped and tormented me so much that in the end I was glad to hear somebody call, "Surrender!" And surrender I did, at once! An ant of impressive size approached; he greeted me politely and even reverently, recommending himself and his people to my favor. I learned that my father-in-law had made peace with the ants, the dwarf folks' eternal foe. The ants had set out at once to find and catch me, and to bring back the truant. Thus poor little me was at the mercy of still smaller beings. I had to face the wedding, and I had to be grateful if my father-in-law was not angered, and if my fair lady was not annoyed with me.

Well, we were married right away.

Court life turned out to be very gay and lively, yet there were lonely hours when I sat and brooded.

My surroundings were pleasant and the newness of my princely life made everything attractive. Everything was in proportion to my present size and present wants. I enjoyed the dainty tidbits; bottles and glasses were just the right size for the wee wine-sipper, a kiss from my little wife's tiny red mouth was still a most enchanting pleasure, but . . . unfortunately I had not forgotten my former state!

In my heart I had a vision of former greatness which made me restless and unhappy. Now I understood, for the first time in my life, what the philosophers mean when they talk about ideals that so torment the mind of man because they are unobtainable. I had a vivid ideal of myself, and in my dreams I appeared to my present tiny self as a giant. Enough of that! All these bonds—the ring, my wife, my dwarfish figure—made me utterly unhappy. Soon I thought seriously of escape.

I was sure the whole secret lay in the ring, and I decided to file it asunder. Therefore I secretly took some files from the court jeweler. It was my good luck that I was left-handed; indeed, throughout my whole life, I have never done anything right.

I worked hard to set myself free again. It was not easy, for the gold ring had grown very thick when it contracted, but doggedly I kept on working at all hours, whenever I was unobserved. Finally I had nearly cut through the metal and, thank goodness, I was thoughtful enough to step out of doors. For, as the golden fetter sprang and fell from my finger, I shot aloft with great violence. I actually thought I would dash against the sky! Most certainly I would have bolted through the roof of our palace; I might even have destroyed the new summer residence altogether.

There I stood once more in my proper size, much larger than the dwarfs, but also, it seemed to me, dumber and clumsier.

After a while I recovered from my shock and saw a strongbox at my side. I picked it up; it was rather weighty as I carried it down the path to the stage house. My coach was waiting there, and I ordered horses and drove away at once. In the coach I found a key fitting the strongbox, which contained gold and jewelry.

As long as these riches held out, I drove in my carriage

and traveled in style, but bit by bit the money dwindled away. I sold the carriage and had to use the public coach. I always expected the strongbox to be refilled once more, but that did not happen. Finally I lost hope and sold it, and ere long I rode on shanks' mare again.

My adventure had caused me quite a detour, that is true, but at long last I found myself at the inn, wheedling myself into favor with a cook, and all was with me as it had been when you first met me.

The Invisible Kingdom

*

RICHARD LEANDER

Dreamer George was a young peasant who lived with his old father in a little house not far from a mountain hamlet. In the evening when the numerous chores on the small farm were done—the old black horse curry-combed, the cream-colored oxen fed and watered, the gentle cow milked, the noisy chickens fed and sleeping on their rafters—George would go into the garden. After the day's work he loved to sit there on a boulder and look down into the beautiful valley. He did not care much for other people's company and was always quiet and withdrawn. People jestingly called him "Dreamer George," but that did not bother him.

After his father died, George drew away even more from the villagers and hardly ever went down into the valley. Every evening he sat on his lookout and watched the clouds drift through the valley, saw the fog rise from the meadows, saw darkness blot out all colors till moon and stars in silent splendor wandered across the night-blue vault of the sky; and his heart was filled with a serene joy. He listened to the murmuring of the river in the valley as it sang about the mountains whence it came, about the faraway ocean to which it flowed, about the nixies who lived in the clear depths. The trees joined in the songs and told tales full of marvels and wonder. It was an extraordinary valley, filled with secret life.

The stars high in the nocturnal sky trembled with joy, they wanted to dive down into the green forests and the blue waters. But the angels who stand behind each star held on to them, saying, "Stars! Stars! Don't commit such foolishness, you are much too old for that—thousands and thousands of years! Now stay here and shine!"

Yes, it was a marvelous valley! But only Dreamer George heard and saw all this. The village folks did not know anything about it for they were just ordinary people. When they saw how brightly the stars sparkled and glittered, they only said, "It's quite cold tonight, hope the potatoes won't freeze." The trees in the green forest were just good for firewood, and the river was handy for washing their linen —everything had to be useful. Sometimes Dreamer George tried to tell them about the wonders that were all around them, but they only laughed at him. They were just ordinary village folks.

One evening George fell asleep in the garden and had the nicest dream. He dreamed he saw a golden swing hanging from the sky. Each rope was fastened to a star, and a beautiful princess sat in the swing and swung from sky to earth and from earth to sky. Each time the swing came near the earth the princess clapped her hands with joy and threw a rose to George. But suddenly one rope broke, and the swing with the princess flew up into the sky, farther and farther away, till at last he could see her no more.

Dreamer George awoke and rubbed his eyes: at his side lay a bunch of roses. Next night he dreamed the same dream, and sure enough there the roses were when he awoke. Thus it went for an entire week.

"There must be some reason for that dream," George said to himself. "Maybe it's a message."

Next morning he closed his house and set out to find his dream princess. He wandered for days and days, and finally he saw from afar a country where the clouds touched the land. "That must be Dreamland," George thought, and went on with new strength.

He was just crossing a dense forest when suddenly he heard groaning and whimpering. He rushed to the spot from where the pitiful moaning came, and there he saw an old man with a long silvery beard lying on the ground. Two ugly, loathsome, stark-naked men were holding him down, trying to strangle him. Excited, George looked around for a weapon, and for want of something better he broke a large branch from the nearest tree. He ran toward the ugly men, who were so taken by surprise at his assault that they jumped up and ran away. He helped the old man to his feet, asking why those two fiends had tried to strangle him.

"I am the King of Dreamland," said the venerable old man, "and by mistake I entered the land of my greatest enemy, the King of Reality. As soon as my eternal foe noticed my presence, he sent two of his creatures to kill me."

"What have you done to the King of Reality that he wants to kill you?" Dreamer George asked, astonished.

"God forbid that I ever do ill to anybody," replied the old king, "but my enemy is aroused very easily. That's his disposition, and he hates me like sin."

"Why were those two scoundrels stark naked?" asked Dreamer George after a few moments of pondering.

"That's the custom in the Land of Reality," answered the king. "Everyone walks around without a bit of clothing on, even the king. They have no modesty! It's outrageous, they are not even ashamed of themselves." The old king was getting quite excited. "The Land of Naked Reality is harsh and ugly. I love to throw a shimmering veil over its bareness and drabness, to add a dash of color, a touch of Dreamland, to the bare facts—even a bit of self-delusion."

George stared at him in great astonishment. "But are we not supposed to stand with both feet on the firm ground of reality?"

"Well, my boy, since you are a mortal, maybe that is best for you. But I am the King of Dreamland, for me the world is bright and rainbow-colored!" He smiled. Gently he touched George's shoulder. "It wouldn't hurt a mortal, though, to know there is more to the world than just what he can see and touch." Then he took George's arm. "Now come, you saved my life, and I want to show my gratitude. I'm going to show you my country. It is the most beautiful land in the whole world, and the dreams are my subjects."

Soon they came to the country where the clouds touch the earth, and the king opened a well-concealed trapdoor under some brushwood. They entered and descended five hundred steps, till they came into a wide, brightly lit grotto

which stretched as far as one could see. It was so beautiful no description can do it justice.

There were immense gardens filled with fantastic flowers in dazzling colors, redolent with sweet fragrance. Jewel-colored birds poured out their melodious songs. There were lovely islands in a large azure lake. Lofty castles were set on the shimmering green islands, and the isles drifted through the pure blue waters. If one wanted to enter such a castle one had only to call:

> Dream castle, come and float my way,
> I want to enter your halls so gay.

And the castle would come swimming to the edge of the lake.

There were also castles built in the clouds; radiant with rainbow colors, they sailed slowly through the air. And if one called:

> Castle in the clouds, come down to me,
> Your marvelous splendor I want to see,

then they slowly descended.

There really was more to be seen than one person can dream in many a night!

"Now I will show you my subjects, the dreams," said the king. "I have three kinds," he explained as they walked on the silver paths, "good dreams for good people, bad dreams for bad people, and then there are goblin dreams. Sometimes I amuse myself and send goblin dreams to people. Even a king has to have a little fun once in a while."

They entered one of the castles. It was built in such a crazy way that one became befuddled just from looking at it.

"This is the goblins' castle," said the king with a twinkle.

"They are a saucy and insolent lot. They enjoy teasing people but they are really quite harmless. Come here, little one," he called to a fidgety manikin who came running at once, with grotesque jumps. The king turned to Dreamer George. "Once in a great while he gets permission to go up to earth. And you know what he does when he gets there? He runs into the first house he sees. If he finds a man peacefully asleep, he drags him out of bed, carries him up the staircase of the steeple, and then drops him from the very top. Then helter-skelter the goblin races down the stairs. Just in the nick of time he catches his man unharmed, carries him home, and throws him into his bed so that the whole bedstead creaks. The sleeper awakes, sits up in bed, rubs his eyes, and says to his wife, 'Dear me, what a dream I had! I just dreamed I tumbled down from the steeple—thank goodness, it was only a dream.' "

"I know that imp!" cried Dreamer George. "He has visited me too. Now if he dares come back to me, we'll see if he can bounce me around again!"

The king laughed. "Maybe you gobbled down your dinner too hastily. My goblin dreams are just waiting for that!"

Another goblin crept out from under a table. He wore a shaggy coat and looked almost like a dog. A little red tongue protruded from his mouth.

"This one is not any better," said the king, and he chuckled. "He barks and howls like a dog, and when people become afraid and want to run away, he holds them down by their arms and legs, and they can't move the tiniest little bit. He is as strong as a giant!"

"I know that one too," George said, looking disgusted. "He's awful! And sometimes he isn't a dog, but a bear or something like that—and one can't get away from him no matter how hard one struggles."

"Well, I'll forbid them to visit you again, my young friend," the king said comfortingly. "But now let's have a look at the bad dreams."

They came to a huge castle surrounded by high walls. The entrance was locked and barred by a heavy iron grating, and through the iron gate George saw a throng of ghastly monsters milling around.

"You don't have to be afraid, my boy," remarked the king as he saw Dreamer George shudder. "They are only for really bad people."

They were the most revolting fiends: some of the brutes looked to be half-man, half-beast, frightful to behold. There were also men so terrible and evil-looking that George shrank back.

"Don't you want to see how bad people have to suffer in their dreams?" The king waved to a monstrous giant who carried two millstones under his arms.

"Tell me where you are going tonight," he asked sternly.

The giant grinned a hideous grin that split his ugly face from ear to ear. He shook with horrid delight.

"I'm going to visit a rich man who let his old father go hungry. Once the father came asking for help but the man said to his servants, 'Chase him away, that good-for-nothing!' Now I visit him night after night and squeeze him between my millstones till he feels as if every bone in his body were broken. And when he is good and pliable and jerks and kicks around, then I'll pick him up and shake him and say, 'Now look how you sprawl and kick, you good-for-nothing!' He wakes up, with his teeth still rattling, and he is so shaken up that he calls out, 'Wife, bring me another featherbed, I'm as cold as death!' And as soon as he is asleep, I start my little game again."

George listened with mounting terror. He gripped the king's sleeve.

"Please, oh please, let's get away from here! I can't bear to look at them any longer."

"All right, but you'll never have to fear them," the king said kindly. "Come, let us go to the good dreams now."

They wandered then through the enchanting gardens where the paths were made of silver, the flower beds of gold, and the flowers of cut jewels. Here the good dreams walked around. Their shimmering garments shone like the sun, like rose petals were their sweet faces. One dream wore a glistening star in her night-dark hair. Another dream had a wreath of radiant flowers, and a third one a jewel-studded crown. In the distance George saw Prince Charming on his white charger. Then he saw a handsome knight in gold-embossed armor lifting his blue-gleaming sword to slay the dragon. Now there was an angel with strong, dazzling-white wings carrying a pale child to his mother who was waiting for him at the Golden Gate of Paradise. George suddenly spied a jolly little old man who seemed very familiar to him, carrying a sack of sand on his bent back. Who could that be? Then he remembered: of course, it was the Sandman, getting ready to go up to earth.

There were more and more dreams the farther they walked. A shimmering world of beauty and peace unfolded before Dreamer George's eyes: he saw the dreams of mankind!

It was quite an experience to see the loveliest and boldest dreams come true. Many of them he recognized, but still he looked around eagerly. Suddenly he stood stockstill.

"There she is!" he called aloud, and all the dreams turned and smiled at him. He grabbed the king's arm excitedly.

"What's the matter, George?" the king asked, astonished.

"There is my princess! My very own! I saw her in my dreams!"

"Indeed!" The king laughed aloud at George's delight. "Didn't I always send you sweet dreams, my boy? She is one of my most beautiful subjects."

George hardly listened. He rushed to the princess who was sitting dreamily in her golden swing. When she saw George coming, she leaped down with a delighted little gasp, right into his arms. He put her down gently, took her hand, and led her to a marble bench. They sat down, they smiled, and then they told each other how wonderful it was to meet again, and when they finished they started all over again.

Meanwhile the King of Dreamland paced the silver paths in his realm. His hands were folded in back of him, and once in a while he looked at his watch hoping that the two young people would get finished with their exciting and remarkable story. But there seemed to be no end to it for them.

Finally he came over to the bench and patted George on the shoulder. "Well, well, children. This will have to do for the time being. Dreamer George, you have a long way home. Sorry I can't let you stay here, but I don't have a single bed in my country because all my dreams leave for the night. You have to go home, George. And you, princess, go and change. Wear something pink tonight, apple-blossom pink, and then I'll tell you whom you have to visit."

When George heard this his heart leaped within him, and he felt more courageous than ever before in his life. He got up from his seat and said in a firm voice:

"Your Majesty! I'll never leave my princess again as long as I live. Either you have to keep me here forever, or send her up to earth with me. I cannot live without her. I love her so, I love her so!" And his eyes filled with tears, for he was very emotional.

"But, George, George, what are you thinking of!" the king replied. "This is really the prettiest dream I have in Dreamland."

Two sparkling tears as big as hazelnuts ran down George's smooth cheeks. The king shrugged his shoulders, but he had to smile at George's desperation.

"All right, my boy. You saved my life, you shall have your wish. Go home and take your princess with you. As soon as you are back on earth, take the silver veil and throw it down through the trapdoor. Then your princess will turn into a girl of flesh and blood. Now she is only a dream!"

"A thousand thanks, Your Majesty!" Dreamer George was overwhelmed with joy. He took his dream princess by the hand to rush home with her, but then he stopped short. Hesitantly he said, "I ought to be ashamed to ask for more favors after you granted me my heart's desire. But, oh, King, look at my situation! Now I have a princess but no kingdom, and I think it is impossible for a princess to live without a kingdom. Could you not provide me with a kingdom? A very little one would do."

"I don't have real kingdoms to give away." The King of Dreamland shook his head and looked amused at the eager young man. "I have only invisible kingdoms, but I will grant you one. One of the largest and most marvelous kingdoms that I still own, I'll give you. Mostly they go to poets, you know."

"What is an invisible kingdom?" George asked. He was a little taken aback. It seemed very strange to him.

"You just wait and see, and you will be surprised. An invisible kingdom is quite wonderful and much better than an ordinary one. For, you see, if you are a real king in a real kingdom, you might experience all kind of troubles. An empty treasure house, for example, or even worse problems. You might wake up in the morning and find someone had declared war on you, and you'd find yourself most horribly involved. You might even be defeated and thrown into a dungeon, and the victor might marry your dream princess. All this can't happen in an invisible realm."

"That sounds all right," Dreamer George answered,

a little doubtfully, "but what good is a kingdom if we can't see it?"

"Oh, don't be so slow-witted!" The king was getting quite impatient by now. "You and your princess will see it all right. You will see the woods and fields, the meadows and castles, the streams and flocks. You'll live in it, and you can do in it as you please. Only ordinary people can't see it."

"That's just fine with me! I was already beginning to worry about what people in my village would say when I come home with a princess and become a king myself. But what they don't know won't hurt them."

He took the princess's hand again; they waved goodbye and left Dreamland. They climbed the five hundred steps till they saw daylight again. Then George tenderly loosened the veil from her hair and let it flutter down into Dreamland. He was going to close the iron trapdoor, but it was too heavy and slipped from his hand and snapped shut with a terrific BANG! It was as loud as a cannon shot, and for a moment Dreamer George lost consciousness.

When he came to himself again, he was lying in the grass in his garden, and at his side was his princess—flesh and blood like any other human being. She caressed his hand and said, "You darling, foolish man! How long you hesitated to tell me that you loved me. Were you afraid of me?"

The moon shone and its beams silvered the rippling wavelets of the sleepy river. The forest stirred softly, and George and his princess sat and talked and talked. Suddenly they saw a very small, very black cloud darken the moon, and then something fell at their feet. It looked like a folded cloth. The moon shone brightly again, and they picked up the cloth and started to unfold it. It was a very filmy material, strong and thin, and it took a long time till they had it all straightened out. It looked like a huge map: a river parted it in the middle and there were towns and forests and fields on both sides. Then they recognized it. It was a kingdom! The good King of Dreamland had dropped it for them out of the night-blue sky. George's humble hut had changed into a splendid castle with marble walls, glass staircases, and blue turrets. He took his princess by the hand and they entered the castle together. Their subjects were waiting for them and bowed deeply. Trumpets and drums resounded, pages sprang before them strewing flowers. Then and there they were King and Queen.

Next morning the news ran like wildfire through the village that Dreamer George had come back and had brought home a wife.

"Well, you know how Dreamer George is," people said to each other. "Do you think he married somebody smart and thrifty?"

"I saw her this morning, when I went to work," a peasant remarked. "They were standing before the door of his hut. She is nothing special, just an ordinary person and too slightly built for my taste. Heaven knows whether she's a good worker." The man shrugged. "She was dressed rather poorly," he added as an afterthought.

"Well, how else could it be!" said his neighbor. "He has nothing, and I guess she hasn't a penny to her name either."

So gossiped the stolid villagers, for they could not see that she was a princess. In their simple-mindedness they did not even notice that the little hut was transformed into a most splendid castle. For, you see, the hut belonged to the Invisible Kingdom in which Dreamer George reigned as a king. He did not mind living and working like any other peasant now that he had to provide for a family. But he felt like a king, and he never lost his dignity nor his queen her charm.

George did not bother to explain to the dull people that he was a king now, but lived happily with his queen in their own realm. They had six children, and each one was more beautiful than the others, and they all were princes and princesses.

But nobody in the village knew that.

You see, they were just ordinary village folks and much too thick-headed to understand such things.

The Spendthrift

*

FERDINAND RAIMUND

Ilmaha is the name of the Queen of Fairyland.

In eternal youth she governs her many-splendored kingdom in the clouds. Happiness, youth, and beauty reign
there forever, but Ilmaha, the wise, knows about human
suffering. To ease the human burden, she sends her fairies
down to earth.

One day she called Cheristane before her throne. Putting a crown of pearls on the head of the ever young and
beautiful fairy, she said solemnly:

"Go down to earth, Cheristane, and use these pearls for
mankind's welfare. A magic power is enclosed in each
pearl, and you may release this power as you choose. When
the last pearl is spent, your reign ends, and you must return to me to receive your reward or punishment. Woe
betide you if you spend this treasure on the unworthy,
thus depriving the needy. Go now, and do not abuse your
power."

Joyfully Cheristane left Fairyland in the encircling clouds high in the sky, and descended to the world of man. She roamed the earth, spending her pearls wisely and helping people in their distress. She still had many pearls left, when one day she saw a motherless boy of seven playing in his father's garden. The boy looked lovely in his unsullied youth, and Cheristane could not take her eyes from him. She had seen too much suffering in her futile attempts to help mankind, and her heart went out to him. "One day he will suffer, too," she thought sadly. She had become a little weary. What had she achieved? She had dried the tears of some men, but millions still wept.

A strange idea occurred to her. Here was a happy, healthy, beautiful child. She would see to it that one human being should have a perfect life!

She removed a pearl from her crown and spoke:

> No sorrow shall touch you,
> Luck shall follow your every step,
> Fate shall never cross your path.

With these words she waved her magic wand over the child.

As she had wished it, so it happened. Julius, the boy, grew up in perfect health, in perfect ease, in perfect happiness. No wish was ever denied him; he knew no suffering, no longing, no painful struggle for achievement. Cheristane showered blessings on him. His father became extremely rich and success crowned his smallest efforts, for Cheristane did not spare her pearls.

Julius von Flottwell became a handsome young man.

When he was twenty years old, his father died and left him an immense fortune. The fabulously rich young nobleman soon enjoyed quite a reputation as a seeker after new pastimes. The Flottwells' ancestral castle in the Alps was always bustling with life, for young Flottwell put himself out to offer his friends all the pleasures he could think of. With open hands he squandered his money. He never doubted life would go on this way forever, and his flattering friends strengthened him in this belief. He was king in a realm of endless joy. He was happy, and he wanted to make everybody else happy. Did he succeed?

One fine summer morning, Valentine and Fritz were busy in the great entrance hall of Flottwell Castle. They wore the rich livery which Flottwell had designed for his servants. The hall was deserted, though the castle was crowded with guests.

"The master will not be hunting today, it seems," remarked Valentine, while he was busily cleaning rifles.

"What did you expect?" answered Fritz with a mocking smile. "He played faro with his fine friends till three in the morning. They never know when to stop. Last night they robbed our master quite nicely." Fritz laughed slyly.

"It always makes me mad to see that," murmured Valentine as he peered down the rifle barrel to check that it was clean.

"Why? Let the rich pay for the trouble they cause other people," was Fritz's reply.

"I suppose you're right. But there is nothing wrong with our master. He really is a noble man!" answered Valentine. Fritz shrugged, and Valentine went on somewhat angrily, "All right! He entertains his friends in grand style. But his peasants, I hear, pay him hardly any tithe. Don't you know that?"

Patronizingly Fritz patted Valentine on the shoulder. "Of course, he supports the whole world—including you and me!" With a grin he added, "I'm not doing badly myself with Flottwell's famous generosity. The only trouble is that he's too hotheaded. Did you ever see him in a rage? Everything can go to ruin then, as far as he's concerned."

"I know he's spoiled," Valentine admitted, "but after he calms down, he makes up for everything doubly and triply."

"Yes, he thinks he can straighten out everything with money. You know how rich people are! Well, life usually deals out measure for measure," Fritz said wisely. "I'll make hay here as long as the sun shines. But this won't go on forever, mark my words."

Valentine was quiet for a moment, then he said thoughtfully, "He is just too lucky for his own good, that's the trouble. He has everything a man can wish for: wealth, good looks, wisdom . . ."

"Wisdom? That's a great joke! He's the greatest fool ever, he lets himself be cheated by everybody. His friends don't care a jot about him, they just sponge on him. We all stuff our pockets here—and why not? But when I see how he is taken in by that cunning sneak, his secretary Wolf, then I really must say he's stupid!"

"Wolf is a villain, all right." Valentine sighed. "His famous good luck has made our master blind. Of course, he's never known trouble. People say he has a charmed life."

"There you have it! How can he distinguish good from

evil if he has never met with evil? He gives me the shivers, to tell you the truth."

"It's a shame! And he's a good fellow at heart, but . . . 'All too good is slovenly,' that's what my grandmother used to say. Guess she was right."

So his servants gossiped. They did not respect their master, for Flottwell seemed to have nothing to his credit but his father's money and his generous disposition.

With increasing anxiety Cheristane had watched the development of her experiment. How happy she had been the first few years! She was sure she had done right in creating one life radiant with bliss.

But as Julius grew older, there seemed to be no fulfillment of what the beautiful child had promised. He never got into trouble, but that was not because of his own merits—it was a result of Cheristane's gift. Of course, nobody, least of all Julius himself, knew that he was the chosen protégé of a fairy, that he, indeed, had a charmed life! He took it for granted that life was just a round of pleasure.

To turn his shallow mind to beauty, Cheristane had assumed human form. For three years she lived in a hut near the castle. The rocky place was transformed into a Garden of Eden. Cheristane hoped he would learn peace of mind and real happiness in her loving presence, but beauty and love seemed not to be enough to strengthen his character. Her lovely flowers blossomed in vain. Young Flottwell wanted life to be an eternal feast, with the whole world invited to his golden tables.

Julius enjoyed the fairy's unwavering love without questioning or doubt. She had asked him not to ask her who she was, and he had obeyed her wish. He took it for granted that he was loved by everybody.

But Cheristane's time had now run out and sorrow overwhelmed her heart, for the fairy had fallen in love with the mortal. She was deeply concerned about his shortcomings. Had she harmed the one she loved?

She had one pearl left. When that pearl was used up, her reign would end and she would have to return to the Fairy Queen. But her heart would remain on earth.

In her anxious desire to protect Julius longer than she really could, she had found a clever way out. From her last pearl she created a good genius to watch over Julius' future life.

She removed the last pearl from her crown; she waved her magic wand, and Azure, spirit of the air, appeared. She entreated him to watch over her darling's life and heard the strange verse:

> You freed him from all human grief and strife,
> It's up to him to master now his life.
> He has the strength to master his emotion,
> All I can do is—warn him—teach him caution.

"Oh, that is a grave sentence," sighed Cheristane. "You lend wings to a child while you deprive his guardian angel of them."

"This is what is written in the Book of Future," was the unmoved answer of the aerial spirit.

Cheristane, in her disguise of a lovely young girl, was waiting in the mountain hut for Flottwell. Sad was her heart, for today she had to part from him forever, and tell

him that she was Cheristane, the fairy, a being from another world. At first Flottwell was unbelieving when the
beautiful maiden, the joy of his restless life, said the
strange words:

"My realm is in the clouds. It was not a human being
whom you loved. My time on earth has run out and I have
to return to Fairyland."

She told him about the crown of pearls and her destiny to bring happiness to mankind. Flottwell was too
dumbfounded to understand her fully. But then she said
gently, "The fairy fell in love with a mortal, and lavished
every pearl she had left on one single human being. Oh,
Julius! Did I waste my treasure? Did I deprive the needy
for one who is unworthy? My dream is over, all my pearls
are gone. Today I sacrificed the last one for your welfare.
My reign here ends, and you must make your own way."

"Cheristane, I cannot let you go. You take my life away
if you leave me forever," the man said urgently. "I'll give
up everything, but stay with me, stay a mortal woman,"
he pleaded. But the fairy shook her head.

"I must go. It grieves me that I cannot help you any
more, can only warn you. I must not reveal your future,
for it is left to you to choose your way. Grant me one
wish, my beloved."

Julius nodded; he was too shaken by all these strange
revelations to speak.

The fairy said, "Grant me one year of your life, a year
that I may choose myself, my friend."

"Take them all!" he burst out. "Take them all, for un-
happiness will rule my life without you, dearest treasure
of my heart."

"One year I'll take to save you from disgrace," she said

earnestly. "Do not let me down, sweet friend. I loved you more than all the world."

Flottwell listened as a man in his dreams listens to the strange words of an enchanting vision. A golden haze rose, turning everything solid into shadowy, indistinct clouds. A warm golden mist enshrouded his beloved, and she seemed to float away in a wavering radiancy that blinded his mortal eyes. He stretched his arms out to hold her, but all he embraced were shadows.

"Farewell," he heard her whisper.

He cried out, "Do not leave me alone!"

From afar her silver voice came floating back once more.

"Farewell, my beloved, remember me."

Then the vision was gone, and he stood alone in a desolate mountain area.

Three years passed. His youthful infatuation with a fairy soon seemed a lovely dream to Flottwell. How far away it was! She was only a shadow now, the shadow of a flower in a golden mirror.

Life was very different from the way he had seen it in his youthful dreams. The enchanting glow had gone from his life since he no longer lived under Cheristane's silken veil. He had not suffered as yet, but he knew boredom, disappointment, dragging hours. He was not acquainted with sorrow, and small hardships seemed unbearable. It meant little to him that he was still a very rich man.

"I wish I could deal out kingdoms to my friends," he used to say with a laugh. "I'll never be weary of giving," and with open hands he dealt out gifts and favors. His soft-tongued friends praised him to the skies—"The noblest friend, the greatest soul," they said, burning their heady incense before him. It turned his head, it was so wonderful to be loved by everybody.

He frowned at the well-meant warnings of his old steward, who had been in the Flottwell's service since the time of Julius' father, and who thought it his right and his duty to warn the heedless young man. "Sir, you'll give so much till you give yourself away to poverty," the old man said, looking at Julius with concerned affection. "Believe me, it is not befitting for man to deal out favors like a god."

Julius only laughed at him. "My good luck is a challenge to me," was his reckless answer. "I want to enjoy the unlimited pleasures life has in store for me, and I want to share my joy with others."

"Sir, there is a limit to everything. Even the greatest fortune . . ." Angrily Julius interrupted. "I don't like it when my servants think they have to act as my schoolmasters," he snapped at the faithful steward. "Kindly keep your disapproval to yourself." The old man withdrew into a hurt silence, and did not offer his advice again even when Julius overstepped all limits of good sense.

The old ancestral castle in the mountainous area seemed too small for the gay crowd that lived with young Flottwell, and Julius had a splendid palace built in the rolling hill country of the Lower Alps. There was no end to the resplendent festivals he gave.

Then his life changed again, for he fell in love. Amelia was in his every thought. The golden fairy veil was there

again, enhancing his days, covering all difficulties. Life was good once more; he loved his friends and wished to see only happiness around him.

Amelia's proud heart yielded to his ready charm. Who was more lovable, more brilliant, more manly than young Flottwell? But her father was not blind to Flottwell's weakness. He was a rich man himself, and for his only daughter he wanted not the glittering moods of a spendthrift, but peace and security. He was convinced no fortune could outlast the young man's wastefulness, and he was strongly opposed to their marriage. This was the first real obstacle that Flottwell had ever encountered, and he could not endure that things were not going his way. He did not understand how anyone could oppose him. Amelia's father seemed to him just a stiff-necked old man who was making his daughter the victim of his stubbornness.

Today was Amelia's birthday, and Flottwell had invited her and her father to a magnificent party. He was determined to overwhelm the old man with such a sumptuous display of his wealth that he would gain Amelia.

It was morning. Flottwell was waiting impatiently for the arrival of the jeweler. He had ordered a most elegant necklace as a birthday present for Amelia. Restlessly he paced his study. As he looked out the window, he saw a beggar sitting at the foot of the wide staircase which led to the portal of the palace. A chill fell upon his heart. The man looked strangely sinister.

"What are you writing in the sand?" he called to him.

"I count the sums of gold I once possessed," came the beggar's hollow voice.

"You were rich then? What is your name?" Flottwell asked in surprise.

"My name? I have forgotten it. Forgetfulness is the beggar's only remedy against despair. Once I was as rich as you are now."

Flottwell was taken aback. He threw a gold coin into the beggar's hat. The man jumped up, he stretched his thin arms to Flottwell. "Give more, give more, oh, gracious sir!" he implored the surprised Flottwell.

"Eat and drink and be merry." He tossed him another coin. "That should feed you well and chase away your sorrow."

"Sorrow is not chased away as easily as good luck."

"Hold your ill-humored tongue!" was Flottwell's impatient answer. He felt almost frightened by the weird old man. Was he a bad omen on this day which should bring him the most important news of his life? He turned away and heard the beggar wail, "Give more, give me much more. Give, to ease your heart. It's not a beggar's trick, it's not in greediness that I ask for more. Give to the poor for your own sake!" the whining voice continued.

"Go, or shall I have you chased away!" Flottwell called out angrily.

The beggar moaned, "A beggar can but obey," and he shuffled away.

A lackey entered. On a silver tray he brought a letter. Anxiously Flottwell tore it open; his eyes lit up as he read that Amelia had finally made up her mind: "*I entrust myself to you, and promise that I will never desert you. If my father does not change his mind, then let us do as we decided.*"

"She is mine! Amelia is mine, oh, blissful word! The whole wide world shall share my happiness!" he exulted. He turned to the waiting servant. "Bring back the old beggar who just sat there."

"What beggar, sir? We never allow those people near the palace," was the astonished answer.

"What's the matter with you? Are you blind? There he is, still under the trees. Go, bring him back."

The lackey seemed at a loss. "He's already seeing things, from drinking too much," he thought. But he went obediently to the group of trees which his master pointed out to him. "Come back, old man," he called with a trace of mockery in his voice. "Come back," he called as he wandered into the park.

The beggar stood there, visible only to Flottwell.

"I have received splendid good news and you shall share my joy. Here, take this purse, take everything I have on me!" He tossed his costly ring and the other jewelry into the beggar's hat after his purse. Then he hurried into the park, tingling with bliss.

The beggar slowly pocketed his treasures.

"Oh, compassion!" he murmured. "How weak a ruler are you in man's heart. But joy brings easily about a noble action; the beggar's hat is filled now with the spendthrift's gold."

The jeweler arrived with the ordered necklace. Flottwell received him as happy as a child. But after one glance he uttered angrily, "What have you done? It's ugly, it's old-fashioned! And these are not the stones I chose."

"Mr. von Flottwell! You offend me! My honor is involved."

"Mine too! I have no use for this bauble," rashly answered Flottwell.

"A bauble! The necklace is worth two thousand thalers!" The jeweler collected himself and added pleadingly, "Look at it without prejudice. It is a noble piece of art."

"I think it's so disgusting I could just throw it out the window," was Flottwell's vehement answer.

"You won't do that, I'm sure."

"I won't do that?" Scornfully he glanced at the glittering jewels. "There it goes!" Carelessly he hurled the necklace out the window.

"For goodness' sake! You threw away a fortune!" cried the startled jeweler.

"Did I? Are you scared you won't get your money? It's just dirt for the rich Flottwell," was the haughty reply. "Wait here," and he left the cabinet to fetch the money.

The stunned jeweler stared after him. "He's mad, that spendthrift," he thought angrily. "I never heard of such

willfulness." He rushed into the garden to rescue the necklace, but another had arrived first. The beggar caught it as
it came flying from the window. He held it up, the stones
glittered in the sun.

> *My thanks, good sir, for all these treasures,*
> *This gift will lighten my distress.*
> *The prey of grief my heart became,*
> *My own undoing, I confess.*

Flottwell returned with the money. "Forgive my violence, my good friend," he said with his most dazzling
smile. "I ought to be ashamed of myself," he laughed,
self-consciously. The jeweler easily succumbed to the
Spendthrift's famous charm. "I'm deeply touched, sir,"
he murmured as he withdrew, and he meant it. "I'll
always be at your service," he added with a deep bow.

"It's a stormy day today," thought Flottwell when he was alone. "I wish it were all over." From the distance he heard singing and recognized the beggar's voice:

> . . . *the prey of grief my heart became,*
> *My own undoing, I confess.*

Flottwell sprang to his feet. "What a gloomy song! Like a funeral hymn, intended to kill my joy! Where is Wolf?"

Wolf, his smooth-faced secretary, entered with soft steps and listened unmoved to Flottwell's tale.

"I had better look for the necklace," he said cautiously. "It's too much of a temptation to leave it lying around."

"Do as you please," replied Flottwell impatiently, "but chase that beggar away first!"

Wolf was soon back. "I've searched everywhere, but nobody admits to having picked up the necklace. Only Rosa, the chambermaid, was around. Of course, she denies that she took it, but I'm sure she is the thief."

"Rosa? The pretty one? I don't believe that, she's a good girl. She has been in my service for quite a while, Valentine is going to marry her, isn't he? They are all right, leave them alone."

"But I almost saw it with my own eyes!"

" 'Almost,' you say! Let it go. I don't care for it anyhow. But now what present shall I give to fair Amelia?"

"Why not the precious vase you just bought for twenty thousand francs? That would be a present worthy of you!" suggested the sleek secretary with his servile smile.

"Thanks, my dear Wolf! You always give good advice." Flottwell seemed more cheerful. "Her father is a great lover of arts, this will win him for me."

His secretary did not blink an eye as he thought, "How

mistaken he is! His money has rendered him insensitive to other people's sets of value. Amelia's father will be disgusted."

It was as the smart Mr. Wolf had anticipated. The old man was offended by the overcostly gift when Flottwell presented it to Amelia.

"You had better keep that vase. My daughter is not going to accept it," he said coldly. "That's a king's gift, but not a nobleman's."

"That's how I give," Flottwell replied proudly. "I am the king of my property. This vase is only precious if Amelia's fair hand receives it."

"My daughter will not accept it," her father repeated stiffly.

"Well, then I no longer care for the vase." In subdued anger he looked around. His eyes fell on his secretary. "Wolf, you take it, it is yours."

Flottwell smiled haughtily as the other guests applauded him. "Bravo!" they shouted, amused. "That's a millionaire's revenge!"

Among the guests was a young nobleman who also hoped for Amelia's hand. "What an offense!" he muttered angrily.

Flottwell heard it and stepped nearer. "What concern is that of yours, my dear sir?"

"I speak in behalf of my future wife, Mr. von Flottwell," the young nobleman answered.

"Amelia! Is this true?" Flottwell was going to rush to the embarrassed girl, but his rival grabbed his arm. Flottwell hurled him away. Hostilely the two young men stared at each other. The joyful clamor of the guests suddenly ceased. Everybody watched them.

"Satisfaction, sir!" the young man said in a strained voice. "I won't take this from you."

"I'm at your disposal." Flottwell bowed politely. He pointed to the park. "If you please," and they left the room. An anxious silence followed till one of the guests called, "Stop them! They mustn't fight a duel, hotspurs that they are. They will kill each other!"

Amelia had retired to a small drawing room. Her heart was torn within her. She loved her father dearly, and she knew well what he wished, but . . . "It's my own life," she thought rebelliously. "Father can't run it for me." Anxiously she listened. Suddenly she heard two pistol shots, and visions of the wounded Flottwell rushed through her mind. But to her unspeakable relief he soon came softly into the room.

"Thank heavens!" she cried out. "Julius, are you all right?"

He was pale. "I am," he answered quickly. "But my rival is seriously wounded. I couldn't help it! Why did he dare to try to steal you! But now every minute counts, we have to flee this night."

"Tonight?" Amelia said hesitantly. "I cannot leave my father so suddenly."

"Oh, Amelia, if you really love me, you have to forget everything else! We'll flee to England, and how happy we will be, united forever!"

"If I could only live without you," the girl whispered.

"But you cannot! We are as one, my dearest love." He took her in his arms and murmured urgently, "I'll be waiting for you at our old meeting place at midnight. You will not forsake me, my darling?"

"But my father . . ."

"Stronger are the ties of love, deeper is the desire for happiness than anything else in the world. What more can life hold than happiness?"

"And you will make me happy, Julius?"

"I swear by the sun you shall be happy. My love will replace your father's affection, your friendships, your fatherland—everything! I am 'Fortuna's well-beloved Child'! The world does my bidding, trust yourself to me."

Amelia looked at him with admiration. He had never known defeat and she believed that nothing could defeat him, ever; it gave him a strange power over her heart. No duty, no unwritten laws could hold her back. His ardent love had burned away all scruples, nothing was left but the mirage of happiness.

She put her arms around his neck. "I'll follow you," she promised. "My poor father, will he ever forgive me?"

They drew apart, for Amelia's father had entered, anxious about his daughter. He did not speak to Flottwell but silently led her away. Little did he suspect that he had already lost his daughter, lost her to her selfish desire to be happy.

With the determination of a man walking in his sleep, Flottwell made preparations for their flight. Cheristane's dangerous gift had blinded him to reality. He did not know that he really was "Fortuna's Child," as he had boasted. He did not understand the significance of the phrase. He had never understood Cheristane's words when she left him, nor the strange beggar's mysterious warnings. He was completely untried. He had learned nothing, had never performed a duty, never known the serene pleasure of work well done. As he set out now for another land, he valued only two possessions, Amelia and his wealth. All else seemed negligible, and he left everything behind without a qualm. He instructed his trusted secretary Wolf to follow him to London after tending to his master's affairs.

While Flottwell was waiting for Amelia, the sinister beggar crossed his path once more. Suddenly he appeared before him, cringing, begging, demanding, threatening! He demanded half of Flottwell's fortune. What madness!

Flottwell threw a purse at him to get rid of him, fearful lest the beggar's clamor might rouse people and destroy his chance to depart unnoticed with Amelia. The beggar picked it up. "More! Give more!" he shrieked.

Infuriated, Flottwell drew his sword. "If gold can't silence you, steel will!" and he struck a heavy blow at the beggar's unprotected head. But the beggar stood unharmed.

"I laugh at your wrath. Nothing can silence me. You cannot escape your fate, though you flee from here." He vanished. Flottwell shuddered, and was shamed by his uncontrolled anger. Then Amelia appeared, and all unpleasantness was forgotten. Why should he care about specters and premonitions?

They reached England and all went well. They were married, and the pleasurable life in the capital soon occupied all their time. Flottwell's money opened every door to them. Wolf had not come, but Flottwell soon forgot his annoyance over that. After a while, however, the pleasant life became stale to Flottwell. He was restless, he wanted to move on to new adventures, new excitement and pleasures. But now it was Amelia who wanted security and stability. A fine, healthy son gave her deeper happiness than her husband's hectic pleasure-seeking.

But Flottwell would not stand it any longer, and against Amelia's wishes they set out for South America.

Suddenly his good luck deserted "Fortuna's Child."

Soon after their departure from Liverpool they met with bad weather. Fog surrounded them, dark and cold and silent, and their sailing vessel crept forward slowly. But all caution was of no avail. A dreadful crash broke the silence as the vessel struck another ship.

It was dark and confusion reigned, but Flottwell was able to reach the upper deck with Amelia and their son.

"Women and children first!"

The age-old cry of the sea resounded, as it became obvious that the ship was doomed. Amelia clung to Flottwell but a boatswain tore her away, pushing her and her little boy into a lifeboat. Men leaped into the water, swimming away, and Flottwell was among them. He was a good swimmer and tried to follow the shadowy form of the lifeboat bearing his loved ones as it disappeared into the fog. That was the last he remembered.

Flottwell was among the few survivors picked up by other ships. Later on he learned that the lifeboat carrying Amelia and his son had capsized and that none of the women and children had been saved. After his rescue Flottwell was taken to a hospital in Liverpool where he remained a long time, overcome with the shock of his loss.

Back in London finally, he sought diversion. He had loved Amelia and his little boy, and now his heart was barren. Life was senseless, dull! Gambling and speculation became his only interests in life. Nothing held him back any more. He had lost so much, he was sure he had to win again. He still believed in his right to happiness!

Reckless, fearless, he chased after the elusive vision of happiness. Cheristane's favor had deprived him of the fear natural to all mankind. No early disappointments had taught him caution and good sense. He would have ruined himself, and have perished in sordidness, but for the faint memory of his golden youth. A strange awareness of the beauty of life haunted him, and it saved him. But the fairy's golden veil had totally disappeared. Life rushed in on him—pulsating, ruthless, coarse, ugly, threatening. He could not breathe in this surging wave of life, he felt as unprotected as a naked babe under the onslaught of reality.

Why did nobody respect his inalienable right to happiness? As he walked the dreary streets of London, he saw himself with sudden clarity. He saw he was the same as everybody else. Only his failure was greater than most people's failures. A great desperation born of loneliness swept over him.

One desire was left. He wanted to go home. Home, where the world had been golden, and he rich and careless, innocent of suffering!

He sold his last few possessions in London and shipped to Hamburg. But home-coming held no relief, for there was nobody to greet him. He wrote to his old friends, convinced they would be glad to see him again, and happy to help him. Their answers were strangely similar.

"I count it my greatest affliction that I cannot help you . . .", "How unlucky! Just yesterday I bought a house and now I have no means to spare . . .", "What a pity . . .", "So sorry . . .", "I should have wished . . ." He could hardly believe his eyes as he read their letters of regret. He had always felt rich in having so many devoted friends. "I'm still wealthy in my friends," had been a comforting thought. Now he was really poverty-stricken!

He set his teeth; he would not go home a pauper, but would hurry to Wiesbaden and gamble. He won. He won again, and lost. He kept on gambling till all was lost. To whom should he turn now?

There was one last hope. He would approach the owner of his splendid mansion in the Alps and tell him his fate. Surely, this man would be moved by the greatness of Flottwell's misfortune! Was it begging? He cast away that unpleasant thought.

And now he was home after twenty years. His splendid palace, always bustling with life, looked strangely deserted. He stood in front of the wide, curved stairway which lead to the great portal. But he hesitated to enter his former home.

How quiet it was! He remembered it so differently, with laughter and cheerful clamor ringing out, when Joy had spread its glorious wings. "A dismal place," he murmured, "about as forlorn as I." He glanced at his worn-out clothes. The long footmarch from Wiesbaden to the Alps had taken its toll. "I look the beggar I am," he thought in disgust.

He heard footsteps crunching on the gravel and looked expectantly at the gardener who came upon him with his garden tools.

"My good friend," Flottwell asked politely, "can you tell me the name of the owner and if he is at home?"

The gardener glared suspiciously at the poorly dressed, elderly man. "His name is Mr. von Wolf," he answered in surly tones.

"Von Wolf? I never heard of a family by that name."

"Is that so?" The gardener laughed unpleasantly.

"Well, he used to be the rich Flottwell's secretary, the Flottwell who fled to England while Mr. Wolf stayed here."

Flottwell stared at the gardener in surprise. "Wolf? Did he inherit a fortune or how . . ."

"How? How did he make his fortune? He fleeced Flottwell. You know how these rich fellows are; they think they own the world and listen to every flatterer. And Mr. Wolf knew exactly how to soft-soap his master. Well," he shrugged, "the famous spendthrift died in poverty somewhere in America, and Wolf is rich and prosperous. Thrifty fellow too."

With rising wrath Flottwell listened to the gardener. "One more question," he said then in a strained voice. "Is Mr. von Wolf happy with his ill-begotten wealth?"

"Happy? You can see for yourself." The gardener pointed to a haggard, stooped man who was just leaving the house. Two liveried servants were helping him as he moved listlessly toward the staircase. "Even the sun has no warmth," he grumbled. His voice was crabbed and old.

The gardener stepped forward and pulled his cap as he addressed Wolf. "Sir, here is a poor man who wants to talk to you."

In shocked surprise Flottwell gazed at the prematurely aged man who twenty years ago had been his sleek, smooth-faced secretary. "I would never have recognized him," he thought. "Good heavens! I certainly don't feel poor any more. I'll talk to him, but I surely won't ask favors of that man!"

Fretfully Wolf glared at the beggar. "What do you want from me?" he asked crossly. "What's your name?"

"Flottwell is the name," was the cold reply.

A faint flush crept slowly over Wolf's pinched, blood-
less face. "Flottwell? Still alive? And he returns a beggar?" he murmured. "Heaven punishes a spendthrift."

Dumbfounded, the gardener stared at the man in the
worn-out coat. "This is the rich Flottwell? I'd rather stay
a gardener all my life," he muttered under his breath as
he withdrew.

Wolf had collected himself. "I'm greatly honored, Mr.
von Flottwell, that you remember your old servant," he
said smoothly without his old servility. "Unfortunately I
cannot celebrate your arrival as you may have expected.
I am a sick man."

"I don't expect anything from you," was the proud
reply. "I only wanted to meet the owner of my palace."

"It's a strange coincidence, isn't it! It proves my true
attachment to your house." A malicious smile wrinkled
Wolf's thin lips. "Heaven has blessed my enterprises," he
added pompously. "Only lately I suffered some grave
losses. I'm hard up myself now." Peevishly he turned to
his servants. "You know I mustn't stand so long. Take me
to that bench over there." He contradicted himself at once.
"No, that's no good, there's too much sun. Back to the
palace. No, that's too gloomy," he mumbled and shuddered. "I want to go to the park," he finally decided wearily.
"Take me there, you rascals."

Painfully he descended the three wide steps on re-
luctant legs, supported by his indifferent lackeys. He
looked very old as he shambled away, a stricken man in the
last dreary chapter of his life.

Flottwell stared after the woeful procession. "This is
where I used to live, spreading joy and enjoying myself,"
he thought. "Was that a crime? Careless I was, but not

ignoble like this spiteful old man." Wearily he pondered.
"What went wrong with my life? I did not know the
power I held. Is that why it slipped from my careless
grasp? Slipped into these evil hands!" He sighed. "But
it's all over. Why should I torment myself with self-
reproaches? I only wish I knew what to do, where to go."

As he stood irresolute he heard a man singing. Among
the trees he saw a joiner advancing toward him singing
cheerfully:

> *How people argue back and forth*
> *In search for happiness.*
> *But what would be the smartest course,*
> *That's everybody's guess!*
> *This fellow thinks he's much too poor,*
> *That man too rich by far!*
> *But Fate steps in, and with her plane*
> *She trims them down to par.*

Flottwell listened. "Quite a philosopher, that man," he
thought to himself.

> *Youth claims its right for happiness,*
> *Their luck is all they care.*
> *But as we grow a little old*
> *We like our moderate share.*
> *My wife is often scolding me*
> *I let her raise all hell*
> *And shrug. It doesn't bother me.*
> *I work, and I work well.*
>
> *If Death appears—please, do forgive—*
> *And murmurs, "Brother, come!"*

I act as if I didn't hear
And play I'm deaf and dumb.
But he says, "My good Valentine,
You must with me now dwell."
Then I shall put my plane away,
Say to the world, "Farewell!"

The joiner was quite near now. He looked at the poorly dressed old man and fumbled in his pockets. Obviously he was going to give Flottwell a small coin. But then he hesitated. "You remind me of somebody," he said uncertainly, "but what a dreadful idea! Let me see your face."

"What do you want?" asked Flottwell.

The joiner mumbled to himself, "I hardly dare to give him a penny; gives me the creeps, that resemblance." He stood uncertain, and Flottwell, lost in his gloomy thoughts, paid no attention to him.

"Excuse me, friend, I . . ." The joiner's voice trailed off, but then he started anew. "Tell me, do you happen to know this palace?"

"Do I happen to know it?" Flottwell repeated with bitterness. "Indeed, I do! Once it was my own!"

The man stared at Flottwell.

"My gracious master!" he cried happily. Then he repeated in a voice trembling with joy and pain and astonishment, "Oh, my gracious master!" Clumsily he grabbed Flottwell's hand and kissed it.

Flottwell was deeply moved by this unexpected sign of love and loyalty where he had expected to find none.

"Who are you, my friend?" he asked a little shakily.

"I'm Valentine! Don't you know me any more? Valentine, who once was your servant."

"Well, well! Good old Valentine!" smiled his former master. "And are you doing all right?"

"Just so-so. But I make a living for myself and my family. I'm satisfied."

"Satisfied! You are a lucky man!" Flottwell replied enviously. "Satisfied, that's more than I can say!"

"Is it very bold if I ask—Oh, sir! Tell me how you are. I've thought of you so often," Valentine went on. "You look so . . ." He stopped, embarrassed.

"I guess I have changed quite a bit."

"No, no! Not in the least! I'm so glad to see you. But, beg your pardon . . ." Then he rushed on determinedly. "May I take the liberty of asking you to do me the honor to be my guest?"

"I gladly accept it, my good Valentine." Flottwell was touched. He felt a great relief. It was not so much that the problem of his next meal was solved, but Valentine's blundering kindness had dispelled the sense of doom that had settled on him. As they walked on together, he listened to Valentine's cheerful chatter about Rosa, whom he had married.

"She's not so gay and pretty any more, sir," he twinkled, "but she's all right, the missus. Too quick with her tongue at times and, well . . . Of course, she has to pinch every penny to feed our five healthy youngsters on the little I earn." He talked at great length of Hansel and Liese, "a great little helper for her mother," and of Michael, Hiesel, and Pepi, the baby. Flottwell listened with pleasure, till Valentine interrupted himself. "Here I go on raving about my affairs, and you look so tired, sir! But don't worry, you'll stay with us now. As long as Valentine has something to eat you'll be all right too!"

"My dear fellow," Flottwell put in, touched and embarrassed, "I'm a poor man. I couldn't possibly accept . . ."

"But, sir! Don't you see," Valentine explained eagerly, "it's all yours really. You gave me so many presents, two hundred ducats it was altogether! That's how I could start a business, raise a family, build a house. Oh no! It's all settled. You just stay as long as you choose. Rosa will be delighted to have you, I'm sure."

Flottwell listened to Valentine, glad to have reached some kind of a haven. Soon they arrived at Valentine's modest little house, a cheerful place, bustling with children. The little ones were quite taken in by their father's "gracious master," as he proudly introduced Flottwell to them, and made every effort to entertain him. Valentine beamed happily. His awkwardness was outdone only by his eagerness as he tried to make Flottwell comfortable in the workshop, and the children helped as best they could. Hiesel took a big broom and swept the floor covered with wood shavings around the wooden stool on which Flottwell was sitting. Valentine was soon called away to do some work. He left hurriedly. "Rosa will take care of things now," he called cheerfully. "She'll fix us a splendid meal!"

But it turned out quite differently.

Rosa, grown old and coarse from hard work, was far from being pleased at having one more mouth to feed.

"What? The fine gentleman wants to live with us?" she muttered furiously when the children told her the grand news. She went into the workshop where Flottwell still sat.

"Good morning, Mr. von Flottwell," she said crossly. Her arms akimbo, she stood before her former master. "We are surely greatly honored that you found your way to our humble house." She glared at him in defiance and went on, "My husband is a fool, he can be talked into anything! But I'm the one who makes the decisions in this house." With a visible effort to be polite she continued, "We shall be very glad to have you stay for lunch today, and I'll do the best I can. But . . ." Suddenly she flared up; thinking of the extra work, the extra money involved, she snapped at him, "but stay for good? Oh no! Today all right, but never again!"

Flottwell jumped up at this unexpected rebuke.

"No! I did not hear you right! It's a bad dream!" Rosa looked him squarely in the face; he stepped back, cold anger aroused in him by her vulgarity.

"It can't be! She did not speak that way to me, her former master; to Flottwell, who was the praised father of his servants, the very soul of bounty—the great, the rich, the most worthy Flottwell—or whatever sweet flattery I used to hear!" Then humiliation overwhelmed him, he turned his head, so that she should not see the fire of shame spreading over his face. In a stricken voice he murmured, "What have you done! How could you offend me so bitterly!"

He drew himself up and left the house, while the mortified Rosa stared angrily after him, and the children huddled in a corner. The little ones were crying and Liese said sadly, "Oh, Mother! You shouldn't have done that!"

Rosa, glad to have an outlet for her shame and fury, yelled at the girl, "Shut up! And get out of here, all of you!"

The crying children ran into the garden and the maddened Rosa muttered, "What else could I do? If you don't open your mouth, you've got to open your purse, that's an

old story. I'm going to give Valentine a good piece of my mind."

But when Valentine heard that she had turned out his former master, the usually easygoing man exploded.

"You dared to turn out my guest? You dared to offend the man to whom I owe all I have?" he shouted. "I'm going to leave you. I'll take the children with me, and you can stay all by yourself, if you don't want Flottwell to live with us!"

Rosa was shocked. She had never seen him so infuriated.

"You want to leave me for that stranger, that down-at-the-heels good-for-nothing? Take the children away from me?" she raged, but Valentine, who had always been willing to submit to her leadership, stood his ground.

"Either-or," he said firmly. And when Rosa continued to storm at him, "Children, get out of here," he said sternly. After they had closed the door he turned to his wife. "I don't want to shame you before the children as you shamed me. But now listen well! What do you prefer,

Mr. von Flottwell staying with us or shall we all leave you?"

"You are crazy! Whoever heard of such a thing!" Rosa said sullenly. But Valentine repeated firmly, "Either-or!"

In the end Rosa yielded. She was glad, indeed, when she finally gave in, and she looked at her husband with new respect. Valentine's good humor had not deserted him for long. He patted her round shoulder and said affectionately, "Don't worry, old lady. We'll make out all right. I'll work a little harder, and everything will be fine."

He shouted cheerfully, "Children, come back. We won't leave. Father and Mother are reconciled and Mr. von Flottwell is going to live with us. Now run as fast as you can, and bid him come back."

"But where did he go, Father?" Hansel asked eagerly.

"Where? I don't know. We'll have to find him, and quick. Ask the neighbors, they'll help us look for him. Now, let's hurry, he must be somewhere."

Flottwell had left Valentine's house in great anger, but he was soon seized by desperation. He was at his wit's end, and now he came face to face with himself. He thought of the far off days of his good fortune. What good had he done with his immense wealth? His mind had been too shallow to grasp the responsibility his riches had imposed on him.

"I have offended His Majesty King Gold," he thought. "I should have trembled before the power I held, a power which can make black look white; false, good; wrong, right; and I despised the mighty King for the sway he holds over the world. With my money I should have helped the needy. That was my claim to happiness!"

Dimly he recalled Cheristane's words that her destiny was to help people in distress. "I failed her, fool that I was!"

He was so steeped in gloom that he did not notice that his feet had taken him along a well-known path. He was on his way to the ruins of the old Flottwell Castle, way up in the mountains.

"That's where I belong now," he thought as he realized where he was going. As the way grew steeper and the ascent more difficult he put his whole heart into the effort to reach his goal. "My last goal. I'll never return to live with other people. My false friends scorned me, my trusted secretary betrayed me, Rosa sneered at me. Poor Valentine was the only one who stood by me and gave me some hope. But he's too weak, too goodhearted really to be of help."

He felt dizzy and weak but kept climbing doggedly, his thoughts revolving around the reason for his failure. Finally he reached the summit. The old fallen-in tower was covered with ivy; the crumbling walls showed the empty rooms. It was a desolate place, nothing remained of the splendor of the old family. Flottwell looked around desperately, then sank down on a rock.

"Here I belong, and here I'll die! Oh, Death, you are my only comfort! I have no other friends!" he called out in the deep silence. A hollow voice answered:

"But me!"

Flottwell leaped up in fright. "Who answered me?" he called in alarm.

In the crumbling entrance stood the mysterious beggar whom Flottwell had not seen since their last encounter. He looked like a reflection of Flottwell.

"Time has brought me down to your condition!" cried

Flottwell in desperation. "Now I see it clearly—you were sent to me as a warning, a shocking premonition of my fate!"

"That was my aim. You did not recognize me, for passion is not aware of its faults," was the stern reply. "Now I will tell you who I am: I am one year of your wasted life! The fiftieth year I am, which began today and will be ended when the sun sinks down. Cheristane read in the Future's Book that if you did not change your foolish, wasteful life, at fifty you would be a beggar. You presented her with one year of your life, and I am that year. Nothing could warn you. But I am able to prevent your final destruction now and give you another chance to lead a good life. You have not taken alms from anybody, so I can restore to you the gold which I extorted from you with threats and tricks in my disguise." The beggar stepped aside and Flottwell saw a casket filled with gold and precious stones. The necklace glittered atop the heap. "Take back your property. You will appreciate it better now, since you have learned wisdom through your suffering. What you gave to the beggar you gave to yourself indeed. Farewell. My mission is accomplished."

He changed before Flottwell's astounded eyes. The ragged beggar's garments fell from him; now he stood, a wondrous apparition. His body glowed in bluish-silver tints; the classical beauty of his head was fearful to behold, because for eyes he had two glittering stones. Flottwell staggered back at the extraordinary and unexpected vision which slowly faded.

"That was a dream!" he comforted his anxiously beating heart, when everything had disappeared and only the solid rocks and desolate walls of the deserted castle stood before him. But now they seemed to change, to dissolve into clouds. The clouds turned into a rosy mist, and in the haze appeared Cheristane, the fairy. The flame of her beauty made him sink to his knees. Enraptured, he listened to her gentle words:

"That was Azure, the spirit, the last of my pearls. I sacrificed the last one to create him as your protector after my reign on earth ended. Thus I fulfilled my promise to save you from disgrace."

"Cheristane!" whispered Flottwell. "Cheristane, I see you once more, golden dream of my youth! I hardly dare to lift my eyes to your eternal youth. Don't leave me! Overwhelming is my longing for times gone by!"

"Do not despair, my Julius. Your life span is not ended, but one day we will meet in the boundless realm of spirits, where love meets love."

The golden haze curled and rose, turning into rose-red clouds which enshrouded Cheristane's enchanting form, till she had disappeared.

Slowly Flottwell rose from his knees. "I will deserve your love now, Cheristane," he murmured. Then he heard voices, children's clear, excited voices. Liese cried happily:

"Here he is, Father! He's here!"

Hansel and Liese stormed up the height; the boy called out eagerly, "We found him, Father! He's unharmed, and we'll not let him get away!"

Flottwell had to smile. Reality surrounded him once more; he knew he would not drift away again into unreal lands of fantasy and wishful thinking.

Suddenly the lonely place was crowded with people. Led by Valentine, the whole village had set out to search for their well-beloved former master.

"What do you want, Valentine?" asked the surprised Flottwell.

Happily, Valentine gripped his hand. "I want to keep my promise, and I want to apologize for my wife."

Rosa came up behind him.

"Forgive my rude behavior, Mr. von Flottwell, but I'll make up for it," she said, ashamed. "I'll take care of you as if I were your daughter. You must never leave our house again," she added heartily.

"It's all right, Rosa." Flottwell smiled at her to ease her embarrassment. His smile was calm and easy. He turned to Valentine. "I'm no longer a beggar, for I found a hidden treasure that my father buried here for me. I'm very happy that I can now reward your loyalty."

"But I do want to take care of you," Valentine said, dumbfounded.

"It's better this way, my faithful friend. I'll take you and your family into my new home, and I'll provide a good education for your children."

The village folks had pressed nearer while they were listening to this wondrous turn of events. Now they sang out:

"Long live Flottwell, our gracious master!"

And so it was that Flottwell learned the meaning of true happiness, which does not come to anyone without pain.

Nutcracker and Mouseking

*

E. T. A. HOFFMANN

It was Christmas Eve. Fritz and Mary sat huddled together in a corner of the back parlor. All day long they had been forbidden to go into any other room, and now twilight had fallen. No lamp had been brought to them as on other days, and they felt almost afraid in the semidarkness. Fritz whispered to his sister Mary, who was just seven, that he had heard distant hammering, rustling, and rattling all day long in the closed rooms.

"What do you think we'll get for Christmas?" Mary whispered back. "Miss Gretl, my biggest doll, is so clumsy lately. She falls so easily. I don't know what's the matter with her. She looks awful, her face is scratched and her dress is soiled."

"I have no chestnut horse in my stud, and my army of tin soldiers is quite without a cavalry," answered Fritz.

"Did you ask the Christ Child for all that?" Mary inquired wistfully.

"Of course I did," replied Fritz, and added hopefully, "Papa knows it, too."

Mary sat in thoughtful silence, wondering if she and Fritz really deserved all those coveted treasures. Fritz seemed to have some misgivings, for after a while he murmured quietly to himself, "But I do want a chestnut and some hussars."

It was quite dark now. The children sat cuddled together and did not dare to utter another word. They felt as if there was a gentle fluttering of wings around them. They heard faraway silver-toned music. A pearly shimmer flashed across the wall. They knew then that the Christ Child was being borne away on radiant clouds to other happy children. They sat very still, filled with great expectations.

Suddenly a tinkling bell rang out, "Kling-ling, kling-ling!" The doors flew open. A dazzling stream of light came across the drawing room from the large front parlor. "Oh, how lovely!" the children cried out. They clasped their hands and stood entranced at the threshold.

Papa and Mamma came toward them and took their hands. "Now come, darlings. Come on in and see what the blessed Christ Child has brought for you."

The great Christmas tree in the middle of the room bore many silver and golden apples. The branches seemed to bud and bloom abundantly. The buds and blossoms were really sugar almonds, multicolored bonbons, and all sorts of delicious things to eat. But more beautiful than everything else was the light of dozens of candles on the tree, twinkling like stars. The gleaming light shone on so many lovely things! Mary gazed at a beautiful new doll and at marvelous toys. A dainty silk dress hung from a projecting branch so that she could see it from all sides.

"Oh, the lovely, lovely dress!" She clapped her hands with delight. "Can it hang there a little longer? It looks so pretty there."

She was hugging Miss Clare, the new addition to her doll family who outshone Miss Gretl by far. Fritz for his part was trying out his new horse, cantering and galloping around the table.

"I believe it's a wild beast," he said as he stopped, "but that doesn't matter. I can master it already."

He turned to muster his new hussars. They were splendidly equipped in red and gold uniforms with shining swords. They were mounted on white horses that shimmered as if they were made of pure silver. Fritz made his cavalry trot out from under the tree, and in the empty space Mary discovered a little man whom she had not seen before.

He stood there quietly and modestly waiting for someone to take notice of him. He was a queer fellow. His long, stout body seemed to be too heavy for his thin little legs; and his head was much too large. He was excellently dressed in a violet hussar's jacket trimmed with white braid and many white buttons. He wore the most elegant little boots ever! His kind green eyes and sweet smile showed him to be a person of gentle disposition, besides being a man of good taste. It was strange, though, that he wore a short, absurd little cloak which looked as stiff as if it were made of wood.

"Oh, Papa!" Mary cried out at last. "Whose is that darling little man under the tree?"

"That little lad, sweetheart, will have to work hard for the whole family. Look, he's going to crack nuts for you."

The father took the little man, and as he raised the wooden cloak the little fellow opened his mouth. Mary put in a nut and, crack, the nutcracker bit it to pieces. Mary was quite taken with the manikin. She held him in her arm and let him crack nut after nut. Carefully she chose the smallest ones so as not to tire him out too much. But soon Fritz joined them and made her little friend work very hard. He picked out the biggest and hardest nuts. Suddenly there was a crack! crash! Three little teeth fell out of Nutcracker's mouth. His chin became loose and wobbly.

"My poor darling Nutcracker!" cried Mary and took him from Fritz.

"That's a stupid fellow!" Fritz was disgusted. "Wants to be a nutcracker and doesn't know his trade."

But Mary was not listening to this final insult. She picked up the little white teeth and put them in her pocket. Then she bound Nutcracker's poor shaky head with a white ribbon from her dress. She wrapped him in her handkerchief. Cradling him in her arms, she sat down under the tree to look at her picture books. But her mind was more on her little patient than on the new book.

Mary and Fritz used to keep their toys in a glass cupboard in the drawing room. It was late. The children were tired, but still they did not want to go to bed. Finally Fritz started to put his soldiers into the upper shelf where he kept his whole army.

"I'd better go to bed," he said at last and yawned. "I gave them a good workout today. But I know they wouldn't dare to snatch a nap as long as I'm around. I have to give them a chance to sleep." And off he went. But Mary begged to be permitted to stay just a little longer.

"There is so much I still have to do," she said as she put the new doll into bed in the beautiful doll's room in the lower shelf of the glass cupboard. Mary was always a good little girl, and her mother allowed her to remain there a little longer. Her parents blew out all the little candles, then they put out the lights and left burning only the lamp which hung from the ceiling. A soft light shone on everything.

As soon as Mary was alone, she untied the white ribbon and examined Nutcracker's wounds. "Oh, darling Nutcracker," she murmured softly, "don't be angry with Fritz. He is a good boy really, only a little wild at times. I'll take good care of you, and Godfather Drosselmeyer shall fix your shoulder and put your teeth back again. You'll be all right pretty soon."

She was crouching before the glass cupboard. Lifting her new doll from the bed, she said earnestly, "I'm sorry, Miss Clare, but you have to make room for the poor wounded Nutcracker tonight. Look, the sofa is quite comfortable, too. You are rosy-cheeked and well, but he's sick, the poor darling."

Miss Clare looked very elegant and very disdainful sitting on the damask sofa in her Christmas dress.

"I don't think she has a nice disposition," Mary thought, as she took the bed and placed it on the upper shelf near Fritz's tin soldiers. "Nutcracker better stay with these men instead of with that naughty girl." Tenderly she put her little patient into bed and tucked him in. She was just going to close the glass door, when she stopped short.

A soft whispering and rustling started all around her.

The clock on the wall rattled and whirred but could not strike. The big gilt owl which topped the clock had dropped its wings so that the face of the clock was covered. The owl stretched its ugly catlike head forward. The rattling increased. The astonished Mary could make out some words now:

> *Clocks! Clocks! Prrr, prrr,*
> *All ticking stops.*
> *Here aloft,*
> *Low and soft, prrr, prrr, purrr!*
> *Sharp is Mouseking's ear*
> *He will hear . . . Prrrr, purrr, purrr!*
> *The bells soon chime:*
> *　　NOW rings out the fateful time!*

Poom, poom, poom, poom, poom, poom, poom, poom, poom, poom, poom, poommmm.

Mary counted. It struck twelve times. Midnight!

A mad scampering and squeaking started everywhere. Thousands of tiny feet seemed to be trotting behind the walls. Thousands of tiny lights glittered between the chinks of the wainscot. But they were not lights, oh no! They were tiny glittering eyes. Mary saw hundreds of mice squeezing through the chinks. Soon they were galloping and trotting around the room.

Mary was not scared of mice as some people are. She thought it very amusing to see them form squadrons and wheel into line. "Just like Fritz's soldiers when they are being arrayed for battle," she thought. "This is really funny! I have to tell him!"

Suddenly there was a terrible, piercing, piping sound. A crack in the floor split open wide. Seven mouse heads with seven jewel-glistening crowns rose through the floor. They were grown together on the body of one large mouse, which now wriggled out after the seven heads. The whole army of mice squeaked three times in full chorus to greet their king. Then they fell into line and, trot, trot, trot, they advanced right up to the cupboard where Mary was standing.

Mary was startled. She leaned back, and klirr, klirr! There went the large pane of the glass door. The ghastly mouse army took flight before the tremendous crashing.

But what was happening now?

Right behind her in the cupboard it rustled, cracked, and creaked. Mary heard faint voices calling to each other.

> *Arise! Awake!*
> *All is at stake!*
> *This is the night*
> *We have to fight*
> *To left and right!*
> *The foe we'll smite!*
> *This is the night,*
> *The glorious night!*

Bells were pealing. Dolls and all kinds of toys were astir, waving their little arms and shouting at the top of their tiny voices.

Suddenly there was a big commotion in the upper shelf. Nutcracker cast off his bedcothes. He jumped out of bed and called out in a rather gruff voice:

> *Crick and crack!*
> *Stupid mousy pack!*
> *We'll chase them back!*
> *Crick and crack!*

He drew his little sword and, raising it high, he cried:

"Friends and followers, are you willing to stand by me in battle?"

Right away three clowns, a pantaloon, four chimney sweeps, and a drummer cried, "We follow you, oh, valiant sir!" And they leaped down from the upper shelf.

They could jump down easily from the tremendous height of fully two feet, for they were soft and pliable, being made of cloth and sawdust. But poor Nutcracker was carved from lindenwood. He risked arms and legs as he threw himself down, daredevil that he was! But luck was with him. Miss Clare jumped up from the sofa and caught him in her soft arms.

"Oh, darling, beloved Clare," sobbed Mary. "How could I have misjudged you so. I thought you were selfish and disliked Nutcracker because you had to give him your bed."

But Miss Clare, pressing the hero to her silken bosom, whispered urgently, "Do not court danger, sick and wounded as you are, oh, valiant sir! Stay with me and let your vassals fight."

Nutcracker behaved quite rudely. He kicked and flayed around with his arms and legs till Miss Clare had to release him. But well-bred and courteous as he was, he sank on one knee and lisped, "Noble dame, in the midst of strife and battle I shall remember your gracious help."

Obviously Miss Clare was deeply moved. She took off her twinkling belt to fasten it as an officer's sash over Nutcracker's shoulder. But Nutcracker jumped up. Stepping back, he said solemnly, "Do not, most noble dame, squander your favor on me, for I . . . ." He hesitated. Then he loosened Mary's ribbon from his wounded shoulder. He pressed it to his lips, he raised his soulful eyes, he sighed deeply. Then he slung the plain ribbon around himself as a sash. Resolutely he drew his gleaming sword and, quick as a bird, he leaped down the last short step to the floor.

The squeaking and piping started again, worse than before. Beneath the big table the mouse army was gathered under the command of the terrible seven-headed Mouseking.

"Beat the general advance, drummer!" Nutcracker cried. And the tambour major rolled his drums so splendidly that the glass panes of the cupboard rattled.

The martial sound aroused Fritz's soldiers. They jumped out of their boxes; they threw themselves down to the floor and formed squadrons, ready for action. Nutcracker rushed

up and down the eager ranks. Full of fire, he addressed Pantaloon.

"General, I know your courage and your great experience. I entrust you with the command of the cavalry and artillery. Do your duty. Lead the troops to victory!"

Pantaloon put his thin fingers to his mouth and gave a shrill whistle. Immediately there was a great neighing, stomping, and clattering, as Fritz's glittering hussars marched past Nutcracker with flying colors and bands playing. The cannons boomed out, and Mary saw the jelly beans strike in the thick of the enemy, powdering them white. The mice were very ashamed of themselves and greatly harassed by the fierce bombardment. One especially heavy battery on Mamma's footstool did them great harm, pelting them relentlessly with sugar plums and spiced nuts.

But now the enemy came into action. Grimly they charged into Nutcracker's ranks. It was a tremendous fracas that went on! Prrr, Prrr, Poom, Piff, Paff, Puff! BOOMM—BOOOMMMM!!! Squeaking mice, neighing horses, shouting men, booming cannons! But all noise was drowned by Nutcracker's sonorous voice as, fighting coura-

geously, he shouted his orders. But the mouse army continuously displayed more troops. Their ammunition, little
evil-smelling brown pills, pelted the hussars like a hail-
storm. The hussars reeled from this blast of missiles, for
the little pills made very bad spots on their red uniforms. They hung back. The general wanted them to shift
ground, but in the heat of the battle he gave the wrong
command. They all wheeled round and, taking advantage
of his mistake, they marched back into their quarters.

"Bring out the reserve!" called Nutcracker at this critical
moment. And there they came, a marvelous and extremely
colorful troupe. Harlequins, Tyroleans, Turks, Tunguses,
tigers, lions, shepherds, bears, monkeys: they all fought
with admirable courage and perseverance. Valiantly they
strode forward into the welter of mice, led by a Chinese
emperor. But, alas, a madcap of a mouse bit off the Chinese emperor's head! In the ensuing confusion more and
more mice penetrated into his ranks. Soon hideous disorder
reigned. Nutcracker's troops were outnumbered by far.
Besides that, poor Nutcracker was greatly harassed by his
own allies, large clumsy gingerbread dolls with gilt faces
and helmets. They fought very awkwardly. They never
hit the enemy but were in everybody's way. They def-
initely cramped Nutcracker's style!

Soon Nutcracker was hard pressed, surrounded by enemies everywhere. All his troops were withdrawing into
safety. He tried to jump the bottom ledge of the cupboard
but his legs were too short. In desperation he cried out,
"A horse! A horse! My kingdom for a horse!"

Two of the enemies seized him by his cloak. The terrible, seven-headed Mouseking came rushing up to him,
squeaking triumphantly from his seven throats!

Mary could not bear it. "My poor Nutcracker!" she sobbed. She jerked off her left shoe and threw it with all her might and main into the thick of the enemy, aiming straight at the king.

Instantly everything vanished. Deep silence reigned.

Mary cast her eyes around. There stood Nutcracker, his sword in his hand. He fell on his knees before her.

"To you, and only to you, I owe my life, dearest lady!" he said fervently. "It was you who inspired me with knightly courage. And now you have crushed my great enemy! I'll be in your debt until the end of my life. Come with me and I'll show you the marvels of Toyland, a country more beautiful than you can imagine. Follow me, I beg of you! Do follow me!"

"I'll gladly go with you, dear Nutcracker," said Mary without hesitation. "But it mustn't be too far for I haven't had any sleep yet."

"I'll choose the shortest way," Nutcracker. "Just follow me."

They went out into the hall where stood the big old wardrobe. To Mary's surprise the door was open. Nimbly Nutcracker climbed up the wooden tracery till he could reach her father's fur coat. After some bold grabbling he got hold of a big tassel which was fastened to the back of the coat. He gave it a good tug, and the prettiest little ladder of cedar wood descended through the sleeve.

"Will you take the trouble of climbing up that ladder?" Nutcracker said politely. Mary did so. As soon as she had climbed up through the warm, furry sleeve and had reached the collar, a brilliant light was all around her.

She stood in a glittering sweet-scented meadow. Everything was sparkling like jewels.

"This is Candy Meadow," said Nutcracker. "We'll enter Toyland by that gate over there."

A beautiful gateway of white and brown marble arose just in front of them. They went through it, and Mary saw it was made of baked sugar almonds and raisins!

They were in a wonderland. Sweet orange scents surrounded them in the lovely little wood they were crossing now. Gold and silver fruits on multicolored stems were glistening among the dark foliage. The trees were decked out with gay streamers and bunches of flowers. When the sweet wind blew a little stronger, there was such a melodious tinkling, such a dazzling glitter, that Mary turned to her companion.

"Could I stay here a while?" she cried eagerly. "It's so delightful here."

"This is Christmas Wood," Nutcracker explained. He smiled and clapped his hands. Immediately little shepherds and shepherdesses appeared, and hunters and huntresses. They were as white and delicate as if they were made of sugar. They brought a golden armchair for Mary. As soon as Mary had taken a seat, they started to dance a pretty ballet. The hunters and huntresses blew their horns and bugles. It sounded melodious and silvery.

"That was most charming, I'm sure," Mary said delightedly when they had finished. She got up and followed Nutcracker, who obviously wanted to be on his way.

They followed the murmuring brook which filled the air with such delicious scent.

"This is Orange Brook," said Nutcracker. "It's nothing in comparison with Lemon River or Honey Brook. They all flow into Almond Milk Lake."

Lemon River was indeed wonderful to behold, as they

walked along it. The air was filled with a most refreshing perfume. The golden-colored waves rolled proudly between banks of emerald-green bushes. Strange flowers glowed in a green fire. Quite nearby stood a pretty village. Houses, church, parsonage, barns, everything was of a soft brown color. Golden roofs and variously tinted windows and ornaments set off the warm brown very pleasantly.

"It looks lovely, doesn't it?" Nutcracker asked with a smile. "That's Gingerbread Village at the Honey Brook. Nice-looking people live in it, too. But we won't go there. They are very short-tempered, because they all suffer so much from toothache. We have to hurry now. I want to show you the capital."

They rushed on, and before long they reached a great rose-colored lake. Nutcracker again clapped his hands. The rosy waves swirled and swelled. A splendid shell barge approached, drawn by two dolphins with golden scales. Silver-white swans accompanied them as Mary and Nutcracker sailed across the lake. Little fish with glittering jewel-like scales danced around them, the rosy waves splashed, the swans sang a haunting song, the dolphins blew crystal-clear jets of rose-scented water into the air which showered the swans, the fish, the water with rainbow-colored, glistening drops. It was marvelous!

All too soon they had reached the opposite shore. They disembarked and crossed a little wood, even more splendid than Christmas Wood. Then Mary stood stockstill.

A breathtaking sight arose before her. A shimmering, brightly lit castle with hundreds of lofty golden towers loomed before her.

"That's Marzipan Castle in my capital." Nutcracker smiled expectantly. The gates were thrown open, and silver

soldiers presented arms. A little man, splendidly dressed in
brocade, rushed forward. He embraced Nutcracker.

"Welcome home, my prince," he called. "Welcome
home to your kingdom!"

Mary looked in astonishment at her companion. A
clumsy nutcracker being called a prince? Behold! His
awkward appearance had disappeared. His clumsy body had
stretched, his stiff gait was gone. He moved with easy grace,
his dress was superb—he was the most handsome young
man one could imagine! But his sweet smile was as gentle
as ever. With a courteous bow he took Mary's arm, and together they walked up to the castle.

In all her admiration for these astonishing sights, Mary
noticed that one of the tallest towers was roofless. Little
men on a scaffold of cinnamon were working hard at putting it on again.

"What happened to the tower?" Mary asked timidly.

Prince Nutcracker sighed and said, "Marzipan Castle
was in great danger only a short time ago. The giant
Sweet Tooth happened to come along. He bit off the tower
and was just going to devour the star-studded dome. But
the burghers of Toyland sent a petition and he agreed to
be bought off. As ransom he accepted a large section of the
surrounding city and also parts of Candy Meadow. He was
so full then that he couldn't eat any more and went his
way."

Prince Nutcracker looked very sad. But at this moment
resounding music was heard. The doors of the castle flew
open, and out came twelve little pages with lighted clover
sticks that they carried as torches. They were followed by
four elegant ladies, gorgeously attired. They were about

the size of Mary's new doll, but Mary instantly recognized them as royalty. And indeed they were!

They rushed up to Nutcracker, and, embracing him lovingly, they cried out, "Oh, dearest prince! Beloved brother!"

Nutcracker was deeply moved. Then he took Mary's hand and said, "Dear sisters, this is the noble savior of my life! Just in the nick of time she threw a shoe and saved my life. There is nobody who can compete with her in nobleness, beauty, and courage."

"How true, how true!" sobbed the four sisters. Tenderly they embraced the embarrassed Mary, then in triumph they led her into the castle.

Mary was conducted to a soft settee in a magnificent drawing room. The prince sat at her side. The four sisters busied themselves with getting refreshments, while they listened to Nutcracker's weird tale. Oh, how excited they were about the cruel seven-headed Mouseking and the wild battle their brother had fought.

Mary listened contentedly. But Nutcracker's voice grew dimmer and dimmer, everything seemed to be so far away. Soon the lights were hidden by a silvery veil. The translucent mist curled and wafted; it looked as if everything were floating. A sweet humming and singing in the distance drowned out Nutcracker's words. Mary felt she was floating herself. She was drifting on silver waves. Higher and higher up she seemed to float . . . higher and higher . . . and ever higher . . . to the sound of the mellow music . . .

Crash! Poofff!

A crash! A tumble!

Mary opened her eyes. All had vanished. She was in her own bed.

Her mother was bending over her, saying, "Mary, darling! Did you have a dream? You are so hot and flushed."

"Oh, Mother," cried Mary, "I was in Toyland, and Nutcracker really is a prince, and oh! everything was so beautiful! Where are they all now?"

Her mother tucked her in. "Sweet dreams," she smiled, and kissed Mary.

Of course, anyone can understand what had happened!

After all the excitement of Christmas Eve, after all her adventures, Mary had fallen asleep in the castle. The four princesses themselves had carried her home and had put her to bed.

Most certainly the twelve little pages had accompanied them, lighting up the way with their clover-stick torches.

For
Curious
Children
Only

AFTERWORD

"Where magic reigns and wishes come true . . ." Where is that happy land? Has it vanished forever, destroyed by our Atomic Age, our inquiring, practical minds? The longings of mankind are embodied in fairy tales. There is much more to them than a simple escape from harsh realities, for they have their roots in eternal truths. Many of them are unforgettable portrayals of evil powers defeated, of the indestructible strength of love and tenderness.

Fairy tales can be enjoyed by children and grown-ups alike. Most of the famous fairy tales of the world were not originally told for children, but children all over the world have always loved them for their freshness and for the simplicity with which they present the highest goals of mankind. Children may not always fully understand them right away, but then they were not meant to.

There is not only enchantment in fairy tales, but shadows too; shadows of guilt, of disappointment, even of death. In the real world all things cast shadows, and life can be cruel and perilous. Deep in their hearts children are aware of this, and they should not be cheated into believing in a brightly artificial world. In fairy tales they come to grips with real problems and learn that evil must be conquered, even at the peril of life. Love and self-sacrifice will break the wicked spell that has trapped the beloved. Yes, strength is given to him who has a courageous, kindly heart.

May Hill Arbuthnot says in her book *Children and Books:*

Great music and great literature are not easy and never have been. That is no reason why we should confine our offerings entirely to the instantly enjoyed. Children's tastes grow; their appreciation develops upon what it is fed . . . We must find books which help the child to understand his own world today, and sometimes books that help him escape from today by going back to times that were simpler and more understandable. We must find stories as homey and realistic as a loaf of bread, and others as fantastic as a mirage. Above all, to balance the speed and confusion of our modern world, we need to find books which build strength and steadfastness in the child, books which develop his faith in the essential decency and nobility of life, books which give him a feeling for the wonder and goodness of the universe.

I have tried to meet this challenge by presenting some of the great German writers to the English-speaking child. Although I am well aware of the shortcomings that simplification and condensation carry with them, I preferred to retell these stories rather than translate them literally, and I beg to be forgiven for the occasional liberties I have felt justified in taking. Most of the stories are too long in the original, and too involved with subplots for today's young readers. So I have tried to preserve the essential flavor and meaning of the tales so that children will really love and enjoy the beauty and poetry of these great documents of the human soul.

German folklore is a vast domain, and one that attracted many German poets, writers, and scholars besides the Brothers Grimm. The famous brothers were scholars and never intended to *create* fairy tales. They only collected the stories which had been handed down by word of mouth since time immemorial. They did so with a warm heart and a cool mind, retaining the essence of the tales as they were told to them. They caught the idiomatic flavor of the language and greatly influenced European literature at a time when a strong national interest in folklore was awakening throughout Europe.

Their outstanding collection *Die Kinder- und Hausmaerchen der Brueder Grimm,* published in 1812 and 1815, became world famous. For ever after, Grimm's Fairy Tales and German fairy tales were so closely associated in people's minds that they became almost synonymous. But there is a wealth of German fairy tales besides the 741 stories which the Grimms collected.

It is German usage to classify such literary products of the Romantic Period as *Kunstmaerchen* or "artistic fairy tales." These are as different from the older *Volksmaerchen*, or "folktales," as Hans Christian Anderson is from Grimm.

Volksmaerchen tell a straight story with a single theme, without detailed descriptions or development of the hero's character. The hero, or heroine, is more a type than a person. Folktales use symbols to teach a moral lesson that satisfies the basic human need for ethical values. The magic of the style— a folktale was *told*, not read—is one of the charms of this type of story.

Many *Kunstmaerchen* have been written by great poets who have expressed themselves in vivid pictures of deep significance. *Kunstmaerchen* have development of character, appreciation of spiritual values, detailed descriptions of nature, subtlety of style, and, with some authors of the early German Romantic Period, an abundance of magic incidents and complex subplots. The German poets represented in this book did not intend to paint a shallow world. Their fairy tales abound in tragedy and comedy, in basic truth and deep emotion. They are just as timeless in their appeal as the better known folktales. It is one of the purposes of this book to revive a few German classics of the undeservedly neglected group of *Kunstmaerchen,* to make them known and loved in their own right.

I offer this collection now, in all humility, to children and parents alike, hoping to convey some of the enchantment and instruction embodied in their timeless wisdom.

BIOGRAPHICAL NOTES

ADELBERT VON CHAMISSO (1781-1838)

He was the son of French aristocrats who fled to Germany before the horrors of the French Revolution. In his adopted country Chamisso became an officer in the Prussian Army. After Prussia was defeated by Napoleon, he studied botany and joined Otto von Kotzbue on a scientific voyage around the world in 1815. Later on he was custodian of the Botanical Garden in Berlin.

The Wondrous History of Peter Schlemihl is his most famous work. I abridged the story to make it suitable for today's young readers, but hope that I have retained the essence of Chamisso's masterpiece.

The German title is "Peter Schlemihls wundersame Geschichte," published in 1814. After only a few years "Peter Schlemihl" was a part of European literature. Adorned with drawings by Cruikshank he was especially a favorite of the English-speaking world. "Peter Schlemihl" has been adapted for children time and again.

FRIEDRICH DE LA MOTTE FOUQUÉ (1777-1843)

He was an officer in the Prussian Army until he married wealthy Karoline von Briest, and then he devoted his life to writing. He turned out more than one hundred romantic novels and plays, but he is remembered chiefly for the charming fairy tale *Undine*, published in 1811.

Fouqué's *Undine*, which has been the subject of operas, musical compositions, and a recent Broadway play, is book-length. I abridged the original text throughout, since Fouqué writes in the ornate style of early Romanticism. Following the example of Lortzing's opera, I changed the knight's awkward name "Huld-brand" into "Hugo"; and the treacherous Dame "Bertalda" is "Bertha" in my story.

JOHANN WOLFGANG VON GOETHE (1749-1832)

Born the son of a wealthy, patrician family in Frankfort-on-Main, Goethe studied law in Leipzig and Strassburg, and soon settled as an advocate in his native town. As a very young man he started to write beautiful lyric poetry and drama. When he was only twenty-five he gained world fame overnight as the author of *The Sorrows of Young Werther,* a sentimental novel which swept all Europe. In his most important work, the drama "Faust," he expresses his conception of man's place and duty in the world. His long, creative life was guided by the conviction that all being is one organic whole.

Of all modern men of genius, Goethe was the most universal. He stood at the threshold of an era of rapidly growing knowledge. Since his time it has seemed impossible for any single human mind to embrace all domains of human knowledge and undertaking.

Our fairy tale is contained in Goethe's novel *Wilhelm Meister's Travels,* published in 1829. I abbreviated it slightly, simplifying some sentences, hoping to be forgiven for my young readers' sake.

WILHELM HAUFF (1802-1827)

Hauff has written short stories, a novel, and poetry, but he is best known and loved for his fairy tales. He found his material in European, and especially German, folklore, and also in oriental fairy tales. His magic tales lead into the romantic crooked streets of old German towns, woodlands, and mountains, to the rocky shores of Scotland, to sumptuous courts of oriental kings, and to the nocturnal resting places of caravans in the dismal deserts. The creatures of his untiring imagination are very much alive in their humor and lovable originality. Hauff died when he was only twenty-five years old.

ERNST THEODOR AMADEUS HOFFMANN (1776-1822)

Born in Königsberg, East Prussia, he studied law at the famous university of his native town. Hoffmann was an ugly little man; brilliant, with unlimited imagination and a gift for keen observation. Restless and unhappy all his life, this great writer was also a composer, a painter, a theatrical manager, a music critic, and a lawyer. Small wonder that the outstanding fact about his work and character was a startling duality. A strange mixture of realism and grotesque imagination, of minute description and an uncanny faculty for calling up otherworldly thrills, enabled him to write with a startling originality which has greatly influenced his contemporaries.

His bizarre tales attracted the attention of great composers. The opera "Tales of Hoffmann" by Jacques Offenbach, Tschaikowsky's "Nutcracker Suite," Schumann's "Kreisleriana" prove this till our day.

There is nothing of the ghastly horror of his novels in the fairy tale *Nutcracker and Mouseking,* for he wrote it for the children of his lifelong friend, Hitzig. Nutcracker and the other figures in the story are intensely alive as they go about their astounding adventures.

RICHARD LEANDER (1830-1889)

This was the pseudonym of Richard von Volkmann, a surgeon in Halle, a city in central Germany. *The Invisible Kingdom* is one of his most charming fairy tales, and to my knowledge it has never before been translated into English.

EDUARD MÖRIKE (1804-1875)

The Swabian Mörike, a sensitive lyric poet, was a clergyman by profession. His poems are very melodious and many of them were set to music by Hugo Wolf.

Mörike is a magician. With simple words he paints striking pictures of beauty and harmony, or reveals the vague sadness which sometimes rises from the secret depths of man's soul. The little fairy tale, *The Peasant and His Son,* published in 1839, is written in simple and warmhearted language approaching the style of a folk tale. It has not been translated into English before, as far as I know.

FERDINAND RAIMUND (1790-1836)

Born in Vienna, he was a playwright as well as a famous actor. He wrote eight plays which are still favorites with theater audiences in their blending of romanticism and realism. His masterpiece is the whimsical and charming musical comedy *The Spendthrift*, an allegory depicting man's greatness and weakness. Conradin Kreutzer composed the incidental music for the play, which saw its opening night in Vienna in 1834, with Raimund playing Valentine, a great success for him both as author and actor.

THEODOR STORM (1817-1888)

Born at Husum, Schleswig, he studied jurisprudence, entered the judicial service, and became a district judge. Storm is the author of a large number of short stories and knows how to spellbind us with masterful tales. The resignation and "sweet sadness" of his earlier work is largely overcome in his later novelettes.

Storm's down-to-earth fairy tale *Rain Trudy* is free from his usual resignation and melancholia. Deftly he describes the Frisian peasant and the landscape which molds and determines his life. I abridged the story regretfully, dispensing with some of the nature descriptions.

The German title is *Regentrude*, published in 1864. There are several translations of most of Storm's short stories and of his poetry. His four fairy tales, including *Regentrude* have not been translated before, as far as I know.

A CATALOGUE OF SELECTED DOVER BOOKS
IN ALL FIELDS OF INTEREST

A CATALOGUE OF SELECTED DOVER BOOKS
IN ALL FIELDS OF INTEREST

AMERICA'S OLD MASTERS, James T. Flexner. Four men emerged unexpectedly from provincial 18th century America to leadership in European art: Benjamin West, J. S. Copley, C. R. Peale, Gilbert Stuart. Brilliant coverage of lives and contributions. Revised, 1967 edition. 69 plates. 365pp. of text.

21806-6 Paperbound $3.00

FIRST FLOWERS OF OUR WILDERNESS: AMERICAN PAINTING, THE COLONIAL PERIOD, James T. Flexner. Painters, and regional painting traditions from earliest Colonial times up to the emergence of Copley, West and Peale Sr., Foster, Gustavus Hesselius, Feke, John Smibert and many anonymous painters in the primitive manner. Engaging presentation, with 162 illustrations. xxii + 368pp.

22180-6 Paperbound $3.50

THE LIGHT OF DISTANT SKIES: AMERICAN PAINTING, 1760-1835, James T. Flexner. The great generation of early American painters goes to Europe to learn and to teach: West, Copley, Gilbert Stuart and others. Allston, Trumbull, Morse; also contemporary American painters—primitives, derivatives, academics—who remained in America. 102 illustrations. xiii + 306pp.

22179-2 Paperbound $3.50

A HISTORY OF THE RISE AND PROGRESS OF THE ARTS OF DESIGN IN THE UNITED STATES, William Dunlap. Much the richest mine of information on early American painters, sculptors, architects, engravers, miniaturists, etc. The only source of information for scores of artists, the major primary source for many others. Unabridged reprint of rare original 1834 edition, with new introduction by James T. Flexner, and 394 new illustrations. Edited by Rita Weiss. 6⅝ x 9⅝.

21695-0, 21696-9, 21697-7 Three volumes, Paperbound $15.00

EPOCHS OF CHINESE AND JAPANESE ART, Ernest F. Fenollosa. From primitive Chinese art to the 20th century, thorough history, explanation of every important art period and form, including Japanese woodcuts; main stress on China and Japan, but Tibet, Korea also included. Still unexcelled for its detailed, rich coverage of cultural background, aesthetic elements, diffusion studies, particularly of the historical period. 2nd, 1913 edition. 242 illustrations. lii + 439pp. of text.

20364-6, 20365-4 Two volumes, Paperbound $6.00

THE GENTLE ART OF MAKING ENEMIES, James A. M. Whistler. Greatest wit of his day deflates Oscar Wilde, Ruskin, Swinburne; strikes back at inane critics, exhibitions, art journalism; aesthetics of impressionist revolution in most striking form. Highly readable classic by great painter. Reproduction of edition designed by Whistler. Introduction by Alfred Werner. xxxvi + 334pp.

21875-9 Paperbound $3.00

VISUAL ILLUSIONS: THEIR CAUSES, CHARACTERISTICS, AND APPLICATIONS, Matthew Luckiesh. Thorough description and discussion of optical illusion, geometric and perspective, particularly; size and shape distortions, illusions of color, of motion; natural illusions; use of illusion in art and magic, industry, etc. Most useful today with op art, also for classical art. Scores of effects illustrated. Introduction by William H. Ittleson. 100 illustrations. xxi + 252pp.

21530-X Paperbound $2.00

A HANDBOOK OF ANATOMY FOR ART STUDENTS, Arthur Thomson. Thorough, virtually exhaustive coverage of skeletal structure, musculature, etc. Full text, supplemented by anatomical diagrams and drawings and by photographs of undraped figures. Unique in its comparison of male and female forms, pointing out differences of contour, texture, form. 211 figures, 40 drawings, 86 photographs. xx + 459pp. 5⅜ x 8⅜.

21163-0 Paperbound $3.50

150 MASTERPIECES OF DRAWING, Selected by Anthony Toney. Full page reproductions of drawings from the early 16th to the end of the 18th century, all beautifully reproduced: Rembrandt, Michelangelo, Dürer, Fragonard, Urs, Graf, Wouwerman, many others. First-rate browsing book, model book for artists. xviii + 150pp. 8⅜ x 11¼.

21032-4 Paperbound $2.50

THE LATER WORK OF AUBREY BEARDSLEY, Aubrey Beardsley. Exotic, erotic, ironic masterpieces in full maturity: Comedy Ballet, Venus and Tannhauser, Pierrot, Lysistrata, Rape of the Lock, Savoy material, Ali Baba, Volpone, etc. This material revolutionized the art world, and is still powerful, fresh, brilliant. With *The Early Work*, all Beardsley's finest work. 174 plates, 2 in color. xiv + 176pp. 8⅛ x 11.

21817-1 Paperbound $3.00

DRAWINGS OF REMBRANDT, Rembrandt van Rijn. Complete reproduction of fabulously rare edition by Lippmann and Hofstede de Groot, completely reedited, updated, improved by Prof. Seymour Slive, Fogg Museum. Portraits, Biblical sketches, landscapes, Oriental types, nudes, episodes from classical mythology—All Rembrandt's fertile genius. Also selection of drawings by his pupils and followers. "Stunning volumes," *Saturday Review*. 550 illustrations. lxxviii + 552pp. 9⅛ x 12¼.

21485-0, 21486-9 Two volumes, Paperbound $10.00

THE DISASTERS OF WAR, Francisco Goya. One of the masterpieces of Western civilization—83 etchings that record Goya's shattering, bitter reaction to the Napoleonic war that swept through Spain after the insurrection of 1808 and to war in general. Reprint of the first edition, with three additional plates from Boston's Museum of Fine Arts. All plates facsimile size. Introduction by Philip Hofer, Fogg Museum. v + 97pp. 9⅜ x 8¼.

21872-4 Paperbound $2.00

GRAPHIC WORKS OF ODILON REDON. Largest collection of Redon's graphic works ever assembled: 172 lithographs, 28 etchings and engravings, 9 drawings. These include some of his most famous works. All the plates from *Odilon Redon: oeuvre graphique complet*, plus additional plates. New introduction and caption translations by Alfred Werner. 209 illustrations. xxvii + 209pp. 9⅛ x 12¼.

21966-8 Paperbound $4.50

DESIGN BY ACCIDENT; A BOOK OF "ACCIDENTAL EFFECTS" FOR ARTISTS AND DESIGNERS, James F. O'Brien. Create your own unique, striking, imaginative effects by "controlled accident" interaction of materials: paints and lacquers, oil and water based paints, splatter, crackling materials, shatter, similar items. Everything you do will be different; first book on this limitless art, so useful to both fine artist and commercial artist. Full instructions. 192 plates showing "accidents," 8 in color. viii + 215pp. 8⅜ x 11¼.　　　　　　　　　　　　21942-9 Paperbound $3.75

THE BOOK OF SIGNS, Rudolf Koch. Famed German type designer draws 493 beautiful symbols: religious, mystical, alchemical, imperial, property marks, runes, etc. Remarkable fusion of traditional and modern. Good for suggestions of timelessness, smartness, modernity. Text. vi + 104pp. 6⅛ x 9¼.
　　　　　　　　　　　　　　　　　　　　　20162-7 Paperbound $1.25

HISTORY OF INDIAN AND INDONESIAN ART, Ananda K. Coomaraswamy. An unabridged republication of one of the finest books by a great scholar in Eastern art. Rich in descriptive material, history, social backgrounds; Sunga reliefs, Rajput paintings, Gupta temples, Burmese frescoes, textiles, jewelry, sculpture, etc. 400 photos. viii + 423pp. 6⅜ x 9¾.　　　　　　　　21436-2 Paperbound $5.00

PRIMITIVE ART, Franz Boas. America's foremost anthropologist surveys textiles, ceramics, woodcarving, basketry, metalwork, etc.; patterns, technology, creation of symbols, style origins. All areas of world, but very full on Northwest Coast Indians. More than 350 illustrations of baskets, boxes, totem poles, weapons, etc. 378 pp.
　　　　　　　　　　　　　　　　　　　　　20025-6 Paperbound $3.00

THE GENTLEMAN AND CABINET MAKER'S DIRECTOR, Thomas Chippendale. Full reprint (third edition, 1762) of most influential furniture book of all time, by master cabinetmaker. 200 plates, illustrating chairs, sofas, mirrors, tables, cabinets, plus 24 photographs of surviving pieces. Biographical introduction by N. Bienenstock. vi + 249pp. 9⅞ x 12¾.　　　　　　　　21601-2 Paperbound $4.00

AMERICAN ANTIQUE FURNITURE, Edgar G. Miller, Jr. The basic coverage of all American furniture before 1840. Individual chapters cover type of furniture— clocks, tables, sideboards, etc.—chronologically, with inexhaustible wealth of data. More than 2100 photographs, all identified, commented on. Essential to all early American collectors. Introduction by H. E. Keyes. vi + 1106pp. 7⅞ x 10¾.
　　　　　　　21599-7, 21600-4 Two volumes, Paperbound $11.00

PENNSYLVANIA DUTCH AMERICAN FOLK ART, Henry J. Kauffman. 279 photos, 28 drawings of tulipware, Fraktur script, painted tinware, toys, flowered furniture, quilts, samplers, hex signs, house interiors, etc. Full descriptive text. Excellent for tourist, rewarding for designer, collector. Map. 146pp. 7⅞ x 10¾.
　　　　　　　　　　　　　　　　　　　　　21205-X Paperbound $2.50

EARLY NEW ENGLAND GRAVESTONE RUBBINGS, Edmund V. Gillon, Jr. 43 photographs, 226 carefully reproduced rubbings show heavily symbolic, sometimes macabre early gravestones, up to early 19th century. Remarkable early American primitive art, occasionally strikingly beautiful; always powerful. Text. xxvi + 207pp. 8⅜ x 11¼.　　　　　　　　　　　　21380-3 Paperbound $3.50

ALPHABETS AND ORNAMENTS, Ernst Lehner. Well-known pictorial source for decorative alphabets, script examples, cartouches, frames, decorative title pages, calligraphic initials, borders, similar material. 14th to 19th century, mostly European. Useful in almost any graphic arts designing, varied styles. 750 illustrations. 256pp. 7 x 10.   21905-4 Paperbound $4.00

PAINTING: A CREATIVE APPROACH, Norman Colquhoun. For the beginner simple guide provides an instructive approach to painting: major stumbling blocks for beginner; overcoming them, technical points; paints and pigments; oil painting; watercolor and other media and color. New section on "plastic" paints. Glossary. Formerly *Paint Your Own Pictures*. 221pp.   22000-1 Paperbound $1.75

THE ENJOYMENT AND USE OF COLOR, Walter Sargent. Explanation of the relations between colors themselves and between colors in nature and art, including hundreds of little-known facts about color values, intensities, effects of high and low illumination, complementary colors. Many practical hints for painters, references to great masters. 7 color plates, 29 illustrations. x + 274pp.
20944-X Paperbound $2.75

THE NOTEBOOKS OF LEONARDO DA VINCI, compiled and edited by Jean Paul Richter. 1566 extracts from original manuscripts reveal the full range of Leonardo's versatile genius: all his writings on painting, sculpture, architecture, anatomy, astronomy, geography, topography, physiology, mining, music, etc., in both Italian and English, with 186 plates of manuscript pages and more than 500 additional drawings. Includes studies for the Last Supper, the lost Sforza monument, and other works. Total of xlvii + 866pp. 7⅞ x 10¾.
22572-0, 22573-9 Two volumes, Paperbound $11.00

MONTGOMERY WARD CATALOGUE OF 1895. Tea gowns, yards of flannel and pillow-case lace, stereoscopes, books of gospel hymns, the New Improved Singer Sewing Machine, side saddles, milk skimmers, straight-edged razors, high-button shoes, spittoons, and on and on . . . listing some 25,000 items, practically all illustrated. Essential to the shoppers of the 1890's, it is our truest record of the spirit of the period. Unaltered reprint of Issue No. 57, Spring and Summer 1895. Introduction by Boris Emmet. Innumerable illustrations. xiii + 624pp. 8½ x 11⅝.
22377-9 Paperbound $6.95

THE CRYSTAL PALACE EXHIBITION ILLUSTRATED CATALOGUE (LONDON, 1851). One of the wonders of the modern world—the Crystal Palace Exhibition in which all the nations of the civilized world exhibited their achievements in the arts and sciences—presented in an equally important illustrated catalogue. More than 1700 items pictured with accompanying text—ceramics, textiles, cast-iron work, carpets, pianos, sleds, razors, wall-papers, billiard tables, beehives, silverware and hundreds of other artifacts—represent the focal point of Victorian culture in the Western World. Probably the largest collection of Victorian decorative art ever assembled—indispensable for antiquarians and designers. Unabridged republication of the Art-Journal Catalogue of the Great Exhibition of 1851, with all terminal essays. New introduction by John Gloag, F.S.A. xxxiv + 426pp. 9 x 12.
22503-8 Paperbound $5.00

A HISTORY OF COSTUME, Carl Köhler. Definitive history, based on surviving pieces of clothing primarily, and paintings, statues, etc. secondarily. Highly readable text, supplemented by 594 illustrations of costumes of the ancient Mediterranean peoples, Greece and Rome, the Teutonic prehistoric period; costumes of the Middle Ages, Renaissance, Baroque, 18th and 19th centuries. Clear, measured patterns are provided for many clothing articles. Approach is practical throughout. Enlarged by Emma von Sichart. 464pp.   21030-8 Paperbound $3.50.

ORIENTAL RUGS, ANTIQUE AND MODERN, Walter A. Hawley. A complete and authoritative treatise on the Oriental rug—where they are made, by whom and how, designs and symbols, characteristics in detail of the six major groups, how to distinguish them and how to buy them. Detailed technical data is provided on periods, weaves, warps, wefts, textures, sides, ends and knots, although no technical background is required for an understanding. 11 color plates, 80 halftones, 4 maps. vi + 320pp. 6⅛ x 9⅛.   22366-3 Paperbound $5.00

TEN BOOKS ON ARCHITECTURE, Vitruvius. By any standards the most important book on architecture ever written. Early Roman discussion of aesthetics of building, construction methods, orders, sites, and every other aspect of architecture has inspired, instructed architecture for about 2,000 years. Stands behind Palladio, Michelangelo, Bramante, Wren, countless others. Definitive Morris H. Morgan translation. 68 illustrations. xii + 331pp.   20645-9 Paperbound $3.00

THE FOUR BOOKS OF ARCHITECTURE, Andrea Palladio. Translated into every major Western European language in the two centuries following its publication in 1570, this has been one of the most influential books in the history of architecture. Complete reprint of the 1738 Isaac Ware edition. New introduction by Adolf Placzek, Columbia Univ. 216 plates. xxii + 110pp. of text. 9½ x 12¾.
                                    21308-0 Clothbound $12.50

STICKS AND STONES: A STUDY OF AMERICAN ARCHITECTURE AND CIVILIZATION, Lewis Mumford. One of the great classics of American cultural history. American architecture from the medieval-inspired earliest forms to the early 20th century; evolution of structure and style, and reciprocal influences on environment. 21 photographic illustrations. 238pp.   20202-X Paperbound $2.00

THE AMERICAN BUILDER'S COMPANION, Asher Benjamin. The most widely used early 19th century architectural style and source book, for colonial up into Greek Revival periods. Extensive development of geometry of carpentering, construction of sashes, frames, doors, stairs; plans and elevations of domestic and other buildings. Hundreds of thousands of houses were built according to this book, now invaluable to historians, architects, restorers, etc. 1827 edition. 59 plates. 114pp. 7⅞ x 10¾.
                                    22236-5 Paperbound $3.50

DUTCH HOUSES IN THE HUDSON VALLEY BEFORE 1776, Helen Wilkinson Reynolds. The standard survey of the Dutch colonial house and outbuildings, with constructional features, decoration, and local history associated with individual homesteads. Introduction by Franklin D. Roosevelt. Map. 150 illustrations. 469pp. 6⅝ x 9¼.   21469-9 Paperbound $5.00

THE ARCHITECTURE OF COUNTRY HOUSES, Andrew J. Downing. Together with Vaux's *Villas and Cottages* this is the basic book for Hudson River Gothic architecture of the middle Victorian period. Full, sound discussions of general aspects of housing, architecture, style, decoration, furnishing, together with scores of detailed house plans, illustrations of specific buildings, accompanied by full text. Perhaps the most influential single American architectural book. 1850 edition. Introduction by J. Stewart Johnson. 321 figures, 34 architectural designs. xvi + 560pp.
22003-6 Paperbound $4.00

LOST EXAMPLES OF COLONIAL ARCHITECTURE, John Mead Howells. Full-page photographs of buildings that have disappeared or been so altered as to be denatured, including many designed by major early American architects. 245 plates. xvii + 248pp. 7⅞ x 10¾.
21143-6 Paperbound $3.50

DOMESTIC ARCHITECTURE OF THE AMERICAN COLONIES AND OF THE EARLY REPUBLIC, Fiske Kimball. Foremost architect and restorer of Williamsburg and Monticello covers nearly 200 homes between 1620-1825. Architectural details, construction, style features, special fixtures, floor plans, etc. Generally considered finest work in its area. 219 illustrations of houses, doorways, windows, capital mantels. xx + 314pp. 7⅞ x 10¾.
21743-4 Paperbound $4.00

EARLY AMERICAN ROOMS: 1650-1858, edited by Russell Hawes Kettell. Tour of 12 rooms, each representative of a different era in American history and each furnished, decorated, designed and occupied in the style of the era. 72 plans and elevations, 8-page color section, etc., show fabrics, wall papers, arrangements, etc. Full descriptive text. xvii + 200pp. of text. 8⅜ x 11¼.
21633-0 Paperbound $5.00

THE FITZWILLIAM VIRGINAL BOOK, edited by J. Fuller Maitland and W. B. Squire. Full modern printing of famous early 17th-century ms. volume of 300 works by Morley, Byrd, Bull, Gibbons, etc. For piano or other modern keyboard instrument; easy to read format. xxxvi + 938pp. 8⅜ x 11.
21068-5, 21069-3 Two volumes, Paperbound $10.00

KEYBOARD MUSIC, Johann Sebastian Bach. Bach Gesellschaft edition. A rich selection of Bach's masterpieces for the harpsichord: the six English Suites, six French Suites, the six Partitas (Clavierübung part I), the Goldberg Variations (Clavierübung part IV), the fifteen Two-Part Inventions and the fifteen Three-Part Sinfonias. Clearly reproduced on large sheets with ample margins; eminently playable. vi + 312pp. 8⅛ x 11.
22360-4 Paperbound $5.00

THE MUSIC OF BACH: AN INTRODUCTION, Charles Sanford Terry. A fine, nontechnical introduction to Bach's music, both instrumental and vocal. Covers organ music, chamber music, passion music, other types. Analyzes themes, developments, innovations. x + 114pp.
21075-8 Paperbound $1.50

BEETHOVEN AND HIS NINE SYMPHONIES, Sir George Grove. Noted British musicologist provides best history, analysis, commentary on symphonies. Very thorough, rigorously accurate; necessary to both advanced student and amateur music lover. 436 musical passages. vii + 407 pp.
20334-4 Paperbound $2.75

JOHANN SEBASTIAN BACH, Philipp Spitta. One of the great classics of musicology, this definitive analysis of Bach's music (and life) has never been surpassed. Lucid, nontechnical analyses of hundreds of pieces (30 pages devoted to St. Matthew Passion, 26 to B Minor Mass). Also includes major analysis of 18th-century music. 450 musical examples. 40-page musical supplement. Total of xx + 1799pp.

(EUK) 22278-0, 22279-9 Two volumes, Clothbound $17.50

MOZART AND HIS PIANO CONCERTOS, Cuthbert Girdlestone. The only full-length study of an important area of Mozart's creativity. Provides detailed analyses of all 23 concertos, traces inspirational sources. 417 musical examples. Second edition. 509pp.
21271-8 Paperbound $3.50

THE PERFECT WAGNERITE: A COMMENTARY ON THE NIBLUNG'S RING, George Bernard Shaw. Brilliant and still relevant criticism in remarkable essays on Wagner's Ring cycle, Shaw's ideas on political and social ideology behind the plots, role of Leitmotifs, vocal requisites, etc. Prefaces. xxi + 136pp.
(USO) 21707-8 Paperbound $1.75

DON GIOVANNI, W. A. Mozart. Complete libretto, modern English translation; biographies of composer and librettist; accounts of early performances and critical reaction. Lavishly illustrated. All the material you need to understand and appreciate this great work. Dover Opera Guide and Libretto Series; translated and introduced by Ellen Bleiler. 92 illustrations. 209pp.
21134-7 Paperbound $2.00

BASIC ELECTRICITY, U. S. Bureau of Naval Personel. Originally a training course, best non-technical coverage of basic theory of electricity and its applications. Fundamental concepts, batteries, circuits, conductors and wiring techniques, AC and DC, inductance and capacitance, generators, motors, transformers, magnetic amplifiers, synchros, servomechanisms, etc. Also covers blue-prints, electrical diagrams, etc. Many questions, with answers. 349 illustrations. x + 448pp. 6½ x 9¼.
20973-3 Paperbound $3.50

REPRODUCTION OF SOUND, Edgar Villchur. Thorough coverage for laymen of high fidelity systems, reproducing systems in general, needles, amplifiers, preamps, loudspeakers, feedback, explaining physical background. "A rare talent for making technicalities vividly comprehensible," R. Darrell, *High Fidelity*. 69 figures. iv + 92pp.
21515-6 Paperbound $1.35

HEAR ME TALKIN' TO YA: THE STORY OF JAZZ AS TOLD BY THE MEN WHO MADE IT, Nat Shapiro and Nat Hentoff. Louis Armstrong, Fats Waller, Jo Jones, Clarence Williams, Billy Holiday, Duke Ellington, Jelly Roll Morton and dozens of other jazz greats tell how it was in Chicago's South Side, New Orleans, depression Harlem and the modern West Coast as jazz was born and grew. xvi + 429pp.
21726-4 Paperbound $3.00

FABLES OF AESOP, translated by Sir Roger L'Estrange. A reproduction of the very rare 1931 Paris edition; a selection of the most interesting fables, together with 50 imaginative drawings by Alexander Calder. v + 128pp. 6½x9¼.
21780-9 Paperbound $1.50

AGAINST THE GRAIN (A REBOURS), Joris K. Huysmans. Filled with weird images, evidences of a bizarre imagination, exotic experiments with hallucinatory drugs, rich tastes and smells and the diversions of its sybarite hero Duc Jean des Esseintes, this classic novel pushed 19th-century literary decadence to its limits. Full unabridged edition. Do not confuse this with abridged editions generally sold. Introduction by Havelock Ellis. xlix + 206pp. 22190-3 Paperbound $2.50

VARIORUM SHAKESPEARE: HAMLET. Edited by Horace H. Furness; a landmark of American scholarship. Exhaustive footnotes and appendices treat all doubtful words and phrases, as well as suggested critical emendations throughout the play's history. First volume contains editor's own text, collated with all Quartos and Folios. Second volume contains full first Quarto, translations of Shakespeare's sources (Belleforest, and Saxo Grammaticus), Der Bestrafte Brudermord, and many essays on critical and historical points of interest by major authorities of past and present. Includes details of staging and costuming over the years. By far the best edition available for serious students of Shakespeare. Total of xx + 905pp. 21004-9, 21005-7, 2 volumes, Paperbound $7.00

A LIFE OF WILLIAM SHAKESPEARE, Sir Sidney Lee. This is the standard life of Shakespeare, summarizing everything known about Shakespeare and his plays. Incredibly rich in material, broad in coverage, clear and judicious, it has served thousands as the best introduction to Shakespeare. 1931 edition. 9 plates. xxix + 792pp. 21967-4 Paperbound $3.75

MASTERS OF THE DRAMA, John Gassner. Most comprehensive history of the drama in print, covering every tradition from Greeks to modern Europe and America, including India, Far East, etc. Covers more than 800 dramatists, 2000 plays, with biographical material, plot summaries, theatre history, criticism, etc. "Best of its kind in English," *New Republic.* 77 illustrations. xxii + 890pp. 20100-7 Clothbound $10.00

THE EVOLUTION OF THE ENGLISH LANGUAGE, George McKnight. The growth of English, from the 14th century to the present. Unusual, non-technical account presents basic information in very interesting form: sound shifts, change in grammar and syntax, vocabulary growth, similar topics. Abundantly illustrated with quotations. Formerly *Modern English in the Making.* xii + 590pp. 21932-1 Paperbound $3.50

AN ETYMOLOGICAL DICTIONARY OF MODERN ENGLISH, Ernest Weekley. Fullest, richest work of its sort, by foremost British lexicographer. Detailed word histories, including many colloquial and archaic words; extensive quotations. Do not confuse this with the Concise Etymological Dictionary, which is much abridged. Total of xxvii + 830pp. 6½ x 9¼. 21873-2, 21874-0 Two volumes, Paperbound $7.90

FLATLAND: A ROMANCE OF MANY DIMENSIONS, E. A. Abbott. Classic of science-fiction explores ramifications of life in a two-dimensional world, and what happens when a three-dimensional being intrudes. Amusing reading, but also useful as introduction to thought about hyperspace. Introduction by Banesh Hoffmann. 16 illustrations. xx + 103pp. 20001-9 Paperbound $1.00

POEMS OF ANNE BRADSTREET, edited with an introduction by Robert Hutchinson. A new selection of poems by America's first poet and perhaps the first significant woman poet in the English language. 48 poems display her development in works of considerable variety—love poems, domestic poems, religious meditations, formal elegies, "quaternions," etc. Notes, bibliography. viii + 222pp.

22160-1 Paperbound $2.50

THREE GOTHIC NOVELS: THE CASTLE OF OTRANTO BY HORACE WALPOLE; VATHEK BY WILLIAM BECKFORD; THE VAMPYRE BY JOHN POLIDORI, WITH FRAGMENT OF A NOVEL BY LORD BYRON, edited by E. F. Bleiler. The first Gothic novel, by Walpole; the finest Oriental tale in English, by Beckford; powerful Romantic supernatural story in versions by Polidori and Byron. All extremely important in history of literature; all still exciting, packed with supernatural thrills, ghosts, haunted castles, magic, etc. xl + 291pp.

21232-7 Paperbound $2.50

THE BEST TALES OF HOFFMANN, E. T. A. Hoffmann. 10 of Hoffmann's most important stories, in modern re-editings of standard translations: Nutcracker and the King of Mice, Signor Formica, Automata, The Sandman, Rath Krespel, The Golden Flowerpot, Master Martin the Cooper, The Mines of Falun, The King's Betrothed, A New Year's Eve Adventure. 7 illustrations by Hoffmann. Edited by E. F. Bleiler. xxxix + 419pp. 21793-0 Paperbound $3.00

GHOST AND HORROR STORIES OF AMBROSE BIERCE, Ambrose Bierce. 23 strikingly modern stories of the horrors latent in the human mind: The Eyes of the Panther, The Damned Thing, An Occurrence at Owl Creek Bridge, An Inhabitant of Carcosa, etc., plus the dream-essay, Visions of the Night. Edited by E. F. Bleiler. xxii + 199pp. 20767-6 Paperbound $1.50

BEST GHOST STORIES OF J. S. LEFANU, J. Sheridan LeFanu. Finest stories by Victorian master often considered greatest supernatural writer of all. Carmilla, Green Tea, The Haunted Baronet, The Familiar, and 12 others. Most never before available in the U. S. A. Edited by E. F. Bleiler. 8 illustrations from Victorian publications. xvii + 467pp. 20415-4 Paperbound $3.00

MATHEMATICAL FOUNDATIONS OF INFORMATION THEORY, A. I. Khinchin. Comprehensive introduction to work of Shannon, McMillan, Feinstein and Khinchin, placing these investigations on a rigorous mathematical basis. Covers entropy concept in probability theory, uniqueness theorem, Shannon's inequality, ergodic sources, the E property, martingale concept, noise, Feinstein's fundamental lemma, Shanon's first and second theorems. Translated by R. A. Silverman and M. D. Friedman. iii + 120pp. 60434-9 Paperbound $2.00

SEVEN SCIENCE FICTION NOVELS, H. G. Wells. The standard collection of the great novels. Complete, unabridged. *First Men in the Moon, Island of Dr. Moreau, War of the Worlds, Food of the Gods, Invisible Man, Time Machine, In the Days of the Comet.* Not only science fiction fans, but every educated person owes it to himself to read these novels. 1015pp. (USO) 20264-X Clothbound $6.00

LAST AND FIRST MEN AND STAR MAKER, TWO SCIENCE FICTION NOVELS, Olaf Stapledon. Greatest future histories in science fiction. In the first, human intelligence is the "hero," through strange paths of evolution, interplanetary invasions, incredible technologies, near extinctions and reemergences. Star Maker describes the quest of a band of star rovers for intelligence itself, through time and space: weird inhuman civilizations, crustacean minds, symbiotic worlds, etc. Complete, unabridged. v + 438pp. (USO) 21962-3 Paperbound $2.50

THREE PROPHETIC NOVELS, H. G. WELLS. Stages of a consistently planned future for mankind. *When the Sleeper Wakes,* and *A Story of the Days to Come,* anticipate *Brave New World* and *1984,* in the 21st Century; *The Time Machine,* only complete version in print, shows farther future and the end of mankind. All show Wells's greatest gifts as storyteller and novelist. Edited by E. F. Bleiler. x + 335pp. (USO) 20605-X Paperbound $2.50

THE DEVIL'S DICTIONARY, Ambrose Bierce. America's own Oscar Wilde—Ambrose Bierce—offers his barbed iconoclastic wisdom in over 1,000 definitions hailed by H. L. Mencken as "some of the most gorgeous witticisms in the English language." 145pp. 20487-1 Paperbound $1.25

MAX AND MORITZ, Wilhelm Busch. Great children's classic, father of comic strip, of two bad boys, Max and Moritz. Also Ker and Plunk (Plisch und Plumm), Cat and Mouse, Deceitful Henry, Ice-Peter, The Boy and the Pipe, and five other pieces. Original German, with English translation. Edited by H. Arthur Klein; translations by various hands and H. Arthur Klein. vi + 216pp. 20181-3 Paperbound $2.00

PIGS IS PIGS AND OTHER FAVORITES, Ellis Parker Butler. The title story is one of the best humor short stories, as Mike Flannery obfuscates biology and English. Also included, That Pup of Murchison's, The Great American Pie Company, and Perkins of Portland. 14 illustrations. v + 109pp. 21532-6 Paperbound $1.25

THE PETERKIN PAPERS, Lucretia P. Hale. It takes genius to be as stupidly mad as the Peterkins, as they decide to become wise, celebrate the "Fourth," keep a cow, and otherwise strain the resources of the Lady from Philadelphia. Basic book of American humor. 153 illustrations. 219pp. 20794-3 Paperbound $2.00

PERRAULT'S FAIRY TALES, translated by A. E. Johnson and S. R. Littlewood, with 34 full-page illustrations by Gustave Doré. All the original Perrault stories—Cinderella, Sleeping Beauty, Bluebeard, Little Red Riding Hood, Puss in Boots, Tom Thumb, etc.—with their witty verse morals and the magnificent illustrations of Doré. One of the five or six great books of European fairy tales. viii + 117pp. 8⅛ x 11. 22311-6 Paperbound $2.00

OLD HUNGARIAN FAIRY TALES, Baroness Orczy. Favorites translated and adapted by author of the *Scarlet Pimpernel.* Eight fairy tales include "The Suitors of Princess Fire-Fly," "The Twin Hunchbacks," "Mr. Cuttlefish's Love Story," and "The Enchanted Cat." This little volume of magic and adventure will captivate children as it has for generations. 90 drawings by Montagu Barstow. 96pp. (USO) 22293-4 Paperbound $1.95

THE RED FAIRY BOOK, Andrew Lang. Lang's color fairy books have long been children's favorites. This volume includes Rapunzel, Jack and the Bean-stalk and 35 other stories, familiar and unfamiliar. 4 plates, 93 illustrations x + 367pp.
21673-X Paperbound $2.50

THE BLUE FAIRY BOOK, Andrew Lang. Lang's tales come from all countries and all times. Here are 37 tales from Grimm, the Arabian Nights, Greek Mythology, and other fascinating sources. 8 plates, 130 illustrations. xi + 390pp.
21437-0 Paperbound $2.50

HOUSEHOLD STORIES BY THE BROTHERS GRIMM. Classic English-language edition of the well-known tales — Rumpelstiltskin, Snow White, Hansel and Gretel, The Twelve Brothers, Faithful John, Rapunzel, Tom Thumb (52 stories in all). Translated into simple, straightforward English by Lucy Crane. Ornamented with headpieces, vignettes, elaborate decorative initials and a dozen full-page illustrations by Walter Crane. x + 269pp.
21080-4 Paperbound **$2.00**

THE MERRY ADVENTURES OF ROBIN HOOD, Howard Pyle. The finest modern versions of the traditional ballads and tales about the great English outlaw. Howard Pyle's complete prose version, with every word, every illustration of the first edition. Do not confuse this facsimile of the original (1883) with modern editions that change text or illustrations. 23 plates plus many page decorations. xxii + 296pp.
22043-5 Paperbound $2.50

THE STORY OF KING ARTHUR AND HIS KNIGHTS, Howard Pyle. The finest children's version of the life of King Arthur; brilliantly retold by Pyle, with 48 of his most imaginative illustrations. xviii + 313pp. 6⅛ x 9¼.
21445-1 Paperbound $2.50

THE WONDERFUL WIZARD OF OZ, L. Frank Baum. America's finest children's book in facsimile of first edition with all Denslow illustrations in full color. The edition a child should have. Introduction by Martin Gardner. 23 color plates, scores of drawings. iv + 267pp.
20691-2 Paperbound $2.50

THE MARVELOUS LAND OF OZ, L. Frank Baum. The second Oz book, every bit as imaginative as the Wizard. The hero is a boy named Tip, but the Scarecrow and the Tin Woodman are back, as is the Oz magic. 16 color plates, 120 drawings by John R. Neill. 287pp.
20692-0 Paperbound $2.50

THE MAGICAL MONARCH OF MO, L. Frank Baum. Remarkable adventures in a land even stranger than Oz. The best of Baum's books not in the Oz series. 15 color plates and dozens of drawings by Frank Verbeck. xviii + 237pp.
21892-9 Paperbound $2.25

THE BAD CHILD'S BOOK OF BEASTS, MORE BEASTS FOR WORSE CHILDREN, A MORAL ALPHABET, Hilaire Belloc. Three complete humor classics in one volume. Be kind to the frog, and do not call him names . . . and 28 other whimsical animals. Familiar favorites and some not so well known. Illustrated by Basil Blackwell. 156pp.
(USO) 20749-8 Paperbound $1.50

EAST O' THE SUN AND WEST O' THE MOON, George W. Dasent. Considered the best of all translations of these Norwegian folk tales, this collection has been enjoyed by generations of children (and folklorists too). Includes True and Untrue, Why the Sea is Salt, East O' the Sun and West O' the Moon, Why the Bear is Stumpy-Tailed, Boots and the Troll, The Cock and the Hen, Rich Peter the Pedlar, and 52 more. The only edition with all 59 tales. 77 illustrations by Erik Werenskiold and Theodor Kittelsen. xv + 418pp.   22521-6 Paperbound $3.50

GOOPS AND HOW TO BE THEM, Gelett Burgess. Classic of tongue-in-cheek humor, masquerading as etiquette book. 87 verses, twice as many cartoons, show mischievous Goops as they demonstrate to children virtues of table manners, neatness, courtesy, etc. Favorite for generations. viii + 88pp. 6½ x 9¼.
                                           22233-0 Paperbound $1.25

ALICE'S ADVENTURES UNDER GROUND, Lewis Carroll. The first version, quite different from the final *Alice in Wonderland,* printed out by Carroll himself with his own illustrations. Complete facsimile of the "million dollar" manuscript Carroll gave to Alice Liddell in 1864. Introduction by Martin Gardner. viii + 96pp. Title and dedication pages in color.   21482-6 Paperbound $1.25

THE BROWNIES, THEIR BOOK, Palmer Cox. Small as mice, cunning as foxes, exuberant and full of mischief, the Brownies go to the zoo, toy shop, seashore, circus, etc., in 24 verse adventures and 266 illustrations. Long a favorite, since their first appearance in St. Nicholas Magazine. xi + 144pp. 6⅝ x 9¼.
                                           21265-3 Paperbound $1.75

SONGS OF CHILDHOOD, Walter De La Mare. Published (under the pseudonym Walter Ramal) when De La Mare was only 29, this charming collection has long been a favorite children's book. A facsimile of the first edition in paper, the 47 poems capture the simplicity of the nursery rhyme and the ballad, including such lyrics as I Met Eve, Tartary, The Silver Penny. vii + 106pp. (USO) 21972-0 Paperbound
                                                                    $1.25

THE COMPLETE NONSENSE OF EDWARD LEAR, Edward Lear. The finest 19th-century humorist-cartoonist in full: all nonsense limericks, zany alphabets, Owl and Pussycat, songs, nonsense botany, and more than 500 illustrations by Lear himself. Edited by Holbrook Jackson. xxix + 287pp.   (USO) 20167-8 Paperbound $2.00

BILLY WHISKERS: THE AUTOBIOGRAPHY OF A GOAT, Frances Trego Montgomery. A favorite of children since the early 20th century, here are the escapades of that rambunctious, irresistible and mischievous goat—Billy Whiskers. Much in the spirit of *Peck's Bad Boy,* this is a book that children never tire of reading or hearing. All the original familiar illustrations by W. H. Fry are included: 6 color plates, 18 black and white drawings. 159pp.   22345-0 Paperbound $2.00

MOTHER GOOSE MELODIES. Faithful republication of the fabulously rare Munroe and Francis "copyright 1833" Boston edition—the most important Mother Goose collection, usually referred to as the "original." Familiar rhymes plus many rare ones, with wonderful old woodcut illustrations. Edited by E. F. Bleiler. 128pp. 4½ x 6⅜.   22577-1 Paperbound $1.00

TWO LITTLE SAVAGES; BEING THE ADVENTURES OF TWO BOYS WHO LIVED AS INDIANS AND WHAT THEY LEARNED, Ernest Thompson Seton. Great classic of nature and boyhood provides a vast range of woodlore in most palatable form, a genuinely entertaining story. Two farm boys build a teepee in woods and live in it for a month, working out Indian solutions to living problems, star lore, birds and animals, plants, etc. 293 illustrations. vii + 286pp.

20985-7 Paperbound $2.50

PETER PIPER'S PRACTICAL PRINCIPLES OF PLAIN & PERFECT PRONUNCIATION. Alliterative jingles and tongue-twisters of surprising charm, that made their first appearance in America about 1830. Republished in full with the spirited woodcut illustrations from this earliest American edition. 32pp. 4½ x 6⅜.

22560-7 Paperbound $1.00

SCIENCE EXPERIMENTS AND AMUSEMENTS FOR CHILDREN, Charles Vivian. 73 easy experiments, requiring only materials found at home or easily available, such as candles, coins, steel wool, etc.; illustrate basic phenomena like vacuum, simple chemical reaction, etc. All safe. Modern, well-planned. Formerly *Science Games for Children*. 102 photos, numerous drawings. 96pp. 6⅛ x 9¼.

21856-2 Paperbound $1.25

AN INTRODUCTION TO CHESS MOVES AND TACTICS SIMPLY EXPLAINED, Leonard Barden. Informal intermediate introduction, quite strong in explaining reasons for moves. Covers basic material, tactics, important openings, traps, positional play in middle game, end game. Attempts to isolate patterns and recurrent configurations. Formerly *Chess*. 58 figures. 102pp.   (USO) 21210-6 Paperbound $1.25

LASKER'S MANUAL OF CHESS, Dr. Emanuel Lasker. Lasker was not only one of the five great World Champions, he was also one of the ablest expositors, theorists, and analysts. In many ways, his Manual, permeated with his philosophy of battle, filled with keen insights, is one of the greatest works ever written on chess. Filled with analyzed games by the great players. A single-volume library that will profit almost any chess player, beginner or master. 308 diagrams. xli x 349pp.

20640-8 Paperbound $2.75

THE MASTER BOOK OF MATHEMATICAL RECREATIONS, Fred Schuh. In opinion of many the finest work ever prepared on mathematical puzzles, stunts, recreations; exhaustively thorough explanations of mathematics involved, analysis of effects, citation of puzzles and games. Mathematics involved is elementary. Translated by F. Göbel. 194 figures. xxiv + 430pp.   22134-2 Paperbound $3.50

MATHEMATICS, MAGIC AND MYSTERY, Martin Gardner. Puzzle editor for Scientific American explains mathematics behind various mystifying tricks: card tricks, stage "mind reading," coin and match tricks, counting out games, geometric dissections, etc. Probability sets, theory of numbers clearly explained. Also provides more than 400 tricks, guaranteed to work, that you can do. 135 illustrations. xii + 176pp.

20335-2 Paperbound $1.75

MATHEMATICAL PUZZLES FOR BEGINNERS AND ENTHUSIASTS, Geoffrey Mott-Smith. 189 puzzles from easy to difficult—involving arithmetic, logic, algebra, properties of digits, probability, etc.—for enjoyment and mental stimulus. Explanation of mathematical principles behind the puzzles. 135 illustrations. viii + 248pp.

20198-8 Paperbound $1.75

PAPER FOLDING FOR BEGINNERS, William D. Murray and Francis J. Rigney. Easiest book on the market, clearest instructions on making interesting, beautiful origami. Sail boats, cups, roosters, frogs that move legs, bonbon boxes, standing birds, etc. 40 projects; more than 275 diagrams and photographs. 94pp.

20713-7 Paperbound $1.00

TRICKS AND GAMES ON THE POOL TABLE, Fred Herrmann. 79 tricks and games— some solitaires, some for two or more players, some competitive games—to entertain you between formal games. Mystifying shots and throws, unusual caroms, tricks involving such props as cork, coins, a hat, etc. Formerly *Fun on the Pool Table*. 77 figures. 95pp.

21814-7 Paperbound $1.25

HAND SHADOWS TO BE THROWN UPON THE WALL: A SERIES OF NOVEL AND AMUSING FIGURES FORMED BY THE HAND, Henry Bursill. Delightful picturebook from great-grandfather's day shows how to make 18 different hand shadows: a bird that flies, duck that quacks, dog that wags his tail, camel, goose, deer, boy, turtle, etc. Only book of its sort. vi + 33pp. 6½ x 9¼. 21779-5 Paperbound $1.00

WHITTLING AND WOODCARVING, E. J. Tangerman. 18th printing of best book on market. "If you can cut a potato you can carve" toys and puzzles, chains, chessmen, caricatures, masks, frames, woodcut blocks, surface patterns, much more. Information on tools, woods, techniques. Also goes into serious wood sculpture from Middle Ages to present, East and West. 464 photos, figures. x + 293pp.

20965-2 Paperbound $2.00

HISTORY OF PHILOSOPHY, Julián Marias. Possibly the clearest, most easily followed, best planned, most useful one-volume history of philosophy on the market; neither skimpy nor overfull. Full details on system of every major philosopher and dozens of less important thinkers from pre-Socratics up to Existentialism and later. Strong on many European figures usually omitted. Has gone through dozens of editions in Europe. 1966 edition, translated by Stanley Appelbaum and Clarence Strowbridge. xviii + 505pp. 21739-6 Paperbound $3.50

YOGA: A SCIENTIFIC EVALUATION, Kovoor T. Behanan. Scientific but non-technical study of physiological results of yoga exercises; done under auspices of Yale U. Relations to Indian thought, to psychoanalysis, etc. 16 photos. xxiii + 270pp.

20505-3 Paperbound $2.50

Prices subject to change without notice.
Available at your book dealer or write for free catalogue to Dept. GI, Dover Publications, Inc., 180 Varick St., N. Y., N. Y. 10014. Dover publishes more than 150 books each year on science, elementary and advanced mathematics, biology, music, art, literary history, social sciences and other areas.